BOGMAIL

Patrick McGinley was born in Glencolmcille,
Co Donegal. He was educated at Galway
University. Subsequently, he moved to London
to work in book publishing. He now lives in
Kent with his wife Kathleen. His Donegal
childhood and boyhood are described in his
memoir *That Unearthly Valley*. His eight novels
include *Foggage*, *The Trick of the Ga Bolga* and
Goosefoot, which was made into a film.

ALSO BY PATRICK MCGINLEY

Fox Prints
Goosefoot
Foggage
The Trick of the Ga Bolga
The Red Men
The Devil's Diary
The Lost Soldier's Song
That Unearthly Valley: A Donegal Childhood
Cold Spring

BOGMAIL

PATRICK MCGINLEY

Leabharlanna Poiblí Chathair Baile Átha Cliath

Dublin City Public Libraries

APOLLO

An imprint of Head of Zeus

First published in 1978

This edition first published in the UK in 2017
by Apollo, an imprint of Head of Zeus, Ltd.

9 7 5 3 1 2 4 6 8
A CIP catalogue record for this book is available from the British Library.

ISBN (PB): 9781786696618
ISBN (E): 9781786696601

Typeset by Mariel Deegan

Printed and bound by CPI Group (UK) Ltd, Croydon, CR0 4YY

Head of Zeus Ltd
First Floor East
5–8 Hardwick Street
London EC1R 4RG

WWW.HEADOFZEUS.COM

For my grandson William.

ONE

Roarty was making an omelette from the mushrooms Eamonn Eales had collected in Davy Long's park that morning. They were good mushrooms, medium sized and delicately succulent, just right for a special omelette, an omelette surprise. He had chosen the best mushrooms for his own omelette; the one he was making for Eales was special because it contained not only the mushrooms from Davy Long's park but also a handful of obnoxious, black-gilled toadstools which he himself had picked on the dunghill behind the byre. He was hoping that four of them would be enough to poison his lecherous barman; he dare not put in any more in case he should smell a rat.

Eales was a fastidious feeder who never touched bacon rind or pork crackling or the thin veins of white fat that made the best gammon so tasty. He never ate the frazzled fat of grilled lamb chops and sirloin steak, nor the crisp earthy jackets of baked potatoes. Normally, he would not have blamed him for avoiding the latter because the jackets of some farmers' potatoes were rough with scabs and excrescences. Roarty's potatoes, however, were different, grown lovingly in the sandy soil by the estuary and as smooth to the touch as sea-scoured beach pebbles. The man who was not moved to eat the jackets of such potatoes was nothing if not a scoundrel. He was blind to the beauties of life and the true delights of a wholesome table. He was probably a man who harboured evil thoughts against his neighbour, someone from whom wise men all would lock up their daughters, at least those of them who still retained their maidenheads. The outcome was inescapable: Eales must be destroyed.

The toadstools were a brilliant idea, better than the ragwort which was his first thought and which would have had serious shortcomings as a poison. Sergeant McGing had been talking in the bar about its toxic properties only last week, and if traces of the weed were to be found in Eales's alimentary canal by the pathologist doing the post-mortem, McGing might put two and two together.

'How did the ragwort get into the stomach of the deceased?' he would ask with unselfconscious pomposity. 'After all, Eales was not a cow.' Ragwort was not the kind of thing that got into a man's stomach by accident whereas a toadstool might. Eales had picked the mushrooms himself, and it was all too possible that in his haste he had picked a few wrong ones. Roarty would sorrowfully admit to having made the omelette but since a motive for murder could not be pinned on him, he would go free. It would be a perfect murder, executed cleanly with the minimum of fuss and exertion, better than the needless spilling of blood which was for stupid men who could not control their passions.

Eales, in the sickly yellow waistcoat he wore on weekdays, was perched on a high stool behind the bar, reading the racing results to Old Crubog. He was barely twenty, tall, swarthy and narrow faced with an uncommon self-possession that showed in his unconcealed assumption that other people existed only for his amusement. Old Crubog, the sole customer, was listening intently, head tilted and an untouched pint of stout before him.

'Your tea is ready,' Roarty called from the kitchen doorway.

Eales folded the newspaper, placed it on the counter before Crubog, and dived hungrily past his landlord.

'The paper's wasted on me, I'm afraid. I've left me specs behind,' said Crubog, taking a long sip from his glass and smacking two puckered lips that collapsed over his loose false teeth. 'The first this afternoon,' he said, his watery eyes brightening with eager pleasure.

Roarty leaned over the counter and listened to him praising times past while in a remote chamber of his mind he wondered when Eales would kick the bucket. Would he go out like a light after he'd eaten? Or would he struggle manfully through the evening and quietly slip away in his sleep during the night? To get rid of him so easily, so perfectly, seemed too good to be true.

With his hand on the stout pump, he looked out of the west window at the sharp evening sunlight on the sea, a plain of winking water with not even a flash of foam around Rannyweal, the submerged reef that reached from the south shore almost halfway across the bay. It had been a glorious summer, the best anyone, except Old Crubog, could remember. Not a drop of rain had fallen since Easter, and it was now the first week of August. The corn was only half its usual height, and the potatoes, though floury, were meagre in both size and numbers. The farmers had been grumbling since June, and the parish priest, who was a farmer himself, had taken to praying for rain at Mass on Sundays. Only the tourists, turf-cutters and fishermen were happy. It was a good summer for publicans too, however. Never had he seen men so thirsty in the evenings; never had he sold so much ale and stout. There was always someone in the pub from morning to night, always someone with a thirst that needed slaking. Noticing that the stout shelf was almost bare, he brought in two crates from the storeroom and placed the bottles in three neat rows in readiness for the evening swill. Then he poured himself a large Irish whiskey and water and said to Crubog, 'It's a rare day when you don't see it breaking white over Rannyweal.'

'They were good mushroom, those,' said Eales, returning from the kitchen. 'I've never enjoyed better.'

'I thought some of them tasted a bit strong,' said Roarty.

'Imagination. Mine were perfect.'

'Where did you get them?' asked Crubog.

'In Davy Long's park. I picked every one of them myself,' Eales boasted.

'It's the foremost place for mushrooms.' Crubog spoke with authority. 'You'll never find a bad mushroom in Davy Long's park, every one as juicy as a Jaffa orange.'

He left Eales and Crubog to talk and wandered out behind the house, the sight of the withered conifer banishing all thought of mushrooms from his mind. He filled two buckets of water from the outside tap and poured them on the roots of the dying tree. The cracked earth drank the water as if it were a thimbleful, and he carried six more bucketfuls, dogged and determined but with a black sense of hopelessness in his heart. He had planted the supposedly evergreen tree seventeen years ago, on the day Cecily was born and his wife had died. During its first winter a storm from the west uprooted it one night but he put it standing again with a supporting stake, and it grew with Cecily, tall, dark green, and tapering with branches that drooped with a heaviness of needles. He came to associate the growing tree with the changes in Cecily: the subtle change in the shape of her nose at six, which even he could not find words to describe; the darkening of her flaxen hair at nine; the lengthening of her spindly schoolgirl's legs; and finally the bulging of her breasts. She was a sweet-natured girl, not unlike her mother in looks and yet so different. Though he'd never kissed her even as a child, he felt close to her. Now he could not think of her without a twinge of foreboding. He had been right to send her to London at the time. Now he could hardly bear the thought of her so vulnerable and so far away. Since the tree had begun to wither he had been unable to think of her without holding his breath.

As he grasped a branch above his head, brittle needles turned to dust in his hand. The branches had begun to curl while the dark green had given way to lighter green with a yellowy tinge, yet he refused to believe that her tree would die. All the other trees in the garden were thriving, possibly because of their deeper roots. He had chosen to plant a conifer because it was not deciduous. If only he'd realised that it was sensitive to drought. If only he'd noticed the lightening of the dark green in time.

Out of the corner of his eye he saw Allegro, one of Eales's cats, spring onto the low bird table. He bounded across the garden and caught the miserable creature by the neck but he was too late—the sparrow in its mouth was already dead. Eales was evil. He regretted the day he had so innocently made him his barman. His insinuating leer should have alerted him as he sauntered into the bar on a summer evening with a knapsack on his back and a black cat under each arm. He introduced one as Allegro and the other as Andante, thinking it funny, no doubt. The effrontery of him, introducing his cats as if they were people!

'A pint of porter,' he had said. 'And a job if you've got one.'

He should have known then that a man who goes about with two black cats was not a man to tangle with, but he needed a barman and none of the locals wanted the job.

'What brings you to me?' he asked.

'I made enquiries in the pub at the other end of the village and they said you might have work for me. I'm no slouch, I've pulled pints before.'

He was a good barman, quick to read a slow customer's mind and quick to give change on busy evenings, popular with the regulars and industrious even when there was little to be done. But there was something unnatural in the slinky way he looked at you. He was secretive, sharp-tongued, over-confident, without one intimate friend. Though he went out with every girl who would look twice at him, he behaved as if he would not even consider the possibility that one of them could ever become his wife.

He had an unnatural sense of humour as well. On his day off he would put a plate of bread crumbs on the bird table and sit by the kitchen window waiting for Allegro or Andante to pounce. He had deliberately placed the bird table near the flowerbeds so that they might provide cover for his cats. And whenever one of them caught a bird, he would laugh and slap his thigh. Then shaking both fists, he would shout, 'Good old Allegro. Second kill today.'

One evening at the end of May, Roarty had watched him shaking the sycamore until a little nestling fell from an upper branch. The poor bird, paralysed by fright, could make only the most feeble attempt to fly, while the two parents in the nearby ash were scolding furiously and Eales went off laughing to find his cats. Roarty was so horrified that he got out the ladder and put the fledgling back in the nest. He was climbing back down when Eales returned with Allegro and Andante and saw the white and yellow stain on his shirt sleeve.

'That's the thanks you get for rescuing a scaldy, bird shit on your sleeve.'

That was proof enough. Eales was evil. Eales must be destroyed.

Throughout the evening he kept a watchful eye on him but there was not a sign of him weakening. Never had he seemed so alert, pulling pints as if it were a funeral day and joking and arguing with Old Crubog, the know-all fisherman Rory Rua, the Englishman Potter, Cor Mogaill Maloney, and the journalist Gimp Gillespie who could talk the hind leg off a donkey without uttering a word of the truth. It was a good evening for business, though. The bar was packed, the farmers arguing about the storm clouds that were piling up in the east, overloading the air with humidity. Some shook their heads and said they'd expect rain when they saw it, but Crubog with all the authority of his eighty years said that he'd never seen a sky that had the makings of a bigger rain storm.

TWO

The following morning Crubog was his first customer, complaining of the rain storm that never came.

'Did you see what happened?' he said. 'The clouds travelled right across the sky from east to west. That rain fell on the sea where it was least wanted.'

Roarty pulled a pint of stout for him and took a crimped pound note from his trembling hand. After he had given him sixty-two pence in change, he poured out a large whiskey and placed it on the counter beside the pint.

'What's on your mind?' Crubog asked.

'Nothing that can't wait,' said Roarty with a distant look at Rannyweal and the blueness of the bay.

'Whenever you put up a drink on the house, I know there must be mischief on your mind. *Do shláinte, a chailleach!*'

'*Sláinte na bhfear, is go ndoiridh tú bean roimh oíche.*'

Crubog raised the glass and poured the neat whiskey down his throat. The action was certainly one of pouring rather than drinking, Roarty thought. He had watched his Adam's apple, and it hadn't moved.

'There's nothing like neat whiskey first thing in the morning for clearing out the old tubes. If only a man could afford it...'

'You could if you had a mind to,' Roarty confided.

'How?' asked Crubog, flattening the single tuft of hair that sprang from the top of his otherwise bald head. It was like a tuft of withered couch-grass, and he had split it in two and combed one strand down over each ear. He was an uncommon sight, small, thin, and sun-tanned—and cunning as an old dog-fox.

'I've told you before. All you have to do is sell your land.'

'And how much are you offering today?' Crubog showed a sly hint of interest while treating the subject as a familiar joke.

'The same as last week. Four thousand is a fair price. It would keep you in whiskey while there's breath in you.'

'That's a point of view, but I'll admit it's a sore temptation.'

'Then what's stopping you?'

'You're not the only one who's hungry for my land. Rory Rua for one has his eye on it.'

'Rory Rua's a bighead. He's all talk.'

'If I sell, it will be to a farmer, like me and my father and grandfather before me. Land is for tillage and grazing. What would the likes of you be doing with it?'

'And what would Rory Rua be doing with it? He's more of a fisherman than a farmer.'

'He has two cows and two heifers, and he's thinking of buying a bull. A bull needs scope. Will you be buying a bull?'

'I have no plans. I might stock it or use it for tillage, depending on how the cat jumps.'

'If you want to buy it, you must first tell me what you'd do with it. That would be part of the bargain.'

Crubog was impossible. Roarty had been pouring him a morning whiskey for the past four years without extracting even a promise to sell. It made no sense. All Crubog had to live on was his pension, while his land lay under the crows without earning him a penny. He wouldn't mind if it was fertile land. His six-acre farm was a waste land of rocks, but what interested Roarty was the 'large mountain acreage' that went with it. He had heard from a friend in Dublin that the Tourist Board was going to build a scenic road across the hill right through Crubog's land, and he could foresee the day when the roadside would be lined with week-end cottages and tourist chalets. If he owned what Crubog called 'my large mountain acreage' when the road came to pass, he would stand a good chance of making a killing.

'Well, I must collect my pension,' said Crubog, sucking the froth of his pint from the very bottom of his glass. 'You needn't worry, I'll be back to leave some of it with you before dinnertime.'

Roarty poured himself his second whiskey of the morning. The bar was empty, and the demon Eales had gone to Killybegs for the day. He looked out at the sea, which was the same as yesterday and the day before. Bored, he took his glass upstairs to Eales's bedroom. The window was open but there was a smell in the room, not an unpleasant smell but still a smell – the smell of used lotions and talcum powders. Not a wholesome, daytime, manly smell but a smell that brought to mind the reeking manoeuvres of the night. The room was tidier than his own, the low dressing table covered with an assortment of bottles and hair brushes. The vanity of the man! The misplaced conceit! He certainly looked after his mangy carcass. Always washing his hair and having baths, yet his feet smelt like a midden. The toadstools had failed; he was up at six, chirpy as a lark, calling to Allegro and Andante before the dawn chorus had quite ended. What next? Foxglove? McGing had said that you could make digitalis from the leaves provided you gathered them at the right time.

But what was the right time? He felt dwarfed by the height of ignorance; not even *Britannica* had the answer. He would have to think of something before Saturday. Another omelette with a bigger surprise perhaps?

Moving to the bed, he lifted the pink counterpane, then the perfumed pillow. Underneath, rolled in puce pyjamas, was a glossy sex magazine, wherever he'd got it, full of colour pictures of naked beauties in the most inviting poses, offering their air-brushed bottoms and fannies, or swooning with closed eyes as they crushed pneumatic breasts between their hands. His head swam from the jostling of unthinkable possibilities. He glanced at the letters page. Troilism. Fellatio. Cunnilingus. It was all there, the whole mad circus of the aberrant world. Eales was a citizen of that world. Eales must be destroyed.

Guiltily, he put away the magazine and idly picked up a coupon advertisement from the bedside table, which had been filled in by Eales, who else? Incredulously, he read aloud:

> *Increase your partner's pleasure—and your own—at a stroke! Send for our new heart-shaped pillow today, place it under her bottom, and 'feel' the difference! Choice of foam rubber or hot-water filled. Ergonomically designed. Guaranteed success. Order before 3ʳᵈ September and receive free rubber lust finger by return post, a must for the truly modern lover.*

Pondering the meaning of 'ergonomically', he crossed the landing to his own bedroom and took down an old edition of *The Concise Oxford* from the bookshelf but the only word that resembled the word he wanted was 'erg', a unit of work or energy. He would ask Potter. He was an engineer, he was bound to know. Absentmindedly, he opened the fifth volume of the 1911 edition of *Britannica* and extracted a single-page letter from between the endpapers. He had bought the encyclopedia for ten shillings at a jumble sale in Sligo one Saturday afternoon over twenty years ago. It was the bargain of a lifetime and the only literary work he possessed, apart from the dictionary and a biography of Schumann. Holding the volume to his nose, he inhaled deeply. The vaguely sooty smell of the spine always gave him a frisson of esoteric pleasure that was increased by the fact that many of the articles were long since out of date and totally unreliable.

As he read the letter, which he already knew by heart, he could not help wondering at the impulse that made him wish to re-experience the paralysing pain of uncertainty in his chest.

Dear Eamonn,
Only three more weeks, only twenty-one days and nights. How I long to escape from behind these walls, to see you again, to see you every day. I keep thinking of that evening under the Minister's Bridge and the strange thing you did to me. I've been trying to find out if the other girls know about it, but whenever I hint, they look blank. As our English teacher says, I hold there is no sin but ignorance. It's lights out in a minute. I must end. A hundred kisses and one last one from your loving
Cecily

That was before the Christmas holidays, and he hadn't discovered the letter until after Easter. God only knows what strange things he had done to her since then. Mercifully, he was still in time to save her from the unspeakable refinement of the lust finger.

THREE

It was Saturday evening, the pub was crowded, and Roarty was at his most landlordly. After pouring himself the fourth double since dinnertime he had gone with no perceptible outward change through what he called the well-being barrier. It was always the same. The first double had no effect and neither had the second; the third thawed him; the fourth warmed him; and the fifth lit a taper in his mind that penetrated the internal murk, colouring it like a winter moon bursting through heavy cloud. The self-destructive edge vanished from his thoughts, words flowed as bright as spring water, and laughter came easily and for no overt reason. Between the fifth and the eighth double he lived on a plateau of unconsidered pleasure, which he tried to prolong until closing time. The tenth double was always followed by swift deterioration when the commonest words became tongue-twisters and thought came slowly like the last drop from a squeezed lemon. That was to be regretted, and it was a stage he usually avoided. He liked to arrange matters so that his 'tenth' coincided with closing time. Then after he and Eales had washed up, he would scorn the optic and pour himself what Potter called 'a domestic double' straight from the bottle. This he would take to his bedroom and sip as he read his 'office' for the day, an outmoded article on some aspect of science from the scholar's *Britannica*.

Pulling a pint for a tourist in search of local colour, Roarty listened with enjoyment to the never-ending catechetical conversation between Crubog, Cor Mogaill, Rory Rua, Gimp Gillespie and the Englishman Potter who, though new to the glen, was learning fast.

'Why do seagulls no longer follow the spade or the plough?' asked Crubog.

'Because of the lack of earthworms in the sod,' said Rory Rua, who had heard this conversation before.

'And why are earthworms as scarce as sovereigns?' demanded Crubog.

'Because the artificial manure is killing them,' Cor Mogaill sniggered.

'It's time you all found a new topic for conversation,' Rory Rua complained.

'Would you prefer if we talked about you?' Cor Mogaill sneered.

'When we used to put nothing on the land but wrack and cow dung,' said Crubog, 'the sod was alive with earthworms, big fat red ones, wriggling like elvers as the spade sliced them. And the sky would be thick with gulls on a spring day, there would be so many of them. Now you could dig or plough from June to January without even attracting the notice of a robin. The fertiliser has killed the goodness in the soil so that not even an earthworm can live in it. How can you grow good oats in dead earth? Answer me that Rory Rua.'

'You're all mad, the whole lot of you,' Rory Rua said. 'I'm going up to McGonigle's for a sensible conversation.'

'Good riddance!' Cor Mogaill said when Rory Rua had gone. 'He's the ruination of all crack and conversation. He can think of nothing but the price of lobsters.'

'And land!' Crubog put in. 'He keeps pestering me to sell him my large mountain acreage.'

'But to get back to what we were talking about,' Gimp Gillespie, the local journalist, interposed. 'What we need is humus. Science has upset the natural cycle. Render to the earth the things of the earth and to the laboratory the manufactures of science.'

'Who said that?' Potter asked. 'I'm sure I've heard it somewhere before.'

'How many tons of earth does your average earthworm turn over in a year?' Crubog would not be deflected. 'Answer me that, Cor Mogaill. And you can consult your personal library if you like!'

Cor Mogaill, a youth of no more than twenty, saw himself as the village intellectual. He never came to the pub without his knapsack, in which he kept his bicycle pump, certain back copies of *The Irish Times* and *A History of Ireland* by Eleanor Hull. He would then spend the evening trying to start an argument to provide him with an opportunity of consulting what he called his personal library. Now he looked critically at Crubog but the knapsack remained on his back.

'What do you know about the physiology of earthworms, Crubog?'

'I've had it on the best authority. I read it twenty years ago in *The People's Press,* while you were still doing everything in your nappy. The answer is forty tons, not an ounce less. A Bachelor of Agricultural Science could put the spool of his arse out without achieving that. Now I'm going to pay my daily tribute to nature and improve the quality of the soil.'

'I'll join you,' said Cor Mogaill. 'We'll carry on our conversation and kill two birds with one stone.'

'No, we won't. The recipe for a long life is to shit in peace and let your water flow naturally.' Crubog laughed to himself on his way to the outside lavatory.

It was an evening of energetic conversation. Crubog was at his most engaging, full of trenchant anecdotes and antique lore, and Gimp Gillespie and Cor Mogaill drew him out with unobtrusive skill to the evident delight of the Englishman Potter, who presided over the conversation with an intellectual discrimination befitting a man who saw himself as something of a scientist. Their talk took colour from the obscurity of the topics and the need of the speakers to make up for their relative ignorance by embroidering their thoughts with humorous whimsy. First, they considered if a doe hare drops all her litter in one form or if she places each leveret in a separate nest for safety's sake. When they had failed to find an answer, they turned to the trapping of foxes. Here Gimp Gillespie proved the most knowledgeable or at least the most confident of his opinion. He surprised everyone by saying that he would bet the shirt on his back that a dead cat, preferably in an advanced state of decomposition, was the best bait because a fox could wind it even on a windless night. When Cor Mogaill demanded to know the source of this unlikely piece of intelligence, Gillespie told him that he'd had it from Rory Rua, who'd read it in *The Farmers' Journal*.

'You can't rely on Rory Rua! He still counts on his fingers.'

Crubog, however, was not to be silenced. He demanded to know how curlews, when feeding inland, can tell that the tide has begun to ebb and that it's time to make for the shore. And he posed the question with such an air of dark omniscience that Potter said it was just as well they did not have an ornithologist in the company because his specialist knowledge would kill all conversation.

Now and again they tried to draw Roarty into their circle but his mind was anchored elsewhere. This evening the faces on the other side of the bar seemed far away. He longed to be one of them, to share in their easy banter, but the memory of last night's dream occupied the length and breadth of his thoughts.

He was a boy of twelve again, chasing his ten-year-old sister Maureen in a field full of daisies when suddenly she stopped and said, 'Bring me that butterfly.'

'Why?' he asked, sensing that his will wasn't free.

'Because I want to pull its wings apart!'

It seemed such a natural desire that he ran after the butterfly, dizzy with its rise and fall in the sunlight and the whiteness of its wings like the whiteness of the daisies in the grass.

He stopped on the shore of a lake. The butterfly had fluttered over the unruffled surface of the water and rested on a solitary lough lily in the centre.

'You can walk on the water if you don't look down at your feet,' his sister explained from behind.

Reluctantly, he put one foot forward. The water retreated before him, exposing soft peaty mud that cooled the soles of his feet and oozed up between his toes. The earth swallowed the water with a sucking and a gurgling, and the water lily, lacking the support of its natural element, lay besmirched and bedraggled on the dark mud. He examined the stem and the round, dark hole in the heart of the flower. He held it tenderly between his fingers as an ugly green caterpillar poked its head through the hole and crawled over the leaf with odious contractions.

'You've pursued evil to its lair,' Maureen called from the shore.

'And I've found it at the heart of beauty.' There was a lump in his throat as he spoke; he couldn't trust himself to utter another word.

The tenderness he experienced as he held the lily between his fingers and his horror at the ravishment of the flower merged in dark vexation, and he lost count of the number of drinks in a round.

'Roarty will have the answer,' said Crubog. 'After all he's the second best snipe shot in the county.'

'What's that?' Roarty asked, measuring a large Glenmorangie for Potter.

'How does the snipe beat his tattoo in the spring?' Crubog asked.

'What tattoo?'

'How does he drum?' Potter rephrased.

'With his outer tail feathers,' Roarty replied. 'He holds them out stiffly at right angles as he swoops.'

'Wrong,' said Eales. 'Every one of you is wrong.'

'Enlighten us,' said Roarty, reddening beneath his beard.

'With his syrinx, of course,' said Eales.

'Fair play to you, Eamonn,' said Cor Mogaill, enjoying the rising tension.

'With his syringe?' enquired Crubog who was hard of hearing.

'Syrinx,' Eales shouted. 'That's how most birds make sounds.'

'But the snipe's drumming is a horse of a different colour,' said Roarty.

'I'll bet a double whiskey I'm right,' said Eales.

'And I'll bet a bottle,' said Roarty who did not take kindly to being challenged by his Kerry-born barman.

'Can I keep the bets?' Crubog asked hopefully.

'Can you prove you're right?' Eales smirked.

'Not this minute. I'll look it up after closing.'

It was half-past eleven by the clock, and they would expect twenty minutes to drink up. He put two towels over the dispensers and went out the back for a breath of cool air, only to be disappointed. It was a muggy night with a faint breeze that died away every so often, leaving him becalmed by the back door with a constriction in his throat that made breathing difficult. The eastern sky was a mass of inky cloud, a sagging roof that pressed down on the tops of the hills and obliterated both moon and stars. Those rain clouds had come up since dinnertime, and, surprisingly, no one in the pub had mentioned them. He listened to the hum of conversation from the bar, thinking that a pub at that hour was the most unreal place on earth.

'Where is your proof?' asked Eales when they had washed up and the last customer had gone.

'In my encyclopedia. I'll go fetch it.'

He went up to his bedroom and scanned the article on 'Snipe', too distraught to take pleasure in being right.

The house was quiet now; the last few stragglers had taken the country roads home. Sadness and impossible longing choked him as he remembered summer evenings with Cecily at the piano in her room, the whole house flowing with liquid music. 'On the Wings of Song', 'Für Elise', 'Jesu Joy of Man's Desiring': all the old favourites. The purity of those evenings brought a tear to his eye. The purity of those evenings gone forever.

After he had found the letter to Eales in the wastepaper basket, he wrote to Maureen asking her to invite Cecily to London for the summer. It was not what he would have wished but he didn't have a choice. If she came home, it would be to the lust finger; and if he sacked Eales for no good reason, she would never forgive him. Even if he did sack him, he felt certain he wouldn't leave the glen. He was sure to find another job in the neighbourhood and continue to defile Cecily. Now all his precautions had come to naught; Eales was planning to go to London next week. He didn't say why; he didn't have to. Roarty's hands shook with rage and frustration. Eales was evil. Eales must be destroyed.

He found himself halfway down the stairs, clutching the twenty-fifth volume of *Britannica* in his right hand, the fingers opening and closing involuntarily on the spine. Eales was behind the bar, bent over a barrel, examining a length of plastic tubing.

'Now let's see your proof,' he said without looking up.

Roarty raised the book in both hands and brought it down with all his might on the back of Eales's head. The breath went out of him with a reedy murmur as his head hit the edge of the barrel. He grasped the barrel with both hands in an attempt to get to his feet. The barrel rocked. Roarty raised the book again. Eales sank on his haunches and fell back on the floor without as much as a whimper.

Roarty shuddered, more in fear than in horror. He had acted without forethought, on the spur of the moment, not the kind of thing an intelligent man would do. What if someone had been passing and Eales had called out in his agony? Luckily, Eales had succumbed in silence, and as far as he could see, there was no blood to tell the tale. But what if he was just stunned? He placed a newspaper under his head and got a hand mirror from the kitchen, which he held to his mouth and nose, but there was no condensation. Difficult though it was to credit, Eales must have died instantaneously from the severity of the shock. The mirror test was not foolproof, however. According to Sergeant McGing, who was an authority on such matters, the surest indication of death was the temperature of the rectum falling to 70°F or below. He resisted the temptation to fetch the thermometer from his bedroom; there was a limit to what he was prepared to do in the interest of science. Besides, the body was still warm. It might take an hour or more for the temperature of the rectum to drop to 70°F. As an afterthought he felt Eales's pulse without detecting any perceptible stir in the bloodstream. He noticed a trace of blood on the upper lip where it had hit the rim of the barrel. As a precaution, he placed a plastic bag over the head and tied it round the neck with a piece of string. Eales had an uncommonly thick neck, very much like a round of bacon. It was something he had not noticed before, and quite possibly neither had Cecily. Only that could account for her inexplicable infatuation with the newly deceased.

He took the stairs two steps at a time, reaching the toilet not a moment too soon. His bowel movement was the swiftest and most satisfying he had experienced since his mother gave him an overdose of Glauber salts at the age of eleven. She would have been surprised to learn that homicide was an even better physic.

The relaxing effect of his evacuation was short lived, however. He was sweating profusely, a cold clammy sweat that drenched his shirt under the arms and made tickling rivulets down his forehead and into his eyebrows. Descending the stairs, he felt weak at the knees and very thirsty. As he reached for the Black Bush and unscrewed the top, the immensity of the next problem—how on earth to get rid of the body—stayed his hand. He returned the bottle to the shelf and filled a tumbler with water from the tap. Though he felt uncomfortably sober, he could not risk having another drink. If he was to make this a perfect murder, he would have to act with forethought and intelligence. He told himself to collect his thoughts, but when he tried, he found that coherent thinking was beyond him. A hundred random thoughts flashed before him but none remained long enough to connect with any other. His mind was a sieve pouring thoughts like so much water. To encourage concentration he sat at the deal table in the kitchen with an open notebook before him. Thought now came haltingly, and when it did he wrote down eight words before they had time to vanish into the back of his mind:

Fire   ›   *range*
Water   › *sea, lough*
Earth   › *garden, bog*

Burning was impracticable; he had only a range to rely on. And roasting flesh, fat and bone would raise an unearthly stink in the village. That left him with immersion and burial, and of these he favoured the first because it involved less work. He could drive west to the sea cliffs and heave the body over the edge into the water. Or he could tie a weight to the body, row out into the bay, and cast it overboard. As he imagined these actions in detail, he saw immediately that there were snags. He was reluctant to take out his boat in the dark, as he did not know the position of submerged rocks well enough to be entirely confident. Besides, there were houses along the shore, and it was just possible that he might meet someone. And what if the body was washed ashore? In the inevitable autopsy the forensic pathologist would discover that there was no saltwater in the lungs, and that therefore death was not the result of drowning. There would be an investigation into the cause of death, and questions, searching questions, would have to be answered. Of course he could dump the body in one of the mountain loughs, but as they were a fair distance from the road, he would have to hump a twelve-stone carcase uphill for more than a mile. Not an inviting prospect on a dark night and over rough ground.

That left the third possibility: disposal by burial. The easiest course would be to bury him in the garden, possibly under the dead conifer, but if there was to be an investigation, the garden would be the first place McGing would look. He would have to bury him in the bog, the least obvious place he could think of. He would drive out the Garron road for two miles, take the right-hand bog road and bury the body in the centre of the moor, well away from the areas where turf was now being cut. It was a lonely spot. The nearest house was three miles away, and the likelihood of being seen was remote. The only danger was the possibility of meeting another car on the main road, returning perhaps from a dance in Dunkineely. He thumbed hastily through the *Dispatch,* but there were no ads for dances in any of the local towns. Nevertheless, you never knew what late-night straggler you might meet on a country road, and his silver car was known to everyone in the glen. He would need an excuse, and what conceivable excuse could he have for driving towards Garron at one o'clock on a Sunday morning? A sudden gripe, a severe stomach pain occasioned by a Black Bush too many? That surely would explain the need for an urgent visit to Dr McGarrigle. And if he was seen, he could always say that the pain had abated when he was halfway there and that he had come home without seeing the doctor. It was not the best of excuses but it would have to do.

He opened the back door to have a look at the night sky. The clouds in the east seemed darker and closer. The air was still heavy, hanging like an invisible net over his head, laden with the scent of snuff-dry hay from the surrounding fields. Though already one o'clock, there was light in several of the cottages on the south mountain; he would have to wait until two before venturing out. The heavy night air weighed on his shoulders like a burden of unbearable thought.

Ploddingly, he climbed the stairs and opened a volume of *Britannica*. He lay on his side on the bed, sipping an orange juice and scanning a page. *Murder*. See *Homicide*. A failure to call a spade a spade? The article on *Homicide* was disappointing in its lack of detail, probably the work of some verbose criminologist rather than a scholar with first-hand experience. It occurred to him that a discerning news editor might welcome the account he himself could now write—a story that would tell of the murderer's grim sense of inevitability as he looks down on the sprawled body of his victim, the out-going hatred he felt an hour ago now turned inwards on himself.

From youth he has been conditioned by novels, stories, plays and films based on the axiom that crime does not pay; that if anyone pays, it is the criminal himself. Eyeing the cooling body, he cannot help but wonder if he himself will be one of the rare exceptions. Yet he knows that with the aid of the arcane resources of forensic science, his enemy's body could become more formidable in death than it ever was in life. After months of obsession with the victim, now he is truly alone, facing the instinctive condemnation of every decent citizen, the impersonal tenacity of the police in their investigations, and possibly the relentless treadmill of the courts, while all he has to ensure his survival is his cunning and intelligence. For a moment he wondered if he were intelligent enough.

On this night of all nights he needed to anticipate every contingency. Were there possibilities he had not considered, simple things he may have overlooked? He had not taken account of the moon, for example, which was only two days before the full. If the sky should clear, he would have to bury Eales in ghostly but too revealing light. He must make sure to remain on the alert; dig with one eye on the sky. Another indication of his disabling abstraction was the way he had looked up the *Donegal Dispatch* when he should have known that there was never a dance in Dunkineely on a Saturday.

He had written down eight options. Now the intimation of an unknown ninth tantalised him beyond all endurance, his freedom of action circumscribed by his inability to extend through imagination his gamut of choice. The man who is most free is the man who is aware of most possibilities, and in the past he had prided himself on being such a man. Now the effective possibilities open to him had shrunk from eight to one. And the remaining one was not particularly attractive.

For a moment a ninth possibility illumined the internal darkness; he would smash his front window, break open the till, hide the money, and pretend that Eales had been struck down by a burglar. It had the advantage that he could go to bed at his usual hour and get up in the morning at his usual time. He would listen to the radio over breakfast, and after a black coffee laced with a stiff Bush, 'discover' Eales and ring the police. That, however, might lead to awkward questions. Why hadn't he heard the crash of breaking glass and the rumpus that must have ensued? Murder, he remembered, was better concealed than advertised. His ninth possibility had disintegrated like so much gossamer. Again he was back to only one.

Having considered a possible ninth, he was now harassed by the thought that there might be an unknown tenth. In the kitchen he stared stonily at his notebook with its list of possibilities, but they stubbornly refused to multiply. He had always seen himself as bright, at least a deal cleverer than most of his customers. Now when intelligence most mattered, he was faltering. Many people confused intelligence with a retentive memory, or the ability to remember how things are done and imitate or reproduce precisely what they already know. The truly intelligent were a race apart, as distinct from the rest of humanity as a ram is from a ridgel. Their incisiveness went straight to the core of every crux and their capacity for dispassionate reasoning carried them far beyond the bourn of past experience. Their ability could be described in one word—analysis. That in a word was his present failure: an inability to analyse a situation. Or was it perhaps a failure of imagination?

He put a match to the incriminating note of options and ground the ashes into powder with the poker. He changed into an old pair of trousers that he used for painting, a dark shirt that would not show up in moonlight, and a pair of wellingtons that would keep out the bog water.

Remembering the odious lust finger, he went to Eales's bedroom and found it under the perfumed pillow. Now he would sleep soundly. The lust finger would never again agitate his dreams. He took Eales's hold-all from the wardrobe and stuffed into it the glossy sex magazine, the puce pyjamas, Eales's toothbrush, toothpaste, razor and shaving lather, a spare shirt and three bottles of deodorant. This latter, he told himself, was a brilliant stroke because Eales would not have gone as far as the door without his deodorant. Not quite analysis that, he would concede, but rather ingenious, nonetheless.

Premature self-congratulation was to be avoided, though. The time for hubris, if there was one, was tomorrow morning or in three years or so, when Eales would be as remote in history as a fossilised pterodactyl. He would not fossilise, however. Bogs were noted for their powers of preservation. Five hundred years from now some slow-thinking turf-cutter would unearth him with his slane, a time capsule preserved by tannin, the date of the magazine in the hold-all providing a perplexing *terminus a quo* for the rural constabulary. He was pleased by the coolness of his thinking. He knew he should feel remorse but he didn't. All he felt was a nagging worry that he had forgotten something or that something might go wrong at the last minute.

It was two by the clock when he came downstairs again. Time to make a move now that the glen was abed. Quietly, he opened the door of the garage, lifting it slightly in case it should drag on the concrete floor, and put the hold-all and the unresisting Eales in the boot of his car. The body had hardly cooled. Rigor mortis had not yet set in though the skin had already begun to lose its elasticity. It was difficult to believe that this limp deadweight, this inedible carcase, this uneconomic commodity, had once been the man who threatened the peace and sweetness of his mind. It seemed unreal, far too good to be true. He half-expected him to open one eye and recite once more his favourite verse:

If ever I marry a wife,
I'll marry a landlord's daughter,
For then I may sit in the bar
And drink cold brandy and water.

With a sudden chill of the spine he remembered that his car battery was almost flat. If he used the self-starter, the whole village would realise, as they turned in their beds, whose car was giving trouble. He opened the off-side window and pushed the car into the road, facing it down the hill that ran out of the west end of the village. He would have to start it on the run when he was clear of the houses, double back around the Block, and take the Garron road without re-entering the village.

He was about to move off when he remembered that he'd forgotten the spade. Brilliant! He went back to the garage and took a spade and a slane for good measure as well as a torch in case he should have need of it. He put the car in second gear and with his foot on the clutch pedal moved off down the slope. Halfway down as he began to gather speed, he let in the clutch. The engine fired at once, and he was off with a song of achievement in his heart.

The Garron road climbed steeply out of the glen for the first mile. He drove in third with the accelerator to the floor, enjoying the cool rush of the night air though the open window. He looked down on the retreating glen to his left. Not one light along the whole length of the north mountain. The ever-vigilant McGing with his back to his wife was probably dreaming of suggilation, saponification, and a score of other forensic arcana that to his chagrin mattered little in booking men for poteen-making or cycling without a light on their bicycles, offences that he considered beneath the consideration of a serious policeman like himself. If only he knew what a golden opportunity he was missing.

Soon he was making straight for the black clouds in the east, the heathery hills stretching darkly on either side. Once he had to change down to second thanks to two foolhardy wethers asleep in the dead centre of the road. Then suddenly after a sharp bend he had reached the flat plateau of bogland that separated the twin parishes of Glenkeel and Glenroe. He turned off the main road on to a narrow bog road that was little better than a dirt track, the rushes along the selvage brushing the wings and the doors. The swinging rays of headlamps came over the crest of the hill to his left. He stopped and switched off his lights while he waited for the car to pass down the main road to the glen. He had got off the Garron road just in time.

Wondering whose car it could be, he parked where tractors usually turned. As he switched off the engine and the lights, the dense blackness of the night rushed up to his very eyeballs. The moor was quiet, the sky low and opaque, and the air heavy and clammy. He strained his ear to listen but neither animal nor insect stirred. Yet he did not feel alone. It seemed to him that a thousand invisible eyes were staring at him out of the darkness. For reassurance he kept telling himself that the whole bog was asleep; that he alone was abroad.

He took the body from the boot, hoisted it on his shoulder so that the arms dangled at his back, gripped the legs and hold-all in his right hand while holding the spade and slane in his left. He stepped gingerly over the narrow drain that ran alongside the road and set off across the bog, treading slowly in case he should trip over a stump of oak or stumble into a hole or drain. It was so dark that he could not make out the turf stacks until he was right beside them. Soon he was on the open moor, which stretched before him flat and featureless for two miles. He would bury Eales in the centre, in an out-of-the-way spot untrodden by human foot, except perhaps that of a sheep farmer in search of a straying ewe or wether. He nearly jumped out of his skin as a flushed snipe rose with an eerie 'scape'. It was a hard summer on the poor buggers. They favoured damp or marshy ground but even the bogs were now quite dry.

When he had walked about a mile, he tested the ground with his boot and laid down his load with a sense of well-earned relief. After urinating at some length he began paring the top sod from a patch of about six feet by three, just wide enough to allow comfort in the digging. The entangled roots of the mountain grass were so tough that he had to put all his might behind each drive of the spade. Soon the sweat was making runnels down his forehead and into his beard but still he worked like a man possessed until he had dug out two spits and could turn to the slane which he preferred to the spade. In spite of four months of dry weather, there was a surprising amount of water in the lower levels of the bog, and before long his shirt and trousers were filthy from rubbing against the sides of the grave.

When his shoulder was level with the brink, he stopped digging. He put Eales lying on his back on the bottom with the hold-all resting on his chest and the plastic bag still adorning his head. As it would have been hypocritical to pause and say a heartfelt prayer over the remains, he filled the grave and put the top sods back in place. Finally, he tamped down the sods with his boot and stood for a moment over his handiwork, savouring the spring of the earth underfoot. It was one of those rare occasions when a memorable insight might be in order, but all he could think of was that in next to no time Eales would be shooting up the most picturesque of bog cotton.

What he now wanted most was to get home without mishap and pour himself a quadruple whiskey. An overwhelming tiredness had begun to creep up his legs and arms but he made his way back doggedly to the car with the slane and spade on his right shoulder. As he neared the spot where he had parked the car, a ragged splotch of ghostly light appeared in the southern sky. The moon showed a veiled face for a fleeting moment, and something resembling a movement caught the tail of his eye. Had it vanished behind the nearest turf stack? His grip on the spade tightened as he stole across to the spot. He leaned against the stack listening for the faintest stir or sound. He walked round the stack. It was his overwrought imagination. There was no one there. Who on earth would be abroad at this hour? Someone stealing a neighbour's turf? Even that was highly unlikely. With an effort of will he put the disquieting thought from mind. Reaching the car, he changed out of his dirty clothes, stowed them in the boot, and put on a clean shirt and trousers.

It was almost four o'clock when he got home. As he closed the garage door, a great raindrop stung the back of his neck. He took no notice but went straight to the bar and poured himself half a tumbler of whiskey. There were several things he should do; wash the floor where Eales had fallen, have a bath, and burn the trousers and shirt he had worn at the interment. Otherwise, in the event of an investigation he might find it difficult to explain how they had become so turf-caked. However, he decided to put off until tomorrow what he need not do that night. He would get up in time for eleven o'clock Mass and open the pub as usual at twelve, as if it were any normal Sunday, presenting to his customers a picture of composure and light-hearted bonhomie. Then in the holy hours between two and four, when all good Catholics were at lunch, he would attend to what was necessary.

He longed to sleep and forget, but now that the action of the night was over, his mind was racing madly, dwelling on minutiae, and even questioning his good judgement. He put Schumann's cello concerto on the gramophone and lay on the bed, sipping the whiskey and listening to the recurrent sadness of the first movement, wondering if Schumann could have anticipated with eerie insight the entangled state of his thoughts. He needed ambiguous music, sounds that would bring glimpses of heaven while hinting at the darkness in life's bottomless well. In this respect Schumann was the composer *par excellence*, particularly the Schumann of the cello concerto. Never was the struggle between light and dark, between conscious and unconscious, keener than in Schumann; yet it was not expressed as a struggle but as a fusion of opposites that tantalised the mind with the suggestion of other less 'imperfect' musical possibilities. Listening to him was like looking into a well after a pebble had disturbed the water: a precise reflection threatened to form while the water continued to tilt and sway, distorting the image, teasing the mind in search of facile symmetry. Yet as you looked, it was possible to gain an indistinct idea of the reflection. Though the image was broken, it was recognisable as something remote yet deeply personal.

With a gratifying awareness of rhythmic abridgement, he closed his eyes while his fingers clasped the tumbler on the bedside table. He opened his eyes again, aware of nothing but a searing pain in his rectum, a keenly stinging pain that had made him taste salty tears running down his cheeks into his mouth. He must have slept. The record had finished and he could not remember having heard the last movement. He ground his teeth and pressed hard as if pressing would expel the pain. Was this to be his earthly punishment, a summary visitation of the unvanquished enemy, followed by total colostomy to prolong a life no longer worth prolonging? God Almighty! As a punishment, it was more appropriate to buggery than homicide. Bent in two, he groped his way in the dark to the toilet and sat on the naked bowl, too absorbed in his pain to lower the wooden seat. What he now desired was an elephantine defecation, to discharge in one thundering avalanche this fundamental ache that threatened the very roots of his reason. He pressed and pressed to no purpose. Surely no civilised deity would sanction as condign punishment a phantom crap to plague and torture till the end of time! If there was such a thing as divine justice in the world, this wasn't it. He pressed again until the blood rose to his face. Unannounced and unexpected, a blistering fart, like a shot from a gun barrel, ripped through his rear, dispelling in a moment all but the memory of pain. What heavenly relief! It was as if he had been reprieved at the point of death. The absence of earthly pain was paradisal pleasure. Eales would never again feel pain. But neither would he feel this pleasure. What he had done was not a perfect solution. He had placed a greater value on Cecily's purity than on Eales's depraved desires, and what father— certainly not a heavenly father—could blame him? Human life by its very nature was imperfect, as every theologian knew. He had merely taken the least imperfect path.

He was about to go bed when he realised that he was at the centre of a Niagara of falling water. A clap of thunder, a cracking, splintering sound, reminded him of his tree. He went to the window and pulled back the heavy curtains. They were stiff to saturation, and the carpet under his feet was soaking. Rain was falling out of the sky, not in drops but in a splashing stream that came through the open window and poured down his face and neck. The night was shaken by one thunderbolt after another, the sky torn by fleeing light that seemed to have neither pattern nor purpose, neither beginning nor end.

He put on his slippers and went downstairs and out into the garden. It was within half-an-hour of dawn; he could just make out the dark pyramidal outline of the stricken tree. Soon he was soaking from head to foot as if someone had emptied a keeler of water on his head. He stood under the conifer as the rain made rivulets down his face and chest, imagining the heavenly water being absorbed by the tinder-dry needles, into the sapwood, into the very heartwood. Overhead the sky was a cupola of flame. He visualised the darkness over the bog being rent by bluish light, and water flooding in streams where there never had been a stream before, expunging footprints, swelling the surface of the sod, burying his secret deeper and rendering a fathom unfathomable. It all ended as quickly as it had presumably begun. The streaming and splashing dwindled in a flurry of droplets. He became aware of the dripping of the tree like the susurration of blood in his ears.

As the storm receded into the northwest, he went inside, towelled himself with luxurious care, and lay down in his pelt. He woke in daylight, refreshed by a sleep without dreams. After a copious breakfast of black pudding, bacon, eggs and tomatoes, he went into the garden again to savour the freshest, most intoxicating smell in the world, the smell of the earth after rain. Under the heat of the forenoon sun, the flowers, grass and leaves, after a long parching, gave off a subtle odour that cleansed his memory of the remaining shades of agitation. It was as if he had only dreamt of Eales and his obsessions. He was strong and full of purpose again. Now it seemed to him that there was nothing he could not do.

The Vietnam war : a film by Ken Burns and Lynn Novick / directed by Ken

Date Due   **22 Nov 2019**

To renew your items:

Go online to librariesireland ie com

Phone us at (01) 668 9575

Opening Hours Mon & Tue 1pm to 8pm

Wed & Thu 10 00am to 5 00pm

Fri & Sat 10am to 1pm & 1 45pm to 5pm

FOUR

Potter would have liked a bath before dinner but a bathroom was not among the amenities of the cottage he had rented from Rory Rua. As a makeshift solution he had arranged with Roarty to use his bath once a week; and though Sunday was not his regular bath night, he got out his towel, wrapped it round a bottle of bath oil, and put it in the car to have at the ready.

He had been in the glen since May, and after three months he was at last beginning to feel that he was no longer a stranger, thanks largely to Roarty and his pub. For the first month he had done his drinking in McGonigle's at the top end of the village, which was much frequented by sheep-farmers from the depths of the north mountain who talked mainly about yeld ewes, liver fluke, scrapie, and grass tetany. Night after night he had listened to the sing-song of their conversation, regretting that his knowledge of sheep shearing and dipping was so scant, and wondering if they might be interested to hear of the problems of lawn-mowing in the London suburbs. Then one evening he went into Roarty's for a change and he never went back to McGonigle's again.

Roarty's was smaller and smokier with an old-fashioned flagged floor and a bar so arranged that the farmers and fishermen from the shore townlands who drank in it could all take part in the same conversation. Whoever designed it had probably done so unthinkingly but he had created a place of converse for the like of which many a sophisticated architect strove in vain. On his first evening the customers eyed him as he entered and continued their conversation as if they had not seen him. He ordered a large Scotch, and as an afterthought specified a Glenmorangie, which Roarty poured from a bottle that had been collecting dust on the top shelf. A small, hungry-looking youth whom he later came to know as Cor Mogaill looked up at him with a smile and said, 'I've often wondered how many centuries it takes a people to evolve your pronunciation of the word "Scotch".'

'No longer than it took to evolve your pronunciation of the word, I imagine.' He was reluctant to become embroiled in a discussion on social history that might explode in politics.

'You must be English,' said Cor Mogaill. 'Do I detect the tones of the Home Counties in your accent?'

'Yes, I am English. I'm pleased you can tell.'

'Put English on *ruamheirg*, then,' said the youth with apparent innocence.

The other customers turned their heads and looked at Cor Mogaill and Potter with wide-eyed amusement. One or two laughed as they waited for his reply.

'If you tell me what it is, I might conceivably be able to oblige,' he said drily.

'It's a trick question,' said a tall, sad-faced man at his elbow whom he later discovered to be Gimp Gillespie. 'A question without a straight answer.'

'It must have an English name,' said Potter with a hint of chauvinism that was not lost on the company.

'It's the reddish brown water you find here in hillside streams that run over iron ore in the ground. Rusty water, you might say, but the literal meaning of *ruamheirg* is "red rust".'

I'm sure there's an English name for it,' Potter insisted. 'I just don't know it.'

That was how he'd made the acquaintance of Gimp Gillespie, now his boon companion. Gillespie was a journalist who had no illusions about his craft; he used Roarty's not merely to dull his over-active senses but to snap up what little news there was in the glen. Gillespie told him that the hungry-looking youth was the village intellectual and that 'Put English on *ruamheirg*' was a local phrase that meant 'Square the circle'.

'So if I'd known the English word, I'd have become a local hero?'

'We don't take it quite so seriously,' Gillespie explained. 'There are certain key words that occur again and again in conversation here. *Ruamheirg* is one and *cál leannógach* is another. We all laugh whenever we hear them. They keep us amused in the long winter nights. If you wish to enjoy yourself here, you'd better begin finding words like *ruamheirg* amusing.'

He looked at Gillespie's melancholy face, wondering if he had responded correctly. Was all this nonsense an example of rueful Irish humour or was he having his leg pulled, however gently? He couldn't be sure which, and he felt that it did not matter. He was pleased to have met someone whose company he could enjoy.

'Are all your key-words in Irish?' he asked.

'Most are Irish words for which there is no English equivalent. The only exception I can recall is "replevy".'

'Replevy? I've heard of "replevin," a legal term, something to do with the recovery of goods and chattels.'

'Here we use it to mean a loud noise. If you had the misfortune to fart violently in company, Cor Mogaill might say, "Potter discharged a replevy that would wake the dead."'

'I wonder what the Law Society would say to that.'

'I just thought I'd mention it to save you possible confusion.'

'It's very kind of you, I'm sure,' said Potter.

He had been through a form of induction, he realised. Now they saw him as one of themselves, or so it seemed. Whenever he entered the pub, Roarty would pour him his favourite Scotch without waiting to be asked, and the regulars would involve him in their disputatious conversations as if he were a countryman like themselves. Their talk, as you might expect, was of the country, often of subjects that could well form the last item on *The Times* letters page. They would discuss at length whether wild duck feed with curlews because of the vigilance of the latter. One or two of them might contend that the curlews acted as sentinels for the whole flock while the rest would argue that curlews were too restless and noisy to make easy companions for other wild fowl. The essence of these arguments was that no one knew the answers, and for this reason Potter's olympian judgements were much appreciated by the company.

He turned to the kitchen window and gazed down at the rocks and knolls that fell away sharply to the sea. The waves were winking in the descending sun and Rory Rua in a red shirt was lifting lobster creels in the bay. He thought it would be pleasant to sit by the west window in Roarty's, nursing a Scotch while the evening drifted into night. After a drink or two he would have a bath, and after another few drinks he would come home and cook the lobster Rory Rua gave him that morning. He left the door on the latch, pleased that he could do so in the knowledge that burglary was unknown in the glen. It was a lovely evening after the rain of the previous night, and he drove slowly to the village, enjoying the view of the north mountain, a jigsaw of fields, roads and cottages with here and there a straight plume of smoke rising from a potless chimney.

The bar would be empty at this hour; the regulars never came in before nine. Roarty would be alone as Eales always went dancing on Sunday evenings; and if Roarty was alone, he'd be game for an off-beat conversation. Thanks to his encyclopedia, he was a treasury of useless information. He could talk about everything from phlogiston to fish-plates but his favourite topic was drink and all its concomitants, ancient and modern—pins and firkins and hogsheads, faucets, spiles and spigots not to mention the kilderkin, tierce and puncheon. Potter could listen to him for hours theorising about the effect of Irish whiskey on the dark side of the Celtic soul; and as for his knowledge of fishing and shooting, it was unsurpassed.

He parked his car opposite the pub where the road was widest, and bent his head under the low lintel as he entered. Roarty was immersed in the Sunday newspapers while Gimp Gillespie was seated by the west window contemplating a creamy pint on the table before him.

'I wasn't expecting to see you at this hour,' he said.

'I felt like a snifter before dinner, and I didn't have any Scotch in the house.'

He listened pleasurably to Gillespie praising the forbearance of the Irish bachelor in the face of the rapacity of village windows. 'They acquired the taste from their dead husbands, and now they're insatiable addicts,' he said. Gillespie was a good conversationalist; there was a hint of rumination in everything he said, which gave his lightest remark a substance reflecting the melancholy of his long face, which was never far from spontaneous laughter.

Roarty was seated on his high stool behind the bar, holding the newspaper at arm's length as he read. Even in his present hunched position he looked impressive. He was tall, broad-backed, bald and bearded with an air of stillness that put Potter in mind of early mornings on the mountain. Was it the stillness of self-possession or self-absorption, he wondered idly. When you met him in the street, the first thing you noticed was his bow-legged walk; but seated behind the bar, you could only see his top half, and then it was the bulky head that impressed. It was a noble head with a grizzled beard from the depth of which emerged a sand-blasted, straight-stemmed pipe. Beardless, he would have been red-faced. As it was, the brewer's flush of his cheeks showed above the greyness of the beard, contrasting oddly with the pale skin of his bald head. The bushiness of the beard concealed closely placed ears. As you looked him full in the face, you could not see them, and you felt that there was something missing—which gave his head a rare quality that remained in the memory.

Pulling a pint of stout, he would eye the rising froth, his head tilted sideways, the cast of his half-hidden lips betraying serious concern. But when the pint was nicely topped, his eyes would light up momentarily as he placed it before the expectant customer. At such moments one felt that because of some pessimistic streak in his nature, he did not expect the pint to be perfect and that he was continually surprised by the successful combination of brewer's technology and his own handiwork. The pint served, he would reach out a big hand with well-kept nails and take your money with an absentmindedness that robbed the transaction of anything reminiscent of the cold-blooded self-interest of commerce.

In speech and bearing, he was quite different from the farmers and fishermen on the other side of the counter, hardy, bony men who went out unthinkingly in all weathers. They were men who put Potter in mind of bare uplands, grey rocks, and forlorn roads in the mountains. Even in the twilight of the pub they wore their peaked caps down over their eyes, and though they could be seen squinting occasionally from beneath them, there was an unflinchingness in their gaze, as if they believed that looking could change the object looked at. Their lean faces bore spiders' webs of deeply etched lines that branched from eye corners or crisscrossed stubbled chins, expressing a noble stoicism in the face of life's unremitting adversity. Roarty, on the other hand bore the marks of easy living. He was fleshy rather than wiry, a man who had never experienced sun or wind except from personal choice.

'Where is Eales this evening?' Gillespie asked. 'Dancing in Glenties, I suppose?'

'I wish I knew.' Roarty put down his paper with an air of impatience. 'I got up this morning to find his room empty, the bed not slept in. Wherever he went, he took his hold-all with him.'

'You don't mean to say he's done a bunk?'

'I don't know what else to think.'

'And the bugger owes me a fiver!' said Gillespie.

'That's the younger generation! No sense of responsibility.' Roarty said with feeling.

'I should have known better. Never trust a Kerryman, not even if he's been caught young.' Gillespie looked mournfully through his wallet.

'He must have left after I went to bed,' Roarty grumbled.

'He couldn't have walked out over the hill in that rain. He must have got a lift.'

'I wonder what lift he could have got at that hour.' Roarty shook his noble head.

'There's a woman behind all this,' Gillespie said knowingly. 'I've never known a man so given over to women. He couldn't meet a girl on the road without putting the comether on her. Sixty-six equals forty-six equals sixteen: that was his philosophy. They say he even tossed one or two schoolgirls.'

'He's left me in the lurch,' said Roarty. 'If you hear of anyone looking for a job as barman, let me know.'

After another drink Potter went out to get his towel and bath oil from the car, only to find Cor Mogaill with a knapsack on his back looking up the exhaust pipe of his Volvo. Ignoring him, Potter opened the car door but Cor Mogaill still kept his eye to the exhaust pipe. There were certain things about the Irish he'd never understand. He lay in the bath for half an hour looking out through the open window at the evening sky changing from screened to solid pink in the west. Between the sky and the window was a mountain ash, and on its topmost branch a blackbird was whistling his heart out, the sparrows and thrushes mute with admiration. There was magic in the Donegal evenings, in the luminous twilights that were long enough to seem like days in miniature. He soaped his arms and thought of the long evening ahead, knowing that his dinner would wait till after closing time.

'Ireland is full of wonders,' he told Gillespie on his return. 'Just now I found Cor Mogaill with one eye to the exhaust pipe of my car.'

'Cor Mogaill looks up the exhaust of other people's cars as a journalist might look up a word in a dictionary.'

'Or a woman's skirt?' suggested Potter.

'A sexual fixation, would you say?'

'Undoubtedly. How interesting that the love of cars should manifest itself so extremely—and in rural Ireland, too.'

'And in a man who rides a woman's bicycle as well!'

'Now, in England that would never happen. I know several suburban men whose lives are their cars. They talk about them, dream about them, copulate in them, and when they drive into the country on Sundays they sit in them eating sandwiches. Yet not one of them would be seen dead looking up the exhaust of another man's car.'

'You English are so sophisticated!'

'Or sexually self-aware perhaps. Have you ever thought of writing something about our learned friend? A brief study of car love with special reference to exhaust—or should I say, anal?—eroticism.'

'Surely, that would be risking ostracism and excommunication!'

'Cor Mogaill sees himself as the village intellectual but he's closer in my opinion to being the village idiot.'

'He's no idiot,' Gillespie said pensively. 'But he's certainly the village atheist.'

Outside, the sky had darkened except for a lingering streak of pink in the west. The warm breeze coming through the window enclosed them both in a cocoon of comfort. The pub was full without being crowded, and Roarty had half-a-dozen pints of stout lined up for topping.

'Here, have a chew of dillisk,' said Crubog, who had just joined them.

'What is it?' asked Potter half-suspiciously.

'It's dulse. Seaweed that grows on the rocks here.'

'Is it good for the virility?' Potter enquired.

'And what is virility?' asked the old man.

'Does it make you more attractive to women?' Potter shouted in his ear.

'No, but it's great for the worms. You'll never again pass a worm if you eat a fistful of dillisk first thing in the morning and last thing at night.'

'It's got a salty taste,' Potter said. 'It makes me long for another Scotch.'

'That isn't what I wanted to talk to you about,' Crubog confided. 'Keep your wits about you when you're dealing with Rory Rua. He's greedy for land. He wants to buy my large mountain acreage, and he wants it for a song. He may give you a lobster now and again to get round you, but there's wickedness in that red head of his, believe me.'

'Thanks for the tip,' Potter said with a smile.

'Another thing, if he offers you sloke—that's another seaweed—take it but be careful. It makes you fart like thunder.'

'You mean "replevy" of course,' Potter smiled.

'The very word. Stick to the dillisk. Here, have another chew.'

He felt sure that Crubog was angling for a drink, and he was in no mood to disappoint an engaging octogenarian.'

'Can I buy you a drink,' he asked, placing his empty glass on the counter.

'Not tonight, sir. In six months' time maybe, when you know me better.'

'You've made an impression on Crubog,' said Gillespie when the old man had gone. 'It must be your sporting English manner. Crubog, for all his years, is a bit of a snob. He only takes to visitors with the right tone of voice and the right kind of swagger.'

'I don't know whether or not I should feel flattered.'

'Are you sufficiently English to wish not to disappoint him?' Gillespie asked with disarming directness.

'Would it be immodest to say I'm convinced I shan't?'

He regretted having said it. Gillespie's knowing smile told him that his friend had laid a trap for him. Gillespie was like that. After all he was a journalist, cynically convinced of his powers of penetration into other people's minds. He placed a hand on Gillespie's sleeve.

'Now I must deal with a matter of greater urgency,' he said, heading for the back door.

He went out into the garden and stood in the dark under Roarty's dead tree, but try as he might he could not urinate. He leaned against the tree and asked himself why he needed to escape, to be for a moment alone. Tears of longing welled up in his eyes. His loneliness was neither of the glen nor the country. He had felt it increasingly since his fortieth birthday, and the cooling of his relationship with Margaret. Though they weren't married, they had been doing everything together. In the early days she bestowed on him a point of rest from which to confront the world. She had given him form and direction as well as something of the unconsidered gladness of boyhood, and what is more she did it unobtrusively, simply by her presence and conversation.

Then they never discussed their feelings for each other; they talked mainly of the trifles of daily living, clothing them in a magic that was mutual, making them into symbols from which they drew strength and encouragement. Then out of the blue, Margaret became a vivisectionist. In her passion for analysis, she began tearing their lives apart. One day he realised that their powers of transmutation, his as well as hers, had faded. Trapped in their own forms of inner exploration, they were now wanderers in a once common demesne, having mislaid the flint that lights the annealing fires of life to illuminate the way. Margaret suggested they should try living apart for a year.

'At the end of the year we'll meet again and see what happens,' she said.

'Where will you go?' he asked, thinking she would not have a ready answer.

'I'll stay with Poppy until I find a place of my own. It isn't what you think. I just need more space, more time to be myself.'

'You're looking for something—or somebody,' he said.

'I shouldn't like us to fall out. We'll keep in touch. You'll always be part of my life.'

'Is it because you want a baby before it's too late?'

'No, it isn't that. Try to understand, Ken. I must discover what I can do on my own before I can live happily with anyone else.'

Margaret was a girl who liked to keep her options open. Though she had left him for her childhood friend Poppy, she felt unable to turn her back on him entirely. She kept phoning him to ask how he was coping, and to tell him about all the interesting things she'd been doing. She saw him as a backstop who'd never let her down.

One evening a fortnight after she'd left, as he arrived home from the office, she phoned to say that she'd had a brainwave. 'I simply knew this morning that I must cook you dinner for old times' sake,' she added. He told her to come round by all means, that he felt sure she'd find something in the fridge she could cook. He had a bath and put on a fresh shirt, knowing that if he didn't, she would say he was 'reverting to type', the type in question being the male troglodyte. He listened to two Scarlatti sonatas as he waited for her knock, and observed the businesslike way she went straight to the fridge to assess the culinary possibilities of the contents. She was not impressed.

'You're not looking after yourself, Ken. You're quietly going to pot.'

'I thought we might order a pizza,' he said. 'They deliver within half an hour.'

'I'll buy you dinner since there's nothing here worth cooking.' She came across and adjusted his shirt collar. 'We'll go to the Mazzini, and I'll tell you about all the fun I've been having. I had no idea how foolish the world has become.'

'The Mazzini is noisy. You'll find sausages in the fridge. I'll help you make the batter. I fancy toad in the hole, and they don't do it in restaurants.'

The simplicity of his expectations had an extraordinary effect on her. She laughed as she hugged him and gave him a long and, for Margaret, quite passionate kiss.

'I hope you don't mind,' he said. 'It's just that I'm too tired to go out.'

'I know what you fancy, and I know how you like it,' she breathed, touching him lightly. 'We'll go to bed and listen to your music. Then I'll cook your favourite comfort food.'

He couldn't help laughing at her effortless familiarity. Still, he knew that she knew what he liked and how he liked it. What he didn't know and would never know was whether she liked it as well. Sometimes he suspected that in her heart she was just humouring him. At other times he wondered if she enjoyed a sense of patronage and power in knowing him in ways no other woman had ever known him.

In the bedroom he discovered that she'd come fully equipped. She was wearing the bra and knickers he'd bought her for Valentine's Day. 'I thought I'd give you a little thrill,' she smiled, doing a pirouette to demonstrate the sparkle of her armour. He knew she meant it kindly, that it was her way of being romantic, but he thought it a little patronising, nonetheless. What she would never realise was the wounding power of her frilly darts, which defeated her purpose and left him longing for the comforts of what she called 'the feminine touch', which he in his rueful way thought of as the most elusive touch in the long, long history of feminism.

Her unexpected visit was the first of several, after which he began questioning the purpose of their separation, as she apparently saw it. She seemed intent on keeping a foot in his door while denying him an opportunity to keep a foot in hers. He did not wish to offend her, nor did he wish to sever all ties with her. Since he thought it best to absent himself from her feminine touch for a while, the offer of a year's secondment in Ireland could not have come at a better time. It would give him a chance to be alone with himself in the field and perhaps discover things he would never discover in an office or in the bustling variety of an overflowing city. He might even find out how to live with a woman without intruding on her hallowed ground; to live with her in such a way that she would not think of deserting him for the cosy reassurances of a childhood friend.

Margaret's response to the news of his transfer was predictable. 'Poor Ken, I don't envy you,' she said when he told her that he'd been posted to Donegal. 'Poppy's grandmother came from Donegal and spoke an obscure lingo which was neither Irish nor English. You may be understood, but you'll never understand.'

He disregarded Margaret's less than disinterested views, and arrived in Glenkeel determined to make the best of things. He rented a cottage from the fisherman Rory Rua and settled down to a solitary rural life. At first he missed the sexual gratification intrinsic to Margaret's companionship. He found it difficult to sleep at night. He shivered in bed, though the May weather was mild. Gradually, however, he began to savour the pleasures of self-sufficiency. After coming home in the evening he would make himself a bowl of soup and then, as he waited for a simple meal to cook, listen to chamber music, mainly Bach or Mozart, and drink a Scotch or two. The bachelor life was not without its benefits, but now and again the loneliness of the mountains would cloud his day. Then he could only look forward to Roarty's in the evening and a chat with Gimp Gillespie, Cor Mogaill and the others. Margaret still wrote to him but he knew she was unlikely to intrude on him in this most sequestered of outposts.

Roarty was sharing a joke with Gillespie when he returned to the bar, and there was another Scotch waiting for him on the counter. He felt slightly tipsy, though it was still an hour off closing time, and he knew from experience that the next sixty minutes would slip past before he'd had a chance to grasp even one of them.

'Have you had any good rural rides here?' Gillespie gave him a serious glance.

'The last time I rode a horse was in a gymkhana competition twenty years ago.'

'I wasn't thinking of mares,' said Gillespie, pouring a too-high bottle of stout with unavailing care. 'I was thinking of women.'

'Only a journalist could make such an execrable pun.'

'You haven't answered my question.'

'The answer is no.'

'But there have been women in your life?'

'Enough to satisfy my curiosity.'

'Now you've said it. Once a man has satisfied his curiosity, the rest is routine.'

'I'd like to think about that in bed on a cold winter night.'

'I've had only one woman in my time, and that was just to see what it was like. I picked her up in a pub in Shepherd's Bush. An old tart that drank free gin in exchange for a tumble. She must have been sixty, and her reddish hair was so stiff with lacquer that it felt like wire in my fingers. In the bedroom she took off an old pair of stays that hadn't seen the wash since before I was born.'

'What was it like with stays? Was it erotic or did it put you off women for good?'

'It put me off *loose women* but not *a woman*. I've been in love with the same woman since I was fourteen, and I've never had as much as a kiss off her.'

'Surely no woman is worth such devotion.'

'This woman lit a candle in my mind that will never go out. Thinking about her has kept me warm through colder winters than any you've known in London.'

Gillespie was gazing down into his glass as if reading his past in the physiognomy of the creamy top. His long face seemed to grow longer, his lower lip drooped, and for one disconcerting moment Potter thought that he might weep. His heart went out to him as a fellow sufferer in the misconstructions of the sexes. Gillespie looked up with a melancholy smile. 'Without her I'd be a sapless stick,' he said.

'Does she live locally?'

'I see her from a distance at least once a week, at eleven o'clock Mass on Sundays. You're a different case from me. You're still footloose, still capable of fancying a rub of more than a single relic.'

'What is this relic you all keep talking about?'

'It's what you call the leg-over.'

'A bit of the other. Please continue. '

'If you were to have an affair here, what kind would you wish for?'

'Something light-hearted and amusing, something to engage the mind as well as the heart.'

'You mean you want conversation as well as copulation?'

'In a nutshell. I'm over forty, you see, at an age when the demands of the intellect begin to exact their due.'

'Don't say another word. I'll have you fixed up before the night is out.'

He looked at Gillespie to see if he was being serious. Gillespie was drawing on a burnt-down cigarette, one eye closed against the smoke and his right arm resting casually between the bottles on the counter.

'There are three possibilities,' Gillespie explained. 'There's Monica Manus but she's a man-eater. There's Biddy Mhór but I'm told her natural juices are dry, and who wants to be bothered with axle-grease? And then there's Maggie Hession.'

'Who is Maggie Hession?'

'She's the local nurse and a snappy conversationalist. You did say you wanted conversation.'

'Among other things. But what's her age?' Potter asked, beginning to appreciate the humour of his situation.

'She's barely thirty, ripe for the plucking. When she was a girl of sixteen, she dropped her knickers for a kilted Scotsman who was here on holiday, and no mortal man has had any luck with her since.'

'Maybe she's waiting for the return of Sandy.'

'I think he hurt her. He was a bull of a man, you see, and she's only a sliver. Some say he was equipped with a veritable caber.'

'But that doesn't mean a thing!'

'You're a strange engineer. It's a question of volumes, man. You can't put a quart into a pint pot.'

'Now I know why you're still a bachelor.'

'Finish your drink. We'll corner her before bedtime.'

'But it's nearly eleven!'

'No one here goes to bed before twelve. And if we find her in her night dress, so much the better.'

It was a lovely night with cool airs and what sounded like recitatives coming up from the sea. They lingered for a moment in the street, listening to the wild rumble of conversation inside and Roarty shouting 'Time'; hoarse from exertion.

'Roarty is a landlord in a thousand,' Potter said. 'In a sense he is wasted here.'

'He's a spoilt priest, you know. He saw the glory of the Golden City and turned his back on it.'

'This morning he asked me the meaning of "ergonomically designed".'

'I wonder why he wanted to know that. What on earth did you tell him?'

'Designed for efficiency, to minimise human effort.'

'He must be going to install a newfangled stout dispenser,' said Gillespie.

At the crossroads outside the village they turned left onto a fenceless road, and the moonlit mountain before them gleamed with cottage lights. The night was blissfully quiet, except for the deep breathing of cattle in wayside byres, drowned occasionally by the eerie cry of a curlew from the shore. They walked in silence while Potter wondered what on earth he was doing on such an errand. He felt truly happy, replete with the peace of the country and an inviolable sense of detachment. And what pleased him most was that

Margaret would be surprised, even horrified, if she could see him. All in all he felt inspired.

Halfway up the hill Gillespie halted by a blackthorn bush and farted. Potter faced the ditch and waited for his water to come. Holding his insentient penis between his forefinger and thumb, he studied a sky dappled with light cloud; a mackerel sky with patches of empty blue, and at its centre a moon near the full with its rim so bright that he asked himself if such brilliance could be mere reflection. The clouds were so light that you could not see them passing over the moon's face. They looked as if they'd gone behind the moon while the bottomless blue of the night sky lay behind them both. He watched the moon ride high and fast until it sailed straight into a sea of pure blue, in which it lay for a moment becalmed, suddenly bereft of its halo. Wondering if his imagination was wide enough to encompass the true scope and import of what he'd observed, he suddenly thought again of Margaret. She was standing on a cliff edge by the sea. With his camera he had caught her in profile as she faced into the wind, her long, fair hair streaming behind her. He could never look at that picture without feeling diminished. Her beauty was like the night sky, beyond his earthbound comprehension. Now that she had left him, he was like Gillespie or any ordinary man.

'It takes rain to settle the wind,' said Gillespie as his water splashed vigorously against a rock, but Potter, buttoning with deep concentration, did not answer.

'Maggie Hession lives in the groin of the hill. You can see her light from here,' Gillespie pointed.

'I've had second thoughts, I'm going no further. She's bound to tumble to our game.'

'I've got a plan. You pretend you've sprained your ankle and that you've come to have it bandaged.'

'But I haven't sprained my ankle!'

'How is she to know?'

'She's a nurse, isn't she?'

'You're thinking like a clapped-out bachelor. What you need is another Scotch.'

'I don't need another Scotch. I've already had a skinful.'

'A word of advice then. Surrender to the genius of the country.'

They'd already reached the laneway that led to the house. They could see the light from the kitchen window cutting cater across the lawn to the untrimmed fuchsia hedge at the end. They stood in the shadow of the gable, making final adjustments to their clothes and expressions, suppressing laughter like two schoolboys.

'This has got to look good,' said Gillespie. 'Hop up on my back and I'll carry you in.'

'What if you should let me fall? You're not exactly sober.'

'Then she'll have to bandage both of us.'

He bent forward and gripped Potter behind the knees, while Potter placed a hand on each of his shoulders.

'Hup!' said Gillespie, hoisting Potter onto his back.

'If we're not careful, we'll be had up for attempted buggery,' Potter giggled.

'But we'll plead that it was all in the service of heterosexuality.'

With a sway and a stagger, Gillespie rounded the corner of the house into the light from the open door, keeping close to the wall in case he should lose his balance.

'I'm on a mission of mercy. No less than a corporal work of mercy,' Gillespie called from the door.

'Come in, will you, and rest your burden on the settle,' said a young woman who was knitting by the fire.

'My burden is nothing less than an English gentleman. Nora Hession, Kenneth Potter.'

She reached up and took Potter's hand, smiling with small teeth at his obvious discomfort. She wasn't what he had expected; though younger than Margaret, she was not as good looking. About her mouth and eyes were lines of laughter, or possibly sadness, that gave her face a touch of quiet inwardness and told him that she might be a girl who did not take life easy. He had an impression of extreme fragility, of transparent skin and light bone that demanded to be handled with extreme care. For a moment he wondered if she were recovering from one of those wasting conditions that used to beset talented ladies of the nineteenth century. But no, she was probably more like one of those rare water birds that light once in a wonder on some secluded mountain tarn.

'We need a nurse. Where is Maggie?' Gillespie asked.

'She's down in Paddy Óg's—his wife's in labour,' the girl answered.

'What ails you?' She turned to Potter.

'My ankle,' he said, stretching out his leg on the settle and leaning forward to feel the source of his misery. 'I slipped as I was coming up Gara's Brae.'

'Take off your shoe and sock and I'll bathe your foot for you.'

'You mustn't go to all that trouble. I'll take him down to Paddy Óg's to see Maggie,' Gillespie promised.

'The lane is rough, and it's dark under the trees,' Nora advised. 'Stay as you are and I'll see what I can do.'

She put on the kettle, and while she was getting a bandage from the bedroom Gillespie told him that Nora was not the kind of light-hearted girl he'd had in mind, and that Maggie was more his type. He was so eager to take him to meet

Maggie that Potter soon put two and two together. Nora poured warm water into an enamel basin and placed it on the floor beside the settle. He put his foot in the basin as she knelt beside him with a sponge, her black hair, pale complexion, and hollow cheeks forming a picture of light and shadow that reminded him of a figure from El Greco. As she looked up, he felt the light of her smile on his face, a short burst of sunshine on a January day turning all that was mutable to silver rather than gold. She was wearing light-blue jeans and an open-collared shirt of darker blue which crinkled rather than swelled where her breasts were. Her unpolished toenails peeping through her sandals reminded him of Maureen's before she took to reading the fashion pages. He told himself that here was a girl who had nothing in common with any girl he'd ever met, a girl who might unthinkingly lead a lost man out of a labyrinth.

'You're the first girl I've seen here in jeans.'

'It's my day off. I don't wear them usually because Canon Loftus doesn't approve.'

'What's he got to do with you?'

'I'm his housekeeper.'

'Have you sold your soul to him?'

'He's only a parish priest, not the devil.' She searched his face with wide, black eyes.

'You'd make a good nurse, Nora. The pain is going already.'

'All you needed was sympathy,' she smiled. 'Men are like that. Even the Canon likes being pampered.'

She towelled his foot and went outside to empty the basin into the runnel. As she crossed the floor, he noticed that her feet were not white but brown, as if she'd been standing all day in bog water, a thought he found curiously affecting.

'We'll go now,' said Gillespie. 'We'll go down to Paddy Óg's to see Maggie.'

'Enough is enough,' said Potter firmly.

While they were inside, a great continent of cloud had risen in the east, propelled by a wind from the land. Expanding in all directions and thinning at the edges, it passed over the face of the moon which had become a dull plate, all its brilliance gone. The cloud continued to expand until its black heart swallowed the moon and only a few uncertain stars in the west provided what light there was in the sky.

They walked down the lane in silence, surprisingly sober after the evening's drinking. As they reached the road, Gillespie said, 'Now don't get any ideas about Nora, will you? She's my girl and no one else's.'

'Something I noticed about her toes. The third is longer than the second.'

'She's an interesting girl, but wait till you see her sister Maggie.'

FIVE

'Can anyone be happy who thinks of happiness every day?' Roarty asked himself as he polished a pint tumbler.

It was just after opening time and the empty pub looked shipshape to his approving eye: the floor swept, the seats neatly ranged, a clean ashtray on each table, the beer and stout shelves full, and a fresh bunch of ferns in the empty fireplace. Turning to the big west window, he watched an open boat running on lobster creels in the bay. Though he couldn't see the head of the red setter in the bow, he could just make out Rory Rua's red pullover, and he wondered with satisfaction how many of the men who came into his pub could recognise a man on the far side of Rannyweal. For that you needed a keener eye than most men, even most countrymen, could lay claim to. He wasn't boasting but he could count the loopholes and parapets of the tower on Glen Head from where he stood. It was one of the reasons he was as good a shot as Dr Loftus, though Loftus was reckoned to be the best in the county.

His eye wandered over the fields by the sea where men in shirt sleeves were mowing and women in aprons were turning hay with rakes. It was a bright morning; it would be another warm day. And the men bent over their scythes would be sweating and thirsty, imagining a cool pint of ale or stout at the end. There was no denying; it was a great summer for the trade. He looked up Gara's Brae, and sure enough Crubog was already halfway down, keeping to the green selvage with irregular hops, avoiding the rough centre which would irritate the corns and bunions of his old feet. He was always the first customer, apart from the odd commercial traveller who fancied a quick one between calls.

'Can anyone be happy who thinks of happiness every day? Yes,' said Roarty. 'I am happy, and I think of happiness all the time.'

He had the murder to thank for this unaccustomed state of bliss. It was a perfect murder and a triumph of intelligence in the most testing circumstances. And far from falling prey to Macbeth's rooted sorrow or 'that perilous stuff that weighs upon the heart', his perceptions had quickened, his joy in life had intensified. On the morning after the fateful night he had looked at a rose and felt himself being drawn into a dimension whose existence he had never suspected. Its beauty seemed to hint at worlds beyond his wildest yearnings, yet entirely within his grasp if only... He brushed a petal with his forefinger and experienced a pleasure so rare and immediate that it could only have come from having made the world safer for simple innocence. It occurred to him that in ending life he had acquired a keener sensibility and sharper and more subtle powers of penetration.

It had been a week of potential catastrophe but because he had been born with the perception of misfortune he was not unprepared; he'd had the presence of mind to convert possible danger into actual security. On the morning after the murder, as he was enjoying his breakfast in the kitchen, Allegro wandered in, looked at him indifferently, and yawned.

He could barely believe his eyes. How could he have forgotten Eales's cats? Allegro must have been out all night, 'doing what tomcats do best', as Eales used to put it. But where was his comrade in lechery, Andante? And how could he convince anyone, especially McGing, that Eales had willingly left his cats behind? Instinctively, he knew there was only one thing to be done: take the bull by the horns. When McGing came in for his morning pint, he told him that Eales's bed had not been slept in, and asked if he'd heard anything. McGing did not take the question casually. He said it was something that must be looked into.

'He can't have done a bunk,' Roarty said. 'He's left Allegro behind. I don't believe for a moment he'd ever willingly desert one of his cats.'

'You're not suggesting there's been foul play?' McGing said sharply.

'I don't know, but I'm worried. If Eales doesn't come back, I'll be saddled with two cats I don't want. Andante, you see, is missing. Neither cat would desert the other. They were like David and Jonathan.'

You obviously know nothing about cats, Roarty,' McGing assured him. 'Cats are as cold-blooded as mackerel. Unlike dogs, they have no feelings. All they're interested in is where the next saucer of milk is coming from.'

The following morning McGing came in again. Roarty was reading the paper and Allegro was sitting on the counter, rubbing his cheek against Roarty's arm.

'You see what I mean,' McGing said. 'Cats have no morals. They'll cosy up to anyone who gives them milk. As far as that cat is concerned, you're just a substitute for Eales.'

'Now, you're talking nonsense, Sergeant. I used to have a cat that was very fond of me. She used to sit on my shoulder as I sat up reading at night, and she'd tickle my ear with the tip of her tail.'

'I'll prove otherwise. I'll take Allegro off your hands, if you're agreeable. I'll bet he'll be every bit as happy taking milk from me as he is taking milk from you. Cats are like people; they're activated entirely by self-interest.'

When McGing had departed with Allegro under his arm, Roarty couldn't help laughing. It seemed too good to be true, until he began wondering if McGing was about to conduct some kind of clandestine investigation. For a moment he felt distinctly uneasy. He asked himself if in mentioning Allegro to McGing, he'd made a terrible mistake.

The following morning Roarty opened the front door to find Allegro waiting on the threshold. He was pleased that Allegro preferred him to McGing because he'd always seen Allegro as a cat with a distinct sense of intellectual discrimination. On the other hand he suspected that the return of the tomcat might be a deliberate ploy by McGing.

'You haven't seen Allegro?' McGing asked when he came in for his morning black-and-tan.

'He's disproved your theory that cats are without feelings. He was waiting on the doorstep for me this morning. That cat is fond of me.'

'Don't you believe it,' said McGing. 'He just likes the strong smell of stout and ale. Don't think I'm jealous. I couldn't care less. I was only trying to help you out by taking him off your hands.'

He could see that McGing was miffed. Allegro remained in the pub, and McGing never mentioned him again.

Two days later Eales's mother rang from Dingle, and he told her that her son had left without saying where he was going. That was only common sense; what was intelligent was his decision to tell McGing of the phone call, so that when there was an SOS on the radio for 'Eamonn Eales who is thought to be travelling in southwest Donegal and whose father is dangerously ill', he could dismiss it without further thought. He also took certain other precautions: he thoroughly washed the boot of his car as well as the spade and slane, burned his old clothes and wellingtons, and wiped the floor where Eales had fallen. However, he did not clean the whole bar because a pub without the barman's fingerprints would only heap suspicion on his head. He had taken measures against every conceivable contingency, yet from time to time doubts arose to gnaw at the edges of his mind.

Still, the execution of Eales had conferred its own unexpected benefits. It prompted him to think about the world in ways he had not done since he left the seminary over twenty-five years ago. Arguably, it had made him a better man—if a thinking man is better than a non-thinking man. He supposed that a theologian or even a secular humanist would see the execution of Eales as evil but he could not for the life of him *feel* that it was evil. He saw himself rather as a benefactor of humanity; even after much thought he could not find in his heart a scintilla of regret or sorrow for what he had done. And it was the blinding light of his conviction, this unaccustomed lack of shadow, that made him think. Now he wished that he had his annotated copy of *De Malo*, with its simple distinction between moral and physical evil, if only to experience again the divine clarity of the Angelic Doctor. Would Aquinas, who saw the world through God's eyes, blame him for slaying Eales? Would he not concede that the murderous blow had been as involuntary as a patellar reflex? He went upstairs and looked in *Britannica* but there was no article on 'Evil', only a brief entry on 'Evil Eye'.

Susan Mooney, his new barmaid, came in from the kitchen with a mug of black coffee. It was her second day, and already she was bent on pleasing, a willing girl who would improve with tutelage. It was enlivening having a young woman about the house again. She moved in silence, and wherever she went she left her mark. Apart from working in the bar, she scrubbed and cleaned and cooked in the kitchen—a vast improvement on her slovenly predecessor. In time he would instruct her in the essentials of the drinking man's diet and how to make a hot toddy in the mornings and serve it in the bathroom while he shaved. He smiled as he took the coffee and noted her relaxed walk back to the kitchen. She was sturdily built, wide in the beam, with a belly that protruded pleasingly beneath the belt. A pity that he no longer had the old hand pumps so that he might watch her breasts swelling as she pulled. His late wife was light-boned and somewhat lacking in those pneumatic qualities that make for bliss and somnolence simultaneously. His mind was working well this morning; all that was something that had never occurred to him before.

A hawk and a shuffle at the door told him that Crubog had arrived.

'So we live to drink another day,' the old fox croaked.

'It's the only pastime in this weather,' said Roarty, choosing a tumbler.

'There's nothing as heartening as the sight of an empty pub in the morning, the shelves full and everything spick and span before the barbarians come in and destroy it all. Them that drinks bottles ruin the look of the shelves but draught is a different story—you never see the barrel going down.'

Crubog hoisted himself slowly onto a stool and placed his peaked cap on the counter to cushion his rheumatic elbow.

'Four thousand, two hundred and fifty,' said Roarty, placing a pint of stout before him.

'Is it on the house?' Crubog enquired while he fished in his pockets for loose change.

'It is, seeing we're just the two of us alone. Four thousand, two hundred and fifty is what I said.'

'I hate to turn down a friend, but four thousand, two hundred and fifty doesn't tempt me. You see, it isn't the money I'm after; it's a say in what happens when I'm gone.'

'You want to make history after your death!'

'Wouldn't we all if we could?'

'You're a contrary man, Crubog. Your land is lying under the crows, and you won't lift a finger to…'

'Make me an offer I can't refuse. And I don't mean money, I mean a programme. What would you do with the land?'

'It all depends… I'm not short of ideas.'

'It's an unholy nuisance, the self same land. I'd sleep sounder without it, there's no denying. Offers on all sides and ne'er a programme.'

'What do you mean?'

'Last night Rory Rua came up with a bottle of whiskey to buy me out lock, stock and barrel. He came in the door and said he wouldn't leave till we'd made a bargain. He stayed till midnight but he left empty-handed and without his bottle.'

'He's a mean man, is Rory Rua. He bought Nabla Dubh's and Den Beag's, and still he's not satisfied. Can't you see he's just a grabber. He doesn't see your land as special; he wants to buy it just because it's land.'

'And isn't that why he didn't get it! What I'd like to do is sell to a young man with a young wife, a man that would husband it like the snug holding it's always been and raise children that would in their turn look after it. You can see my predicament, can't you? You're a businessman and Rory Rua is a fisherman with a mania for land. What I want is a hard-working farmer.'

Crubog was impossible. He listened to him with increasing impatience until the other village codgers came in for their morning tipple. Even then there was no stopping him. He rambled on about his land as if it were the Duke of Buccleuch's estate. Roarty wasn't sorry when he finally left to collect his pension.

Almost on the stroke of twelve McGing arrived for his only drink of the day.

'And what's on your mind this morning, sergeant?' Roarty asked as he poured him his black-and-tan.

'Ragwort and brucellosis. Here, would you mind putting up this poster?'

Roarty cast an eye over the yellow sheet: Brucellosis Eradication—Controls on the Movement of Cattle. Issued by the Department of Agriculture and Fisheries.

'No mention of ragwort here,' Roarty said.

'Isn't every field yellow with it? Some farmers seem to grow nothing else. They must know it's poison; you'd think they'd do something about it without waiting to be pestered by me.'

'It's the way of fallen flesh,' said Roarty. 'No respect for the law.'

'It's a disgrace that a policeman of my experience should have nothing better to think about than ragwort,' said McGing, hooking his thumbs in the breast pockets of his well-filled tunic. He was a tall man, about six foot two, pink faced and heavily built. Though within two years of retirement, he was still fresh skinned and light on his feet in spite of the miles he had trudged over soft bogland in search of the ever-elusive poteen still and worm. Among the glen people he had a well-deserved reputation for officiousness. He was particularly hard on publicans who failed to clear their pubs at closing time. Some ten years ago he summonsed Roarty for not opening the door to his knock at midnight. He swore in court that he'd heard the hum of drinkers' conversation and muffled laughter inside.

'Did you hear the knock on the door?' asked the judge.

'Yes, your honour,' said Roarty.

'And why didn't you open it?'

'I was sure it must be some drunk trying to get in, and I wasn't having any of that.'

'And what about the hum of conversation?' the judge asked.

'That was me,' Roarty said. 'I always talk to myself doing the washing up.'

'And what about the laughter?'

'That was me, too, I'm afraid. I always laugh at the jokes I've heard during the evening. It's my way of unwinding, you see.'

Sergeant McGing laughed so derisively and dismissively that he was reprimanded by the judge who swallowed Roarty's story hook, line and sinker, and let him off without as much as a warning. Ever since, Roarty and McGing treated each other like two wary antagonists—with polite but distant respect.

'After a month of badgering farmers about their ragwort I sometimes wish I were in London with Scotland Yard solving rape and murder cases by the dozen.'

'But isn't it pleased you should be that we're all so law-abiding!'

'It's a policeman's paradox. His job is to prevent crime but he isn't content unless he's investigating it.'

'Do you think he encourages it by his presence?'

'Not in Glenkeel. In the country, I'm convinced, all crime is imaginary. People don't act out their fantasies as they do in the city. The last known crime in these parts (forgetting after-hours drinking which we won't mention) was five years ago, the Case of the Tumbled Tramp-cock.'

'With the torn knickers?'

'The very one. And who solved it, I ask you?'

'Every Glenkeel man knows the answer to that,' Roarty smiled.

'The other two guards blamed the two young tourists who were camping in the next field but I told them different. Do you know how I solved it?'

'I can't imagine.'

'No semen on the knickers,' said McGing solemnly. 'Some of these young fellows know no forensic.'

'It was a tricky case,' said Roarty who was enjoying the conversation from his position of unassailable security.

'It was an easy one for the right policeman. Look at the facts. Old Crubog wakes up one morning to find one of his tramp-cocks knocked flat, looking for all the world like a makeshift bed with a pair of torn knickers on top of it. It has rained heavily in the night and the hay is ruined, £10 worth, a tidy sum to an old-age pensioner. Young Garda McCoy investigates, finds footprints leading to the next field where two teenagers from Derry are camping in the rain. He comes back to the barracks thinking he has solved the case until I breathe the pregnant word 'semen'.

"But maybe he took her knickers off before he laid her!" says he. "Why should he tear them off", says I, "if they're camping happily in the next field?" "A fetishist," says Garda McCoy triumphantly. "A practical joker," says I, "and a local man, too. This was done to make Crubog think the younger generation are sex maniacs. The lads are always filling his head with stories." And I put my cap on my head and went straight to the man that did it.'

'Cor Mogaill Maloney.'

'Imagination is what a policeman needs, not logic. A born policeman has a criminal imagination. The only difference between him and the criminal is that he uses his imagination to solve rather than commit crime.'

McGing took a long draught from his pint and winked at Roarty.

'A policeman,' he continued, 'feels closer to the criminal than to the most law-abiding citizen. It's the tie between the hunter and the hunted. You're a sportsman. You must agree that a good hunter knows his quarry.'

'A good sportsman is first and foremost a naturalist.'

'And a successful policeman is first and foremost a criminologist—he gives his days and nights to the study of the criminal mind. Though I say so myself, it's a pity I never got a chance. Oh, if only there was a Moriarty in Glenkeel. I've got the nose, you see. But what's the good of a nose if there's no one to leave a…'

'Spoor,' suggested Roarty.

'Spoor indeed,' said McGing, shaking his head sadly.

There was a thud in the hallway as Doalty O'Donnell put down his postbag.

'You're late,' said McGing magisterially.

'A heavy post. It took over an hour to sort.' Doalty untied the string on a bundle of letters.

'Let's see what you've got today,' said Roarty.

'Nothing but bills,' Doalty said apologetically. 'It's something I've been noticing lately, the increase in official mail and the falling off in private correspondence. A postman's pleasure is easily measured when all he delivers is bumf.'

Roarty looked perfunctorily through the handful of brown envelopes. One from a bottling firm, one from the Electricity Supply Board, one from a record club, and a tatty one that had been used before and restuck with sellotape. Though somewhat affronted by the crude script, he tore it open out of curiosity and felt his legs go limp as he read.

'Doalty is right,' said McGing. 'The telephone has murdered the art of letter writing.'

Roarty mumbled a reply and placed a whiskey glass under the nearest optic, his mouth nauseatingly dry. 'That reminds me,' he said, heading for the kitchen. He asked Susan to mind the bar for ten minutes and went straight upstairs. Weak at the knees, he sat on the edge of his bed and reread the letter, pausing unnecessarily over the large block letters, written no doubt with a matchstick:

Dear Roarty
Eales is transplanted but not his magazine which I'm still enjoying.
If you want to keep his whereabouts from McGing pay £30 a week
into Acc No 319291 Bank of Ireland, College Green, Dublin 2.
Pay in notes not cheques and begin in three day's time August 13th
and oblige
Yours sincerely and seriously
Bogmailer

Ps. I'm fond of your pub. It's the best in Tork. It would be such a
pity to lose you.

SIX

Roarty was so shattered that he could not think. He went about in a noonday trance, pulling pints and giving change mechanically, making small talk without knowing what he was saying. He wolfed down his lunch with one unseeing eye on the dead conifer in the garden. When he had finished, he couldn't recall what he had eaten. He left Susan in charge of the bar and went fishing in the hope that it might steady his nerve.

He didn't fancy the river where he'd be bound to run into other anglers. With his trout rod on his shoulder, he climbed the hill towards the more secluded loughs, forcing himself to concentrate on the familiar features of the landscape: grey ditches of lichened stones built in more straitened times, sheep pens and makeshift dipping troughs, clumps of fern and rushes, a solitary foxglove sheltering in a river bank, pools of reddish-brown water where he had fished for eels as a boy. The reddish-brown water was the *ruamheirg* for which there was no word in English, and he listened to its liquid music falling in a miniature cataract on smooth stones. Further upriver in another pool, fronds of brown dirt wavered among the pebbles at the bottom while the surface was speckled with red-and-gold-and-silver scum in a kind of iridescence.

He walked along poached sheep tracks with heaps of sheepshairn like shiny black peas; past a patch of kindly grass near an old lime kiln; past the mound of rushes where a snipe always rose; past spongy hollows lying unexpectedly in firmer ground; past pools with thick foam churned brown between stones, clotted froth, swirling, swirling, froth that would give you warts, or so his mother used to tell him as a boy. Here and there the stones were covered with a green alga, *cál leannógach*, another word that formed part of the comic consciousness of the glen.

Having reached the top, he sat down gratefully on a clump of heather. Beneath him lay the wide open glen—a feast of which he could not partake. He tried to recapture the delight he normally took in the scene, knowing that today he was a mere onlooker, no longer a celebrating participant. The bottom of the valley with its patchwork of fields; the north mountain irregularly dotted with whitewashed cottages; the village of Tork where he himself lived, a sorry straggle of mediocre houses, a blot on the beauty of the landscape; the sickle-shaped strand in the west and the greeny blue of the sea beyond—all were so many disparate parts that failed to come together in a satisfying whole. A wild bee hovering over a clump of heather roused him. He plucked a handful of moss and, putting it to his nose, inhaled the smell of newly cut peat, which he remembered so well from boyhood.

On the hilltop was a plateau where his father used to cut turf before he opened a bog in the Abar Rua. Now it stretched before him, a carpet of light and darker brown streaked by washed-out greens. The ancestral bog was now a waste land, the old sites of turf stacks like raised graves, mounds of peat mould overgrown with rushes while here and there a whitened stump of bog fir protruded above the heather. The bog-face was scarred by winter frosts and running water, and broken down by the hooves of mountain sheep. Tufts of heather grew in crevices and the marks of the slane denoting the different spits had vanished into eternity, blown to dust by Atlantic winds. In a moment of searing lucidity he had a vision of centuries passing swiftly while the long pull of his own desperate existence seemed never ending.

As a distraction he began listing things that caught his eye as he walked. Ahead of him the ground dipped to form twin basins in which lay two lakes, the Lough of Gold and the Lough of Silver. He reached the larger of the two, the Lough of Silver, first. A wind from the west was ruffling the surface of the water, making the waves boil among the black stones on the lee shore, producing a continuous singing that differed noticeably from the rhythmic wash of sea waves. He walked out along a little causeway of stepping stones, keeping an eye on the belt of sunlight that traversed the water to a little inlet on the left full of churned white froth streaked with brown. To his right was a patch of water weed, the leaves pointing with the wind to the eastern shore.

On the far side of the lough a solitary water bird was sailing before the wind, its black body high in the water, its long neck gracefully arched. He retraced his steps to the shore and lay down to watch the bird. It sat too high in the water to pass for a cormorant, and it had none of a cormorant's nervous vigilance. It was drifting peacefully before the wind, looking to neither right nor left, its gaze fixed on the water below its crop. He could not but feel that it was a stranger to these parts, perhaps even a bird of ill omen. When it reached the eastern shore, it rose against the wind and with slow flapping returned to the windward side of the lough. Then, as if whiffing for fish, it sailed back before the wind once more, only to repeat the performance when it reached the eastern shore.

Roarty pulled the letter from his pocket and spread it out before him on the rough sedge. The sense of nausea he experienced on first reading it had gone and in its place was a dull ache of indefinable anxiety, a kind of tugging that distorted his thoughts, making all he laid eyes on as unreal as the false sense of security he had felt talking to McGing about ragwort that morning. His pattern of thought had shattered into a thousand fragments. To survive he must pull himself together and decide before tomorrow on a sensible course of action.

First, he must discover who wrote the note. It wasn't strictly necessary, of course, but he felt in his bones that decision would come easier once he knew the temper of the enemy. For a moment he studied the handwriting but the anonymous block capitals told him nothing. Any clues they contained must lie in the language, in the telltale turn or twist of a phrase. The writer was obviously intelligent, capable of expressing himself succinctly and with dry humour, capable of writing over fifty words with only one error. But perhaps he had written 'in three day's time' rather than 'in three days' time' to put him off the scent. The word 'transplanted' was another clue; it would come naturally to a countryman but it could also come naturally to a city slicker who had met farmers. And what of the word 'bogmail'? Surely, in this rather self-conscious attempt at humour lay the clue that would lead him to the enemy. Judging by the postscript, the writer was a regular customer, someone who had got his hands on an old business envelope with his name and address, someone who lived in Glenkeel and had a bank account in Dublin. In theory such men were few but they were not at all easy to identify. Cor Mogaill had the right sense of humour. Gimp Gillespie was good with the pen. Rory Rua went to Dublin regularly to see his sister. Kenneth Potter, being English, was a dark horse but he couldn't be ruled out. Of the men who drank in his pub, Crubog was the only one he trusted.

Again he went over the suspects one by one. On the internal evidence Cor Mogaill, Gimp Gillespie and Potter were the likeliest suspects. All three of them had the kind of humour that would have enabled them to write the note, whereas Rory Rua, though a great newspaper reader, was stolid and unimaginative, not the kind of man who would think of the word 'bogmailer'. On the other hand he could well have seen him burying the body on the bog. His bog was on the Abar Rua and he was known to get up early from time to time in the hope of catching the thief who kept stealing his turf. Come to think of it, even Potter was a possibility. He was a keen bird watcher, often on the mountain with his field glasses, but was he likely to be bird watching at three o'clock in the morning?

He gazed round him at the bare landscape. He was lost in a labyrinth from which there was no exit. He could spend the day on 'ifs' and 'buts' to no purpose; the only real evidence he had was the letter. He read it again and heard Potter's cynical laugh on the other side of the counter. It was Potter, by God; he was just the kind of man who'd take pleasure in coining a word like 'bogmail'. He would keep an eye on him and listen for the telltale phrase that would transform a hunch into deadly certainty.

Observing the regal progress of the water bird, he pondered the best course of action. He could pay the £30 a week and hope that the bogmailer would not ask for more;

he could go to McGing with the letter in a display of outraged innocence; or he could call the bogmailer's bluff by ignoring him. As he considered the three options, he knew in his heart that the choice lay between the first and the last. He removed his hat and took a Connemara Black from the band. It was a good fly for a cloudy day with the wind blowing against the flow of the water where the stream left the lough in the southwest corner.

His eye travelled over the popply surface, which glinted intermittently in the changing light. Imagining brown trout lurking in the shadows of the peaty bottom, dark and mysterious as their unplumbed home, he attached the fly to the trace and picked up his canvas bag, about to make his way round the edge to the far side of the lough. As he turned, the water bird raised its head and looked him in the eye for a long moment before settling down once more to its unobtrusive whiffing. The long moment changed his mind. His head swam as he recalled the *malocchio* and the article on the Evil Eye. He knew better than to compete with such a seldom-seen visitor, whose origin and purpose was a matter for speculation. He would cross the hill to the more sheltered Lough of Gold and thus avoid needless confrontation.

The wind blew stiffly through the heather and against the back of his legs. Suddenly he was on the other side of the hill without a breath of air stirring. Below him the sheltered lough was a sheet of glass with stooping weeds on one side and a patch of water weed, red and green, near the edge, flat floating circles with missing segments. Just then his eye caught a familiar form: a grey, high-shouldered heron stooping on a stone near the shore. He dropped to his knees in the heather, his eye still on the skeleton-thin sentinel. He couldn't be sure if the heron had seen him. If it had, it refused to give the slightest indication, not even a tilt of its crested head. He gazed at the long beak on the rough breast, gradually becoming aware of the true meaning of immobility. In an instant he knew what he must do. Like the heron he would move neither head nor foot; while presenting a picture of intelligent vigilance, he would affect a masterly inactivity and possibly make Potter think again.

A devilish thought entered his head; he would test the heron's nerve as Potter would undoubtedly try to test his. He got to his feet and began walking straight towards the bird, determined to see how close he would get before she took flight. Would she turn on the stone and fly into the east or would she fly into the wind and turn on the wing? Picking his steps over the rough ground, he made a slow approach with both eyes on the stooped head. A sudden flap made him jump. Another heron he hadn't spotted rose from the reeds, and when his eye returned to the stone, its companion had also risen. It would not have happened to him yesterday. His nerves were on edge; he was too easily distracted. He watched as they flew off in different directions with powerful wing beats and long legs trailing. Somehow he felt pleased when they converged on a hillock to the east of him.

'By your gimp I'd say your bag is light.' The voice came from the hillside behind him. With a tremor of apprehension, he recognised McGing's nasal drone.

'Not a stir on this water,' Roarty said, turning to face the bulkier man.

'Have you tried the Lough of Silver?'

'Yes,' he lied. 'They're rising short, the buggers.'

'Never. Not with the wind in this airt. It's the best airt there is.'

He watched as McGing came down the side of the hill, the deep heather brushing his wellingtons. He was wearing green corduroys tucked into his gumboots and a grey thorn-proof jacket with bulging pockets that made him look even broader and more awkward than he appeared in uniform. His face was flushed, and as he drew level Roarty noticed a tear in his left eye from having been facing into the wind. He was noticeably overweight; he had the look of a man who was heading for an early heart attack.

They stood on the shore facing the quiet water, two once powerful men now past their prime. Roarty felt that if they were to wrestle, there was no telling which of them would win. They would not wrestle, however. Any conflict between them would be one of irreconcilable intellects.

'And what fly did you have on?' McGing asked.

'A Connemara Black.'

'I'll try a Zulu then. Either should be killing on the Lough of Silver with the wind and the sky as they are.'

'You can try any fly you like. It won't make a hap'orth of difference. I did my best but a big black water bird put the evil eye on me.'

'A big black water bird? You mean a *duibhéan*?'

'It wasn't a *duibhéan*. No cormorant ever kept her head so still.'

'It's nothing else,' said McGing. 'Didn't I see her myself last week, a big *duibhéan*, as big as a swan!'

'But you don't find *duibhéans* as big as swans.'

'We'll put her to the test then. We'll frighten her and make her scream.'

Laboriously, they climbed the hill. When they came within sight of the other lough, there was not a trace of the water bird.

'She's gone,' said Roarty. 'You might catch something now.'

'It was a *duibhéan* all right. They come inland from the sea for a change of diet.'

'It wasn't a *duibhéan*, I'm telling you. It was a big dark bird I'd never seen before.'

'You only imagined it.' McGing finally settled the matter. 'Are you going to try your luck, now that you can no longer see her?'

'No,' said Roarty. 'I won't wet another fly today.'

McGing's flat-footed attempt at humour had annoyed him. He set off across the brown bogland, his mind racing ahead. He was still apprehensive but now he had an immediate sense of purpose. This evening he would be as inscrutable as a heron while keeping a wary eye on Potter. His visit to the loughs had not been in vain.

SEVEN

Potter was waiting for Nora Hession at the priest's gate. Earlier in the week he had run into her in the village, gazing into a shop window. When he asked if she was studying her reflection, she told him that she was looking for something that wasn't there.

'If you like, I'll take you shopping to Donegal Town on Saturday. Perhaps you'll see whatever it is you don't see here.'

'What makes you think I want to go shopping?' she smiled.

'Would you like to see a film, then?'

'Wait for me outside, not inside the parochial house gate at five,' she said, turning away.

In the meantime without seeming to, he'd asked Roarty a few casual questions about her sister, and then in the shape of an afterthought a few questions about Nora herself.

'They're an odd pair,' said Roarty. 'Both luckless in love, ill-served by two undeserving men. Maggie, as I told you, is still pining for her Highland gentleman, and Nora, who used to be a schoolmistress, hasn't been the same since she ran off to England with a good-for-nothing scallywag from Glenroe. No one knows what happened between them. She came home after six months looking like a wraith, a ghost of her former self. She couldn't face teaching again, so she ended up as housekeeper to Canon Loftus. Oh, she's a sad girl. You can see it in her eyes even on the brightest day in summer.'

Potter switched off the engine and watched a shower from the sea envelope the shoulder of the bluff to the north. The shower passed along the mountain, a grey veil that dimmed the brightness of the landscape while a few sparkling drops fell on the windscreen of the car. The door of the parochial house opened and Nora Hession came down the avenue, stepping daintily in high heels with all the caution of a heron. He experienced a momentary thrill at the comparison, seeing lakes and moors under an evening sun and a lone heron fishing. In a moment she had filled the car with a fragrance that reminded him of crushed bluebells and a day in Derbyshire as a boy.

'Why did you ask me to wait by the gate?'

'Your car is bigger than the Canon's. He has a worldly streak for a priest. He might conceivably be envious.'

'So you wish to spare him envy?'

'It's one of the seven deadly sins. Though I'm paid to look after his bodily needs only, I consider it my duty not to lead him into temptation.'

'You're a serious housekeeper, not all domestic economy.'

Smiling to himself, he drove through the village, narrowly missing a cockerel at the crossroads, then up the hill behind the village while she told him what the Canon liked on his toast in the morning. Soon they were flying over the Abar Rua, the bogland stretching away on each side with a single yellow boat on a blue lake and the dark bulk of Slieve League on the right. The road was narrow and the bends came up so unexpectedly that his hand was hardly ever off the gear lever.

Leaving Glenroe behind, they drove through more kindly countryside with small cottages at the ends of laneways and farmers and their sons making hay in the roadside fields.

The west coast of Ireland was a landscape of harshness and exiguity, a million miles from the green and pleasant land of England. It was a landscape that had been shaped by a warped history, eaten to rock bottom by the forces of erosion, now almost irreducible in its barrenness. It was a landscape of green patches precariously struggling against the wildness of encroaching heather; drystone walls instead of hedges; stunted trees bending before wet winds; futile roads winding towards long-abandoned homes and bare hilltops; and lonely beaches among black rocks and the tormenting crash of the sea.

It was an alien land that spoke to something fundamental in his makeup. From it he drew an image that brought him not only to the very quick of the country but to the very centre of his own experience as a man: a solitary fisherman in a boat on a mountain lough and night falling, darkness in the hollows of the hills, and streaks of broken light on the dull water. The man and the boat were a mere silhouette, darkly outlined against the play of the water, the surrounding landscape vague in the thickening light. On first seeing this silent figure, an angler no longer fishing, he was moved as he had not been by anything else in the country. And he carried this image with him until he chanced on a more potent one: a grey heron fishing knee-deep in a stony moorland tarn, solitary, statuesque, timeless, signalling that a country has a life of its own, deeper, more mysterious even than the life of its people. Sensing that he had peeled off a further layer of the onion, he told himself that he had discovered not so much a paradigm of Ireland as a paradigm of life, of the dread and desperate loneliness at the heart of it. With a pang of recognition, he noted the faint lines that branched from the corners of Nora's mouth, and he wondered if she dreaded the night.

They were driving between two rows of sad-looking, two-storey houses which he tried not to notice.

'Run-down villages are the ugliest feature of Ireland, warts on the face of the landscape.'

'I've lived most of my life in one,' she said.

'In England villages improve the countryside; they embody for most Englishmen an ideal of life. In fact their most implacable enemies are the townspeople who drive miles every Sunday to have tea and scones in them. I can't imagine anyone driving even half a mile to have tea in one of these hungry straggles. They all look the same, a street with a row of faceless house on each side: a church, two shops, a petrol station, six pubs, and what you call a barracks. Now in England we ring the changes; we have 'square' villages as well as 'street' villages; villages built around a green where people once gathered to play cricket. It's a simple layout, yet no one seems to have thought of it here.'

'If you don't like Irish villages, you'll like those who live in them even less.'

'Have you ever seen an English village?'

'No. My six months in England were spent in London.'

'That was a mistake. You didn't see England.'

'I saw the Serpentine, and I cried when I thought of the Lough of Silver. It was so artificial, so crowded with people heavy from Sunday lunch. It seemed to me that all the ugliness of humanity was there.'

Glancing at her serious profile, he realised that their conversation had taken a wrong turning. He did not wish to talk to her about the Serpentine but to walk with her along the shore of the Lough of Silver and show her perhaps the stillness of a heron. Better still, he would say nothing; he would allow her to reveal her Lough of Silver and perhaps discover something no guidebook could tell him.

'To know the Lough of Silver it helps to have seen the Serpentine,' he said apologetically. 'It's in opposites that we find ourselves.'

'And it's my fate to be taken to the pictures by men with a taste for sophistry.'

'And who is the other sophist in your life, may I ask?'

'Canon Loftus. Like you, he has the knack of making me feel positively simple-minded.'

Donegal Town had the air of a place that contrived to be at once a town and a village. He parked in the Diamond and they had a drink in the permanent twilight of the lounge bar of the Central Hotel.

'What film are we going to see?' she asked, sipping her sherry too daintily, sipping it like a girl who would have preferred to drink it. She had twisted one foot round the leg of the table, which led him to believe that he had made her feel ill at ease. He wondered if his well-meant disquisition on Irish villages had been ill-judged.

'Which film? I had meant to look it up but I forgot.'

'You've gone native already. It's what I would expect from an Irishman rather than an Englishman.'

'You mustn't expect me to be typical of anything. I came here merely to be myself.'

'It's difficult being yourself in a strange country. I know that for a fact,' she said seriously.

'Then perhaps you'll feel able to instruct me.'

'The first lesson is to say as little as possible, and let everyone else do the talking.' She turned to him with a mysterious smile.

They strolled across to the Four Masters' Cinema, pausing on the way to look at shop windows.

'My God, it's *My Fair Lady*,' he said. 'It follows me everywhere.'

'I've always wanted to see it,' she said enthusiastically.

'I've seen it four times already because of girls like you and I've seen *Pygmalion* twice. Let's have another drink in the Central instead.'

'I want to see the film.'

'Surely you don't wish to spend a lovely evening like this in a stuffy flea pit. Come back to the Central and I'll sing you "The Rain in Spain", and I'll do the Cockney better than they do it in the film.'

'No thank you.'

'Is there another cinema?'

'No, there isn't.'

They arrived in time for the main feature. He sat next to her in the darkened cinema wondering if he would pass through middle age as gracefully as Rex Harrison. He asked himself why it was that he was fated to meet girls whose tastes in theatre and cinema weren't his. Margaret's taste in books, theatre and cinema had defeated him utterly, yet he persisted for five whole years, hoping that finally they might 'grow' together, that their lives might somehow entwine like the branches of two contiguous trees. She was first to see the light; she was more decisive, more willing to wound, than he. The way she had left him still hurt, even in the darkness of a cinema and in spite of Nora Hession's company and the pellucid beauty of Audrey Hepburn. It was his disquieting sense of failure, of personal defeat, that had driven him here.

'We'll have supper in the Central,' he said when the film finally ended.

'I don't think I should. I'd be back too late. The stairs in the parochial house are old, and when they creak, they wake the Canon.'

'I don't see why we should allow the Canon to spoil our evening.'

'He hasn't spoilt our evening. At least he hasn't spoilt mine. I'll tell you what we'll do: we'll have fish and chips in Garron on the way back.'

'Aren't fish and chips a trifle sordid after the dream world of *My Fair Lady*?'

'Not as they're cooked in Garron. The fish will have come off the boats this evening still tasting of the sea.'

He did as he was told. They stopped in Garron and joined the queue in the fish and chip shop, which extended to the door.

'I'm not so sure I'm going to enjoy this,' he said, casting a fastidious eye on the noisy teenagers on each side.

'We don't have to eat here. We can eat in the car if you like.'

They drove round to the far side of the harbour and parked on the water's edge. For a while they sat in silence, eating their fish and chips from a newspaper. Feeling somewhat put upon, he told himself that moonlight on water was the same everywhere.

'To me there's nothing more unlovely than a moon four days past the full,' he said.

'Why is that?'

'It's asymmetrical. It looks as if someone has clipped the top off it with a shears.'

'Look at the water instead. It's beautiful. The Canon always takes me here after the pictures. He was born in a fishing village. There's nothing he likes better than boats.'

The lights of the town surrounded the small harbour. Looking at the water, you'd think there was another town beneath the waves. It seemed to him that he was living in a drowned city giving a refracted view of the mysterious life above. For a split second he glimpsed himself through Nora's darkly discerning eyes.

'Do you ever have fish and chips with the Canon?' Waiting for her to reply, he watched the forest of masts on the other side of the harbour and a faint light in the wheelhouse of the nearest vessel.

'We always have fish and chips here on the way back from Donegal. We sit in the car and look at the lights on the water.'

'So our evening has been a replica of all the evenings you've been out with the Canon.'

'Not exactly. Tonight the conversation is different, the feeling that time is passing more pronounced.'

'What sort of man is the Canon? Is he as combative as he sounds in his sermons?'

'He's different when you get to know him. In his sermons he says women are the root of all evil, but he never goes on like that to women in real life. You might say he treats us all with wary cordiality.'

'It's a wise man who respects his enemy.'

'I am convinced he sees me now and again as an enemy, or at least in league with the Enemy.'

'Then why does he pay you to remain with him?'

'He likes my cooking. He says I'm the first cook who's ever been a temptation to him. Before he met me, he says, he ate only to live.'

He scrutinised her profile, trying to make out if she were being serious—always a problem in Ireland. Though her comments were never less than acute, there was a gleam of innocence in the way she expressed herself that gave her conversation the quality of originality.

'What does he talk about when you're with him?'

'Like you, he asks me questions all the time. He's a very holy man, though you'd never think it to look at him driving a tractor in his dungarees. He closes his eyes when they're kissing on the screen. We have an unspoken understanding about that. I give him a nudge when it's safe for him to look again.'

'I wonder why he doesn't want to watch kissing.'

'I think I know,' she said slowly. 'He was a man of strong passions in his youth.'

Putting an arm round her, he drew her dark head onto his shoulder. Her hair was soft against his cheek, and the warm fragrance of her body mingled with the smell of fish and chips in the car. She raised her head to look at him. As he kissed her on the lips, something trickled on his cheek. He touched her face with his fingertips and realised that it was wet.

'Do you always shed a tear when you're kissed?' he asked, giving her his handkerchief in puzzlement.

'I cried the first time but that was ten years ago.'

'Why did you cry just now?'

'I think it was because of the Canon. It was so strange being kissed like that after fish and chips in Garron.'

They drove home without saying much, while Potter wondered why a mature woman should weep on being kissed. It had never happened to him before, and certainly not with Margaret. Was it because of her reluctance to venture out of her shell after six empty years of denial? Or was it because of the tenderness she sensed he felt for her in spite of his earlier frostiness? Perhaps she had seen the parochial house as a refuge from men who made her feel vulnerable. The Canon was a man and yet not a man. She could share his house, cooking and washing and ministering to his whims in safety, and he would never make a demand she could not meet. Now she was faced with a different beast, a stranger who would hold up a mirror to her face and perhaps surprise her into self-discovery.

As he talked to her, he was conscious of choosing his words with care; treading as cautiously as the bearer of a brimming cup that threatens to spill at the slightest stumble. He had become aware of a life of inviolable boundaries, more terrifying in its privacy that any he had previously encountered. Unwittingly, he had wandered into unchartered territory for which his relationship with Margaret had not prepared him. Now he realised how lacking in shadow had been his relationships with the other women he had known. It seemed to him that without shadow there could only be the blindness that comes from excess of light.

He stopped at the parochial house gate and pressed her hand.

'I'll make you flower, wait and see,' he said. 'From now on you will feel only the warmth of the sun.'

She laughed lightly at the foolishness of his self-confidence.

'The sun is never warm here,' she said. 'Even on the finest day there's a breeze from the sea.'

EIGHT

Roarty slept little in the fortnight after receiving the letter, and whenever he did sleep, it was only to be troubled by the same dream. He would find himself wandering in a dark landscape, his hands tied behind his back, his head of flowing hair thick at the roots with wriggling maggots that scurried over his scalp, burrowing under the skin, tapping on the hard bone of his skull. Unable to scratch his head, he would tell himself that what he had experienced was nothing compared with what was to come. What if the maggots were to tunnel through the bone and eat the very marrow of his skull, the brain pith that gave meaning to life and motion? His hands still tied, he would run wildly with the wind and put his head under a tumbling stream until the icy water flowed healingly round his ears. He would look out between his legs at an upside-down landscape and an upside-down cow at a pool below drinking floating maggots from his infested hair.

Looking out on Rannyweal from the west window, he wondered how long these terrifying nightmares would pursue him. Having ignored the bogmailer's demand for payment, he now found that forgetting was not so easy. Forever there at the back of his mind was an opaque black cloud pressing down, forcing on him the knowledge that among the men who laughed at his jokes in the bar was one who...

Though he noted every word and every nuance of their conversation, the moment of certainty, the revelation that he craved, continued to escape him. After a fortnight all he had to show for his alertness was his earlier vague suspicion that Potter was the man to watch as well as a growing fear that McGing would call one morning with the dreaded evidence.

He was capable of bearing fear and uncertainty at least for a while. What was more difficult to endure was the loneliness of suspicion, of a mind forever in doubt, peering at the world through the wrong end of a telescope. It was a pity that it had to be Potter because Potter was potentially a friend. He was an unknown quantity, as mysterious in his ways as the wildlife he watched through his field glasses, and for that reason he would befriend him, extend a hand across the deep ravine of human loneliness that threatened what creature comforts man could muster. He would invite him out for an evening's fishing in his boat, and perhaps as they talked and joked, out of casual camaraderie mutual trust might take root. Even a single glimpse of Potter's purpose would set his mind to rest. Furthermore, it would be a farsighted act to make friends with him because, if ever it became necessary to 'delete' him, a friend would be last to come under suspicion.

He turned to Gimp Gillespie, his only customer.

'I hear Potter is courting Nora Hession,' he said, hoping that Gillespie's unavailing infatuation with Nora might lead him to divulge his true feelings about his rival.

'So they tell me.' Gillespie spoke without interrupting his contemplation of his glass.

'He's a rare man is our Potter.'

'He's a straight shooter, I'll say that much for him.'

'Have you ever seen him shoot?' Though he could see that Gillespie had no taste for the conversation, Roarty still persisted.

'What I meant was that he knows his mind and speaks it.'

'He's very English. He has no sense of indirection—he comes to the point too quickly.'

'We all have our faults, I suppose.' Gillespie smiled wanly to himself.

'He's different from you and me. He's forever on his guard, even when he laughs, and he never laughs longer than he considers strictly necessary. I once heard him say that laughter interrupts the breathing, that a yawn is better medicine.'

'He said that to take a rise out of Cor Mogaill. He's too intelligent not to recognise the therapeutic value of a laugh.'

'Have you ever noticed how he speaks?' Roarty asked hopefully. 'You could write down everything he says without changing a word, as if he'd thought it all out in advance. No spontaneity, that's his problem.'

'He speaks as you or I might walk on thin ice, picking his way cautiously between words. It's a habit I've noticed in men who have no natural way with words.'

'It may be an English trait, of course,' Roarty tried to encourage.

'I don't see Potter as typical of his class. Potter may be English but he was taught by Jesuits.'

'A potent combination,' Roarty said thoughtfully. 'No wonder his conversation is so tortured.'

'As a journalist, I wouldn't call it "tortured".'

'I meant tortuous.'

'I don't find it tortuous either,' Gillespie said. 'I find it very much to the point.'

'Well, now you know what hooked Nora Hession.'

Roarty turned to the window again, thinking that Gillespie was being disingenuous. He was obviously jealous of Potter, yet here he was taking his part. Perhaps Gillespie himself had something to hide. Turning from the window, he found him sunk in the deep, deep introspection of a man with a guilty conscience.

Canon Loftus, who was coming up the avenue with a load of hay behind the tractor, stopped as Nora Hession emerged from the parochial house. They conferred briefly, while Roarty wondered if the Canon might conceivably be envious of Potter. After all, he was a man with a man's susceptibilities, and he was closer to Nora than anyone else in the glen. Fascinated by the thought, he watched her jaunty gait as she came up the Ard Rua in flat shoes and a loose dress, the very picture of quiet self-possession on the empty road. A rare girl. *A rara avis*. Had she at last found the man for whom she'd been waiting? A potent combination, a mystery within an enigma. Perhaps Gillespie really saw him with a forgiving eye. Potter was a chameleon, appearing in different guises and speaking in different tongues to different people. A man to be watched; a man out of the ordinary run of men. He would see him this evening and mention the boat. They might even make a habit of going fishing together. There was nothing more natural on this rough coast than a drowning accident in a small punt.

'Good morning, Mr Roarty.' He didn't have to look. He recognised the mockery in the lilt of the voice.

'Good morning, sergeant. You're early, it's only half-past eleven.' He reached for a pint tumbler.

'No, don't get me a drink,' said McGing. 'I'm here on duty. I want you to come with me to the barracks to make an identification.'

'Of what?' asked Roarty, his mouth going dry.

'If I knew, I wouldn't be asking you. I hope you don't mind helping a policeman with his enquiries.'

'If you wait a minute, I'll get Susan to mind the bar while I'm out.'

He went straight to the kitchen, cold sweat prickling his forehead. As soon as he had got rid of Susan, he went to the dresser and got out the gin. He poured a quadruple shot into a pint tankard and topped it up with half a pint of Guinness and a good splash of ginger beer. It was an elixir he kept in reserve for catastrophe, and he drank half of it at a draught in case sipping might dissipate the effect. He would go with McGing to the barracks, as if he were keen to do him a good turn. McGing was headstrong; he was not a man to cross without good reason. His treatment of the local tailor last Hallowe'en was typical of a man who must have his way even in the smallest things. The mummers had pinched the tailor's smoothing irons as a joke, and the tailor, being a serious man, reported the theft to McGing.

'The mummers have stolen me two geese,' he said.

'How fat were they?' asked McGing, pulling out his notebook.

'I don't mean birds, I'm talking about me smoothing irons,' the tailor said in exasperation.

'You're talking about gooses then, not geese,' said McGing.

'No, it's geese I said and it's geese I meant.'

'I'll gladly look into it for you,' said McGing. 'If it's geese you've lost, it's missing birds I'll investigate. But if it's gooses, then that's a different story. Now, which do you think you've lost, gooses or geese?'

'Gooses,' said the tailor in bewildered resignation.

Roarty had found the incident funny at the time, but thinking about it now no longer amused him. He drained the half-empty tankard and mopped his brow. Fortified, he returned to the bar to find McGing stroking Allegro's back while Gillespie did his best to get him to reveal more than he should.

'Is there a story in this for me? That's all I want to know.'

'It could be the biggest story that's ever broken here. Mark my words, we'll have the Dublin dailies round our necks before tomorrow evening.'

'I'd better come along with you then,' said Gillespie.

'Not now,' McGing said firmly. 'Duty before journalism is what I always say. But if you come down to the barracks this evening at seven, I'll give you a statement. You'll be first with the news, I promise.'

'What's happened?' asked Roarty.

'I won't prejudice you by telling. I want you to see for yourself.'

Roarty drove to the barracks about a quarter of a mile outside the village while McGing regaled him with snippets of police lore gleaned from long immersion in what he called 'the classics of criminology'. Roarty listened in uneasy silence, anxious not to say the wrong thing. He kept reminding himself that there was nothing to worry about, that McGing was an ass, every bit as stupid as Buridan's.

When they reached the barracks, McGing led the way into the kitchen and sat down at a bare table in the centre of the room.

'What now?' asked Roarty.

'Take a look in the fridge.' McGing pushed back his policeman's peaked cap from his broad forehead.

Roarty opened the fridge door but as far as he could see the shelves were bare.

'There's nothing here.' He turned to McGing, wondering what on earth he could be up to.

'Look in the icebox.'

McGing was treating him like a child, and he resented the implication. Still, he opened the icebox, which was empty apart from a white polythene bag. He turned to McGing, who was observing him with an attitude of exaggerated relaxation.

'Open the bag and look at the contents.'

Roarty had begun to feel foolish, but when he opened the bag he felt positively ill. It contained a frozen human foot, severed three inches above the ankle.

McGing got to his feet, took the bag from Roarty, and put it back in the icebox. Weak at the knees and with his tongue too dry to speak, Roarty sat at the table and began filling his pipe without first raking out the dottle.

'What do you make of that?' asked McGing.

'Maiming or murder,' Roary managed to answer. 'It could be either.'

'Did you recognise the foot?'

'How should I recognise a foot? One looks more or less like another.'

'It's the foot of a friend—an absent friend, I might add.'

'I don't understand.'

'Eales,' said McGing with self-conscious superiority.

'How do you know?' Roarty enquired, less from curiosity than a desperate desire to keep the conversation flowing.

'There was a luggage label tied round the ankle. It said, "Eamon Eales passenger to Hades via Sligo".'

'A grim humorist,' said Roarty.

'But a humorist who's left me with a clue or two to follow.'

'His handwriting?'

'He wrote with a matchstick and in capitals, and with his left hand, I suspect. But he made the mistake of spelling "Eamon" with one "n", the way Dev used to spell his name.

Now in Donegal most people would spell it with a double "n" because that's how it's spelt in Irish. And which farmer would call hell "Hades"?'

'I wouldn't be too sure of that,' Roarty said slowly. 'The young curate often calls it Hades in his sermons, ever since the bishop ordered priests to stop preaching hellfire.'

'Be gob, you're right,' said McGing. 'Two heads are better than one, even a good one. Now I want you to think carefully. Was there anything distinctive about Eales's feet?'

'They stank—not to hell but to high heaven. He was a great one for lotions and perfumes but he never did manage to mask the smell of his sweaty feet.'

'And what did they smell of?' McGing pulled a notebook from the breast pocket of his tunic.

'Overripe gorgonzola on good days and rotten fish after a week without a bath.'

'Would you care to smell the foot in the fridge? After all, identification by smell must be as acceptable in law as identification by sight.'

'Surely there's a limit to a citizen's duty in helping the police. I draw the line at smelling dead men's feet.'

'Very well, then. I must tell you I smelt it myself in the interest of science and found it odourless. What do you say to that?'

'It may not be Eales's foot after all.'

'You're on the wrong tack. The reason it doesn't emit the characteristic odour of putrefaction is that it has been frozen. My guess is that it was sawn off shortly after death and that it's been in the freezer ever since. Another clue, you see. Not everyone has a fridge around here, and even fewer people have freezers.'

'That limits the list of suspects for a start,' said Roarty, who didn't have a freezer and was now beginning to enjoy the flavour of his pipe.

'We can limit it further,' McGing reasoned. 'We can limit it to men—and possibly women—who live on their own.'

'I don't understand.'

'Only a man living on his own could store the foot in the house. What if he had a wife and she found it in the freezer when she went to get out the Sunday joint?'

'A good point.'

'Somehow I feel I'm dealing with a highly sophisticated intelligence, possibly an Irish Moriarty, a man who thinks he can trick me with red herrings like "Sligo". Yet this subtle humorist cut off a man's foot. He's two men in one, civilised but brutal.'

'Just what I've been thinking,' said Roarty, realising that the sergeant in his flat-footed way could have been describing Potter.

'The pity is that he's sent a foot rather than a hand. A hand, you see, would have been of more interest to a forensic scientist. In the death struggle it could have grasped a button, a few loose hairs, or a few fibres from the attacker's clothes. A foot by comparison tells fewer tales, but it will tell the pathologist enough to lead us to the murderer. It will tell how long after death the body was so brutally butchered. I know myself, and I'm no scientist, that Eales could not have died of carbon monoxide poisoning.'

'Well, I must be getting back,' said Roarty. 'Susan will soon be putting the dinner on the table.'

'You're not squeamish, are you? You're a cool customer, and I admire you for it. You've just been handling a dead man's foot and already you're looking forward to dinner.'

'Will you be going without?'

'First things first. Now I must phone the homicide squad. No doubt they'll want to talk to you. After all, you're the last person who saw Eales alive and still in possession of his foot.'

'I don't think I can be of much help, but I'll do my best.'

'You've helped me without knowing it. You helped to clear my mind. This could be the making of me, Roarty. I've got the nose. Now at last I've got the spoor. I can smell the murderer in the air. All I need do is to trace the features of his face.'

McGing raised his head and sniffed the air between himself and Roarty.

'Incidentally, how did you come on the foot?'

'I was wondering when you'd ask. After all, it's the obvious question. It was hanging there from the door knocker when I got up this morning.' McGing, who had accompanied him into the hallway, grabbed him by the sleeve as he reached for the latch.

'You've seen the foot. Now tell me, was it a right or a left.'

'A right, if I remember correctly.'

'You're wrong, Tim. Eales, wherever he is, is no longer a left footer. And now a final question: if you'd killed a man, where would you bury his body?'

'I have no idea.'

'Think. The success of this murder hunt may well depend on your answer.'

'Murderers on the whole are not very intelligent. In murder they show their failure to solve their personal problems by use of reason. Whoever did it is not a thinking man. He probably went no further than his back garden.'

'We'll start with your back garden, then.'

'Thank you very much, sergeant.'

'No offence. We'll search every garden in the village, and every garden in the glen if necessary.'

'Feel free to begin with mine.' Roarty got into his car.

'Don't tell anyone about anything you've seen or heard. I promised Gimp Gillespie he'd be first with the news but only after I'd informed the homicide squad.'

So far, so good, thought Roarty, relieved the ordeal was over. Saying the right foot rather than the left was a brilliant stroke. Looking forward to dinner after handling Eales's foot was another. He had played it cool, he had given nothing away. However, the real test was still to come: the investigation, the inevitable suspicion, and the endless round of questions.

He parked the car outside the pub and waited for Doalty O'Donnell, who was coming down the street, late yet again with the post. He handed him a tatty brown envelope stuck with sellotape, which Roarty took upstairs to his bedroom. With mounting nausea, he read the letter, which had been written in capitals with a matchstick on a crumpled page from a cheap jotter:

Dear Roarty,
The trotter is just an antipasto. If you wish to be spared the agony of the entrée, pay £50 a week (note the higher tariff) in banknotes into Acc. No. 31929, The Bank of Ireland, College Green, Dublin 2, by 1ˢᵗ September. Otherwise I will arrange for McGing to discover a severed head (just the thing for brawn) in your garden. Your far from sleeping partner in devilry,
Bogmailer.

He made straight for the bathroom and, bending over the washbasin, retched in dry but painful spasms with tears of stress in his eyes. At last he felt able to return to his bedroom and wait till the wave of nausea had passed.

Judged on internal evidence, the letter was even more of a conundrum than the previous one. A local man would surely have said 'crubeen' for 'trotter', and neither would he have said 'antipasto'. Both 'trotter' and 'antipasto' pointed to Potter, but not 'brawn' which was more likely to come from a rustic than a *bon vivant* from the London suburbs. On balance then, it was Potter; but whoever it was must be stopped immediately. The only way to keep him quiet till all the fuss died down was to stump up. He would put the first £50 in the post tomorrow, thereby purchasing the time he needed to extirpate the eagle now tearing at his liver.

He lay on the bed with his eyes closed and for the first time in years thought of Dusty Miller, a student he knew as a young man in London. He was working in a pub in Fitzrovia at the time, and the student used to come in at weekends to help in the saloon bar. He and Roarty were the same age. Soon they were the best of friends. They would go to continental films together, and Miller would turn up at Roarty's bedsit, waving a bottle of cheap wine. They would sit up drinking and talking into the small hours while the student told story after story and Roarty marvelled at such a treasure-trove of human experience in a man so young. Perhaps because he himself, having come straight from the seminary, was still unformed, he soon began to think like the student, sensing the dark ambiguities of a life he had yet to live. And whenever Miller, laughing with devilish glee, reminded him that Dante conceived the idea of Beatrice in a moment of cunnilingus with a slut, he would not know whether to be horrified or overawed by the student's emancipated intellectual world, so capacious and all-accepting compared with the Jansenist narrowness of his own.

Miller had told him that he was reading French at Bedford College but it seemed to Roarty that he read nothing but Rimbaud. He quoted him or claimed to be quoting him a hundred times an evening, and one night when he'd had too much to drink, he confided that he had made a discovery that would ensure his literary reputation and possibly make his fortune as well. Rimbaud, he said, had disappeared into the heart of Africa at the age of twenty-one, never to return to France again.

'He died there in 1891, the year Conrad returned from the Congo. Does that mean anything to you?'

'No,' said Roarty.

'It's simply this. Rimbaud met Conrad in the Congo and became Mistah Kurtz in "Heart of Darkness". No one suspects it but me. As soon as I've published my thesis and made my name, I'll vanish one day like Rimbaud, cock a snook at the world, and never be seen again.'

Not long afterwards that was more or less what he did. He disappeared one weekend with the contents of the pub till, and Roarty never laid eyes on him again. Though not lacking in boon companions, for months afterwards he felt truly alone in London. He could hardly believe that one man could pine so keenly for the company and conversation of another. He stayed in the same bedsit, hoping that Miller would turn up one night with a drunken laugh and a bottle of cheap Spanish wine.

Years later he came on a life of Rimbaud in a public library and could not resist the temptation to read it. To his amazement he discovered that Rimbaud had spent his time abroad in Ethiopia, and that he returned to France before he died. He could not believe that such an elementary fact had escaped a student of his poetry. Was Miller a student at all?

Or was he a literary fantasist who found in a naïve Irishman the eager audience of his dreams? And what of his claim about Dante? Was that imagination too?

The student had marked his life, though. He never again had such a close friend. In many ways Potter reminded him of Miller. He had Miller's frosty objectivity and a reductive capacity that enabled him to scotch the imponderable with the chop of logic. He longed to know what it must feel like to be Potter. He did not wish for his form, the slope of his shoulders, the thrust of his chin, or the look he had of being pampered by history, remote from the brute centre of himself. No, what he wished for was his detachment, which he would never have, not until he'd plucked out the thing within that nagged and nagged, wasting his every thought on the commonest trifles when he should be reclining like a god, contemplating the capricious tides of life with a Jameson in one hand and his Peterson in the other.

'If only I could be friends with Potter,' he muttered on the way down to dinner.

NINE

Potter was leaning over the parapet of the Minister's Bridge, gazing at the breakwater splitting the flow between two brown boulders. The river came down the glen out of the mountains, those melancholy uplands that sat brooding one above the other, regardless of summer or winter. He crossed to the opposite parapet and faced downriver towards the estuary, noting the movements of a solitary angler working the left bank.

It was evening. The angelus bell had just sounded in the meagre village of Tork behind him. The air he breathed was heavy with the smell of peat fires and the fragrance of gorse blossom from the hillock to his right. It had been a warm and satisfying day. He had spent it on the sea cliffs with his binoculars, watching guillemots, shags, cormorants, gannets, and any other bird that flew his way. A scarf of summer mist had blown in from the sea, wrapping the face of the north mountain, obscuring the middle but not the crest. An eerie and suggestive scene which the half-forgotten William Allingham had observed before him:

With a bridge of white mist
Columbkill he crosses,
On his stately journeys
From Slieve League to Rosses

A sandpiper came up the river, gliding low without touching the surface. Ignoring his presence, it disappeared with a swoop under the arch of the bridge. Hearing a whistle while expecting a 'twee-wee-wee', he turned as Cor Mogaill and his dog Sgeolan came round the bend.

'What were you looking at?' Cor Mogaill asked.

'The stones in the river. The peaty water has washed them all a uniform brown.'

'I've been carrying hay to the road since eight o'clock this morning, and I'm buggered for want of a drink. Would you be coming for a jar?'

'I had intended going out to the loughs for an hour before sunset. Roarty tells me there's a strange water bird on the Lough of Silver.'

'I remember five years ago I went out to the loughs and came back again. And it was a very cold day.'

'What did you see?' Potter looked at Cor Mogaill's sad grey eyes and the black curls on his forehead matted with the sweat of the day. They both stepped aside as a stooped old man with an ass-cart of turf and a bag of flour on top passed with a crunching and a clacking of iron-shod wheels.

'I'm buggered with the drouth,' said Cor Mogaill. 'I'll be lucky if I make it to Roarty's.' And off he went up the hill, whistling after his yellow sheepdog.

'I remember five years ago I went out to the loughs and came back again. And it was a very cold day.' What could he have meant by it? Did the incident have some significance in his life that words failed to convey? Or had he in the extremity of his thirst omitted unwittingly the kernel and pith of his story? So much that happened between these two ranges of hills was a mystery, he thought, watching the angler playing a trout and listening for the whirr of the reel. There was mystery and melancholy but also spiritual peace. Never before had he been so close to the true centre of himself; so aware of half-thoughts and blurred intimations, the vague nudgings of the unconscious in the blood. Was that perhaps something he owed to Nora Hession?

Canon Loftus's car came round the corner, powdered with the white dust of mountain roads. The car stopped on the hump of the bridge and the Canon looked him up and down through the open window.

'Are you the Englishman who's in charge of the prospecting?' He had a rough voice like that of a farmer who is hoarse from hay dust.

'Yes, I'm Kenneth Potter.'

'I'm Canon Loftus, your parish priest while you are here.'

'So I see.' Potter could not but be aware of the force of the other man's scrutiny, which he found somewhat overbearing, if not ill-mannered.

'You're going out with Nora Hession, I believe.'

'Correct.'

'Do you realise that she is my maid?'

'I have no objection to maids.' Potter laughed in spite of himself.

'That is not what I meant.'

'She has already told me that she is your housekeeper.'

'That's a complication, a factor to be considered. Have you considered it?' The Canon, having spoken, thrust out a darkly stubbled chin. One of those men, Potter thought, who should shave at least three times a day.

'Are you concerned that you may have to find a new maid?'

'No,' said the Canon with annoyance. 'I mean that I'm responsible for the girl and therefore an interested party. Are your intentions serious?'

'How should I know? I've only known Nora for a fortnight.'

'She's a sensitive girl and I won't have her hurt. Are you a Catholic?'

'You know I attend your church, so why do you ask?'

'But you're an English Catholic, a different species from us Irish. You've got different standards. Are you married?'

'What is this? The Inquisition?' Potter's laugh was not good humoured.

'Most Englishmen are married by twenty-five, and you will never again see thirty-five. I must be satisfied for the girl's sake that you are bona fide.'

'Your question is an unpardonable impertinence.'

'A typically English stance. No Irish Catholic would dream of addressing his parish priest in that tone of voice.'

'In England there would be no need. English rectors mind their own business which, if they're good rectors, is God's.'

Conon Loftus flushed a deep crimson while a knot of blue veins swelled in his trunk-like neck. Potter felt pleased that finally he had roused him.

'Don't try to teach me my business,' the Canon spluttered. 'As an English Catholic, you're in no position to. You belong to a rump, less than a minority, a sect with neither temporal nor spiritual power, remote from the ideals that give life to the English nation. Yet you, one of these rag-tag Irregulars, come over here and tell me, a Regular, how to behave in my own parish. I call it cheek, damn cheek.'

'You talk a lot of nonsense, Canon. In a word, bullshit.'

'I'll ask you a question to which the answer is bullshit: what have English Catholics contributed to English culture?'

'We've had Alexander Pope and Gerard Manley Hopkins to name but two.'

'They wouldn't be missed if they'd never written a line. The trouble with you English Catholics is that you are sunk in respectability, a namby-pamby respectability which is merely an expression of your awareness that you are aliens in your own country. A word of fatherly advice in your eye: go back to England and take up Protestantism. You'll find it more sympathetic to your way of life.'

'You are holding up the traffic, padre.'

'Don't call me padre. I don't like it.'

'It's a term of manly camaraderie but that may not be the response you as an Irish parish priest wish to invite.'

'It's barrack-room insolence, but if you had fought with the Chindits, I might have taken it from you.'

'There are three tractors behind us waiting for you to move.'

'I know.'

'And not one of these drivers has the courage to blow his horn.'

'Faith overcomes even courage.'

'How typical of Irish Catholicism! What these wretches lack is the defiance of English Lollardism, a stage you have yet to reach in this priest-infested country.'

'Let's keep them waiting another three minutes to test their faith. Have you ever considered what might have happened if you English Catholics had had a Cambridge rather than an Oxford Movement?'

'As a Cambridge man myself, it's never been too far from my thoughts.' Potter smiled with covert irony.

'It's a measure of the aridity of English Catholicism that such a question can be taken seriously.' And with a puff of black smoke and a crunch of pebbles, the Canon, having had the last word, was gone.

He's burning oil, thought Potter, climbing over the sod dyke by the bridge. He set off along the river bank towards the sea, his peace of mind and pleasure in the evening perceptibly diminished. He told himself that the Canon was a figure of fun and therefore not to be taken seriously. The glen people saw the comic side of his excesses. As Cor Mogaill was in the habit of saying, 'the Canon is larger than life in no eye except his own'.

Cor Mogaill wasn't being entirely fair. The Canon was a local 'character', the kind of man who inspired so many apocryphal anecdotes that it became nigh impossible to distinguish between the reality and the legend. Even the scrawny Cor Mogaill would admit that the Canon was a horse of a man, tall, craggy, and powerful in every limb. More farmer than priest on weekdays, he was a pastor only on Sundays. He would spend the week among his cows and bullocks, driving the tractor that was his latest toy while leaving the parish work to his pious young curate. A local farmer in a moment of diagnostic acuity said that the Canon had picked up foot and mouth disease from his herd, which would account for his reluctance to visit the sick and preach for more than five minutes on Sunday.

In fairness to the Canon, he always marked the Lord's Day in his own way. At ten o'clock he would drive to the village and toll the bell for five minutes as a warning to those who lived in outlying townlands that it was time to get up for eleven o'clock Mass. His great strength was evident even in his bell-ringing, which did not go ding dong, ding dong, but dong-bling, dong-bling, dong-bling. Like the interpretation of English history, the art of campanology was quite beyond him. Try as he might, he could never manage a single stroke, only a double of such power that the sexton feared that one day he would pull the bell from its housing and wreck himself as well as the belfry. After the first bell on Sundays the Canon would hurry home to fodder his cows. At ten minutes to eleven he would return to ring the second bell, which, as he put it, was purely for the benefit of those who lived nearest the church and therefore furthest from God.

In the pulpit his appearances were brief but telling. With enormous fists tucked like breasts underneath his chasuble, he would preach a five-minute sermon with all the confidence of a seventeenth-century parson. He not only told his flock what to do but where they would go if they did not do it. He had two heroes among the popes; Julius II, whom he revered as a builder, and Leo XIII whom he admired as a writer of encyclicals. One Sunday he went so far as to say that the prose style of *Rerum Novarum* was superior to that of *De Senectute,* and he said it with the confidence of a man who did not fear even a murmur of contradiction from his congregation.

Though he never spelt it out in words, he believed that the miseries of men were to be laid at the door of womankind, and one of his favourite axioms was that 'whenever a man falls, you may be sure a woman has fallen first'. Needless to say, the men of the parish held him in high esteem. They called him a man's man, and most certainly a man's confessor. Where he'd give a woman five Rosaries for fornication in a haystack, he would let the man off with six Our Fathers and a warning. Understandably, women seldom entered his confessional; instead they told their tales of erotic adventure to the effeminate young curate who was said to have a more sensitive understanding of their spiritual needs.

The Canon's ambition was to go down in the history of the parish as a great builder. On coming to Glenkeel six years ago, his first thought was to replace the old chapel with a new one. As his parishioners were far from wealthy, collecting money for the undertaking was an uphill task. The Canon was not to be deterred, however. 'God did not make you rich,' he told the men folk in his sermon one Sunday, 'but he made you sound of heart and strong of limb. If you can't give money towards the building of the new chapel, give your time and labour instead.' And that was how the new chapel was being built—by 'voluntary' labour.

The Canon employed a Dublin architect to design what he called a post-Vatican II church to meet the requirements of the new liturgy. It was a square building of forbidding blue-black brickwork with a flat roof surmounted by a tiled cone in the centre, which horrified everyone except the Canon and the schoolmaster. The farmers and fishermen building it shook their heads in disbelief as it took shape under their hands. The Canon assured them that it conveyed the austerity of true spirituality, something of the spirit of early Irish coenobitism; and that the cone was an ingenious attempt to translate into modern idiom the corbel-vaulted stonework of renowned Skellig Michael.

Potter had come within sight of the sea. The tide was at low ebb, the shore bare. He took off his shoes and socks, rolled up his trousers, and walked out over the furrowed sand to the little lagoon of slack water on the landward side of the sandbank. He paddled in the lukewarm water, listening to the crash of the Atlantic on the far side of the Oitir. He had the lonely sea and shore to himself, and he stood with his back to the sun gazing at a farmer in the triangular cornfield on the slope above. The farmer was bent over his shearing sickle, touched by the gold of evening light, and it occurred to Potter that another eye might also be looking and marvelling at how a lone figure on a bare beach could be so transformed by the same magical light. The thought of a series of eyes appealed to him.

'He must be taught a lesson,' he said aloud. 'A priest who has the nerve to speak like that to a compatriot of John Wycliffe is deficient in a sense of history let alone temporal reality.'

He walked back up the beach and wiped the sand from his feet with his socks.

'I must talk to Roarty,' he said firmly, as he laced up his shoes.

TEN

Roarty was late. He had promised to be at the slip at six, and it was now half-past. Wondering about the likely effect of Irish whiskey on memory in middle-aged men, Potter leaned against an upturned boat and cast an impatient eye over twisted rocks, grey-blue beach stones, lengths of rope and bleached timber, heaped nets, rusty anchors, and the debris of crab shells broken for lobster bait. It was a lively evening with a wind from the south and a slight swell on the sea, enough to give the impression of rise and fall even though it was now slack water. Ignoring an occasional whiff of rotting crabmeat, he studied the ragged goat that was straining its neck to reach a kindly tuft of grass on a ledge of the bank opposite. He wondered how the goat had managed to climb down to the ledge as there was no visible path. Again, that disconcerting smell of decomposing fish. To distract his mind he tried to work out how the goat would climb up again.

Roarty came down the path in waders, carrying the outboard engine, a blue reek rising from his pipe.

'Sorry I'm late. A commercial traveller called just as I was about to leave.'

'I've been trying out my new fishing rod. It casts well.'

'Solid fibre glass and a multiplier reel—just the thing.'

Roarty clamped the outboard on the transom and went back to the car which he'd parked at the top of the path. When he appeared again, he was carrying his fishing rod, rifle and woollen pullover.

'What are you going to shoot?' Potter asked.

'I don't know yet. I just like having my rifle at the ready.'

'I can't think of anything you could shoot at sea this time of year.'

'We'll see,' said Roarty. 'Or as Abraham said to Isaac, "God will provide…"'

They pushed the boat down the slip into the water. Potter jumped in first, sat on the centre thwart, and got out the oars. Roarty gave the boat a shove and climbed nimbly aboard, while Potter rowed out through the inlet which was wide enough to take the oars with a yard or two to spare on either side. As they cleared the mouth and the wind caught the bow, Potter looked over his shoulder and pulled with the left oar, as if about to set a course. Roarty stood up in the stern, wound the starter cord round the flywheel and pulled. The engine spluttered and died. Roarty removed the pipe from his mouth, while Potter wondered if he had let himself in for an evening's rowing. On the second pull the engine caught, and immediately they were under way.

Potter shipped the oars in an unexpected surge of happiness. He and Roarty had never before been together in a boat and, though no word was uttered, each had performed his task as if rehearsed to perfection. His happiness came from the knowledge that he was a practical man in the company of one of his peers, someone who could be trusted implicitly to do the right thing in a tight spot. For some curious reason he thought of Margaret up to her ankles in the sea at Whitstable, because she could never bring herself to wade deeper. And it came to him that a man who lived without the company and conversation of a woman missed half the pleasure of life, but that a man who did not enjoy male camaraderie and manly pursuits missed the other half.

They headed up the bay, the wind astern and white clouds above racing into the north. The glen opened before them; they could now see houses and roads that had not been visible from the shore.

'I always have a feeling of freedom on the sea,' Roarty said. 'Of being away... away. Is there anything at all on your mind out here?'

'Not much. I was just thinking what a lovely evening for sailing.'

'She'd run faster than she'd motor this evening. If we weren't droving for pollock, I'd put up the sail. Pollock, you see, go for a slow-moving bait.'

'There's nothing slower than rowing,' Potter said, getting ready to cast.

'It's too much like work for a man who's past his best. I wouldn't begin yet if I were you. We're still over the bare sand. Wait till we're above the wrack; that's where the pollock feed.'

They were approaching a blunt-headed rock that rose darkly out of the waves beneath its white cap of bird droppings. Potter was sure they were making straight for it until he spotted the entrance to a narrow channel between rock and land.

'This is Éaló na Mágach, the Channel of the Pollock,' Roarty explained. 'If you don't stick in one here, we'd better go home.'

Roarty took the way off the boat and set up his fishing rod against the gunwale with his foot on the butt so that the feather jig he was using as a lure trolled behind them. He then put the drag on the reel so that it wouldn't yield line except to a hooked fish. Potter cast astern and sat with his rod over the gunwale while Roarty opened the throttle gently so that they glided through the channel at the right speed for pollock whiffing. Disappointed, they emerged at the other end without a bite.

'They must be feeding deeper, now that the tide is flowing,' Roarty said.

He released the drag and paid out more line, while Potter did likewise.

'We'll go up north, said Roarty. 'If nothing else we'll enjoy the scenery.'

Just as he spoke, Potter's rod dipped while the reel responded whirringly to the rush of a pollock. The power of the dive electrified his wrist, concentrating his mind on the fight and the moment.

'It's a monster,' he said through his teeth.

'You'd be surprised how much fight there is in a small wrack pollock,' Roarty said slowly. 'He's making for the wrack. I should have warned you that the bottom here is snaggy.'

'I've got him,' Potter said, turning the fish's head.

No sooner had he spoken than Roarty's reel sang out, yielding line to a diving pollock. Each of them concentrated on his own fight, countering dive after dive until they brought their fish to the boat simultaneously.

'Two good-sized pollock,' Roarty said, dropping his fish on the floorboards at his feet.

Potter unhooked his catch more slowly. As he watched the dying pollock gasping for air, he could not but acknowledge a sense of life's imperfection. It was a handsome fish with a dark-green back and olive sides and just a glint of reddish-brown that showed more clearly as it came up out of the water. Noting the perfect curve of the lateral line and the long lower jaw moving pathetically with each gasp, he felt, perhaps a trifle piously, that a sportsman's life is not made simpler by his love of his quarry. Still, he did not take his reservations seriously enough to reel in his line.

'The pollock is a bonny fighter if you take him near the surface,' Roarty said. 'If you hook him in deep water, he puts up less of a struggle. After the first dive he's exhausted—his swim bladder inflates if he's hauled up too quickly. The only way to fish pollock for pleasure is with light tackle. It makes the struggle less unequal, but don't tell that to Rory Rua. I've seen him fishing trout on the Lough of Silver with a wooden otter trailing ten or twelve baited hooks. Now that is something I could never bring myself to do.'

They were now out of sight of the glen; the scenery had become wilder and more magnificent. The sea cliffs towered above them, great striated faces of dark and creamy rock with contorted seams that spoke of mighty geological upheavals. As he looked up at them, Potter experienced a rare sense of exhilaration, as if the cares of life lay full fathom five beneath him. The perpendicular cliffs inspired in him a sense of soaring. He inhaled deeply as if he could not get enough of the salty air.

They continued northwards for another mile until they had come to a deserted village on the far side of the mountains, but neither of them had got as much as a bite. Potter felt that it did not matter; he was enjoying the play of sun and wind on the green-blue water as well as the dozing seagulls and vigilant cormorants they passed on the way. Roarty spent the time pointing out rocks and coves and recounting the legends enshrined in their names, while Potter listened with the kind of attention he might have given to the Ancient Mariner.

'We'll try drift-lining for a bit,' Roarty said, cutting the engine. He filled his pipe and stretched his legs, one on each side of his rifle, as if he were savouring the delights of heaven. Meanwhile the boat drifted with their lines trailing on the tide but both reels remained silent.

'What did you make of the murder hunt?' Roarty asked between puffs.

'It's all rather unreal. I can hardly believe such a crime has been committed here in remote Glenkeel. The superintendent who interrogated me seemed to take the same view. He asked me a few perfunctory questions and then thanked me for my help.'

'And yet there *was* a human foot. I saw it with my own two eyes.'

'I've heard about that, a frozen foot in good condition. McGing was puzzled to know if it constituted a sufficient proportion of the human body to warrant Christian burial. He threatened to ring up the bishop after Canon Loftus refused to give him a straight answer.'

'McGing is a fool—worse, an officious fool. He is taking it all too seriously.'

'It's meat and drink to him. He's been waiting all his life for a mystery only he can solve.'

'If he doesn't solve it, no one else will. The homicide squad have gone back to Dublin. We've seen the last of them, I'll warrant.'

'What I can't understand is why a man who presumably had committed the perfect murder should stir up trouble for himself by presenting the police with his victim's foot.' Potter spoke as if he had been giving his deepest thought to the matter.

'I think myself it's the work of a hoaxer bent on showing up McGing for the ass he is. The foot may not be Eales's after all. It may well have come from the body of someone who died a natural death. I'm half-expecting Eales to turn up one of these mornings looking for his cats. If he's still alive somewhere, he'll be back to collect them.'

'It's possible, but unlikely,' Potter said after a moment's reflection. 'Alternatively, the murderer may have wished to leave McGing with a mystery he would appreciate as a change from ragwort and brucellosis. Who knows, the foot may only be a first instalment. A hand or head may follow. Only time will tell.'

Potter was aware of Roarty's scrutiny in the sharp evening sea light. It was a pensive scrutiny as he puffed at his pipe and jerked the line to give the lure a semblance of life in the water.

'It's hard to imagine why anyone should wish to kill poor Eales,' Roarty said slowly. 'Indeed it's hard to imagine whatever it is that makes one man kill another.'

'Some men are more inclined towards evil than others.'

'It isn't man who is evil, it is God.' Roarty spoke with surprising vehemence. 'He created an imperfect world in which evil regularly triumphs. How can such a world be the work of a good deity?'

'Perhaps he is more complex than you imagine, not merely a 'flat' character in a Dickens novel. Perhaps he is both good and evil, like his creation. Perhaps he is at war with himself, just like the rest of us. Forever at loggerheads, never at peace.'

Roarty studied Potter's clean-cut jaw, wondering if he were being serious or just talking for his own entertainment. There were such men. Men who talk and talk and can never be serious about anything.

'Consider his much-vaunted ecological system,' Potter continued blithely. 'Herbivores eating plants and carnivores eating herbivores—that makes sense only to scientists.

Consider it for a moment as a sentient human being and it becomes an obscenity.'

'Are we saying the same thing?' Roarty was trying hard to ignore his suspicion that Potter was taking him for a ride.

'No, you say that God is evil but I say he is both good and evil. While you merely see the disease-bearing viruses, I also see the benign micro-organisms that enable us to make strong beers and delectable wines and provide you with a livelihood and now and again alcoholic bliss in the evenings.'

'If he isn't wholly good, why believe in him? Why not simplify your life by wiping him off your map? It isn't difficult. I've done it and I don't regret it.'

'I'm afraid his absence would raise too many questions. A godless world is a world without music, and that is for simple souls, men who live by mensuration, men without a sense of the numinous, which ultimately is a sense of poetry. Do you lack a sense of poetry, Roarty?'

Now he was fully convinced that Potter was riling him. Potter was so convinced of his own intellectual superiority that he refused to engage in anything except the most inconsequential conversation.

'There's more poetry in mathematics than in the collected works of Shakespeare, Milton and Dante put together,' Roarty said. 'I'm fully convinced that in a thousand years' time all serious poets will be mathematicians and their poetry expressed not in words but in mathematical formulae.' He turned on the thwart, galvanised into life by the whirr of his reel.

Potter watched him playing the fish with all the unobtrusive skill of a man who has done something more times than he cares to remember. He was puffing at his pipe as if he were back in the bar, as if a tussle with a pollock was no more arduous than pulling a pint of stout. A glint of red showed in the water, and the exhausted pollock came up over the gunwale to beat a weakening tattoo on the floor. It was a large wrack pollock, seven pounds if it was an ounce, and Roarty appraised it with lofty objectivity.

'He was a stout fighter,' he said. 'His first rush was like a mad bullock on a tether.'

'We had come a long way from Eales's foot in our conversation,' said Potter.

'So we had.' Roarty picked up his rifle and took aim with lightning speed. Potter, turning, caught sight of a bull seal sliding off a rock about sixty yards off the starboard bow.

'A heart shot. He didn't feel a thing.' A little diversion to jolt Mr Potter out of his complacency, thought Roarty.

'It was rather unnecessary.' Potter was seriously taken aback.

'If God is evil, why be good. For a moment I felt I was he, remote, capricious, death-bestowing. What happened to the seal happens every day to innocent children, except that they suffer before they die.'

Potter was perplexed to discover a side to Roarty that he had not previously noticed. He hadn't seen him as a man of lightning impulse; he had always found him unhurried and considered in thought and movement.

'It was far from godlike. However impressive the marksmanship, it entirely lacked reason and purpose.'

'It was a fair cull. And I did it from the highest of motives —to improve the flavour of the cod you and Nora Hession eat in Garron on the way home from the pictures.'

'What nonsense!'

'It may interest you to know that the cod in these waters are seriously infested with parasites that hatch from the eggs of worms in the stomach of the seal. Next time you have fish and chips in Garron, think of that.'

'Blarney and balderdash,' said Potter, getting to his feet. Facing downwind with his back to Roarty, he unbuttoned and got ready to send a virile spray over the gunwale. The boat was bobbing, and every time he tried to pass water the dip of the boat made him tighten his grip on himself.

'I can't do it. It seems ridiculous but every time the boat pitches I tighten.'

'There's a knack in pissing in a swell. Here, sit on the thwart and do it into the bailer.' Roarty handed him a rusty tin can. Potter faced forward and held his penis in one hand and the bailer in the other, but try as he might he could not pass a drop.

'It's no good,' he said.

'We won't be going home for another two hours. Since I don't carry a catheter, I'll have to put you out on that rock there instead.'

Potter rowed across to the flat rock where the seal had been sunning itself. Roarty held the boat firm against the side while Potter climbed out. He stood on the rock with the wind on the back of his neck and enjoyed the relief of release onto the froth-flecked water below. It was a strange sensation standing on a rock the size of a dining-room carpet with the sea all around and tentacles of floating wrack along the sides. At the edge of the rock was a small pool of seal's blood, and Roarty, a bald-headed man in a boat a hundred yards away, was playing another fish.

He noticed the white bird droppings at his feet and realised that the rock would be awash again before high water. There was no one in sight on the bare cliff tops above. The only sign of humanity was the row of floating buoys marking the position of lobster pots. He and Roarty were all alone in this wilderness of cliff and water. At dawn the fishermen would come to lift their pots. By then the rock would be bare once more and the bird droppings and seal's blood washed away. He remembered a story he'd heard about Cornish criminals and how they were given a jug of water and a loaf and left on a rock at low water to wait for death by drowning. It was a cruel way to go, watching a rising tide with no possibility of rescue. Roarty unhooked his fish, looked over his shoulder and waved. Potter watched as he rowed to the rock with deliberate ease, and again sensed the overwhelming freedom of the evening.

'The human mind is a mystery,' he said, getting into the boat. 'For a moment on that rock I found myself in the mind of a marooned man who sees the tide rising and not a boat in sight.'

'You and I are two of a kind. We have what I call the perception of catastrophe. Without it you can go through life as if it were an acre of garden with a six-foot fence. With it the experience of all human life is yours. Without leaving your hearth you have been with the Persians at Salamis, with Leonidas at Thermopylae, and with the Highlanders at Culloden.'

'You make it sound like a coward dying many times before his death.'

'No, with this capacity you can forestall disaster by spotting it on the horizon. You can foresee another man's mistake before he makes it.'

'But can you foresee your own?'

'Good lord, will you look at that *gliobach* of sea fowl! They've come down out of the empty sky.'

'What are they diving on? It can't be pollock.'

'Mackerel. What they're really after is the small fry the mackerel force to the surface.'

'Let's not hang about,' said Potter.

'Mackerel are not much sport with our tackle but if you want to try your hand, you're welcome.'

Roarty, having restarted the engine, was making straight for the cloud of screaming sea fowl. Within minutes the water around them was boiling with playing fish and glinting with the silver scales of ravaged sprat. Roarty, skirting the school, steered around the outside so as not to drive them under, thus allowing Potter to troll on the inside. With the double tug of the first mackerel, Potter glimpsed the metallic side of the fish sheering in the water as he reeled it in. It was a new experience. Unlike the pollock, the mackerel came at the lure with the speed of an arrow, surrounded by scores of open-mouthed rivals.

'You're not going to try your luck?' he said when he had bagged about two dozen.

'There's no need for luck here. They're practically leaping in over the gunwale. What are you going to do with them? There's a limit to the number you can eat before they go off.'

'I'll take them back to your pub. Some of your customers might appreciate a fish supper.'

'It will do wonders for my trade.'

'You're a hard man to fathom, Roarty. You'd kill an uneatable seal and turn your back on a juicy mackerel.'

'My forefathers may have killed to eat. I kill for sport, and the essence of sport, be it with rod or gun, is skill of eye and arm. There's no skill in killing mackerel except with light trout tackle. On an evening like this they'd go for a bare hook. The only thing that determines the size of the catch is the speed with which you unhook them. Now a seal is different. Would you be ashamed of a heart shot from a rocking boat at sixty yards?'

'I shouldn't be ashamed of the shot. I've culled deer in the Highlands. I think I know what I could do at sixty yards. In culling deer the shot that kills comes at the end of a long and skilful stalk. It's the logical outcome of a whole afternoon's endeavour. But shooting a seal while he is sunning himself on a rock is like shooting a sitting duck. It shows no sense of sportsmanship or fair play.'

'It shows a sense of humour,' said Roarty, drawing a hip-flask from his pocket. 'Will you be having a swig?'

'No, thank you. I don't drink Irish whiskey and, besides, I've had the forethought to bring my own.'

'The perception of catastrophe again. Can it be possible that we're both pessimists?'

'We're sceptical realists, my dear Roarty. We see each other as we are.'

Roarty cut the engine and they both enjoyed the contents of their flasks while the ravenous mackerel and terror-stricken sprat played all around them.

'I'd swear my Redbreast tastes stronger out here. It must be the air, heady with the smell of fish oil.'

'I've seldom seen an evening as glorious as this.'

'It isn't over yet. We'll go back to Éaló na Mágach with the thickening of the light, when the pollock will be feeding on the surface.'

'So the light-shy pollock turns pelagic in late evening?'

'Now that's a new one on me,' said Roarty. 'I hadn't thought of the humble pollock as a headstrong heresiarch.'

'Pelagic, not pelagian.'

'*Touché*,' said Roarty.

The sun was going down behind them and the wind had acquired an edge that prompted Roarty to put on his Aran pullover.

'Look at that sky; there are weeks of fine weather ahead of us.' Roarty picked up a mackerel and took a knife from his hip pocket. Holding the mackerel in his left hand, he cut a long thin strip of skin with the edge of the knife held towards the tail. Then he took a cork from his trousers pocket and laid the piece of mackerel skin on the cork with the skin side down. Finally, he put the point of the hook through the thin end of the strip, and held it up for Potter to see.

'A work of art,' Potter said. 'You could easily mistake it for a silver tadpole.'

'It will be very killing in about twenty minutes.' He handed the cork and knife to Potter and restarted the engine. They both trolled their lines on the surface without the leads as they made for Éaló na Mágach. The sun had set and the darkening water flickered uncertainly in the afterglow. Roarty was right about the feeding habits of pollock in late evening. By the time the light had begun to fade fast, they had caught four or five each, most of them good-sized fish between four and six pounds.

'Not a bad evening's work,' Roarty said, setting course for the slip with open throttle. The shoreline in front of them was dark and the last dregs of pinkish light in the west were draining away.

'There is something I've been meaning to bring up,' Potter said, having abandoned his struggle to light his pipe. 'Everyone I meet here has one thing on his mind, the new chapel, an unsightly cube with a cone on top in a village that should have a traditional church with a spire. Everyone thinks it's an eyesore—a disgraceful monstrosity—but no one has the courage to say so out loud. We've had crude geometrical architecture in London for the last forty years, and Londoners have learnt to live with it. London is not Donegal, however.

People who make a living from land and sea, in step with the swing of the seasons, have a right to better. Londoners have been brutalised by an anonymous bureaucracy that has fallen prey to every current and eddy in fashionable architectural "thinking". Here, thank heavens, we live in a place whose only connection with the world of ideas is your *Britannica*—'

'The 1911 edition,' Roarty emphasised.

'Here the villain is not faceless but larger than life. And we—you and I—can bring him to heel. The cube and its cone are already standing, and now it's too late to pull them down. But we can still do something about the limestone altar, which is yet to come. The wooden altar from the old church is good enough for this "new gazebo", to use Cor Mogaill's favourite phrase. It was carved by craftsmen in an age of craftsmanship, so why discard it for a block of cut limestone that no one wants except the Canon? The wooden altar goes back to the time of the Famine. It was paid for with money that could have been used to buy food for the starving and dying—I am only quoting local gossip—yet this memorial to the inhumanity of organised religion is to be put on a fire while a block of polished limestone—a convenient *tabula rasa*—is to be erected in its place. Everyone knows this, everyone says this, yet no one has the courage to say, "Enough".'

'So what are you proposing?'

'What we need is leadership. We must insist that the old wooden altar be preserved, if only as a reminder of more austere and possibly truer times, and as a memorial to craftsmen who lived on diseased potatoes. There is plenty of feeling. There is plenty of tinder. All we need do is to set a match to it.'

'I'm with you all the way, but have you considered the Canon?'

'He is the villain. It is his mania for building and his obsession with Pope Julius II, the employer of Raphael and Michelangelo, which has made the village of Tork look like a Bauhaus exhibition.'

'He's a crafty old fox. We'll have to tread carefully.'

'That's why I've confided in you. I'm a stranger here. If I organise the opposition, he will brand me an English communist and discredit what we're trying to achieve. I'm only too willing to help, but I mustn't be seen to lead.'

'And what would you have me do?'

'Call a meeting and get all your regulars to come to it.'

'We'll need a committee.'

'You and I will direct without seeming to. As a sop to democracy, we'll rope in Gimp Gillespie, Cor Mogaill—I wish you had more pronounceable names—and Rory Rua.'

'I don't think Rory Rua would make a good committee man. He's too opinionated to listen to anyone. Just because he takes *The Irish Times* every day, he thinks he knows it all.'

'In that event it may be politic to make sure he is one of us. Better to have him pissing out of our tent than into it,' Potter said.

'I bow to your superior sense of strategy.'

Roarty cut the engine and Potter rowed slowly into the darkened cove. Having winched up the boat, they put the fish into two sacks and carried them up the steep path to the road.

'See you at the pub.'

Potter drove off, pleased with the evening's work. He was now on the way to giving the Canon his comeuppance in accord with the reforming spirit of English Lollardism.

ELEVEN

After closing time he and Susan gutted the pollock in the kitchen. Though Susan had never cleaned a fish before, she was quick to learn. Before they had finished, she could dispose of a backbone and swim bladder as readily as Roarty.

It had been an instructive evening for him as well. Now he felt certain that Potter was his man, if only because of his reference to a hand or head as a further instalment, which tallied with the threat in the blackmailer's second letter. It was all such a pity. He liked Potter for his intelligent and entertaining conversation; and good conversationalists were sufficiently rare to make one reflect before reducing their number. Sadly, their number would have to be reduced, simply because he could not afford to pay £50 a week forever more.

Already he had considered staging an accident should an opportunity arise. However, Potter's perception of catastrophe might make an 'accident' difficult to contrive. He could have left him stranded on the rock if it had been closer to nightfall. To have done so with two hours of daylight to come would have been nothing less than idiotic. A sheep farmer might have spotted him from the cliff tops, and anyhow the villagers knew that they had gone fishing together. He was fully aware that expunging Potter wouldn't be easy. He could not poison his drink without risk of exposure, and he was unlikely to get a chance to hit him over the head with a volume of *Britannica*. The murder weapon would have to be a rifle or shotgun, and because bullets bore rifling marks and cartridges the mark of the firing pin, he would have to find a gun other than his own. Better to wait for a week or two until the shooting season began in earnest, by which time an 'accident' would fall within the bounds of possibility.

He was pleased about Potter's interest in the old altar, though he could not imagine how it had arisen. He did not believe for a moment that Potter merely wished to commemorate 'craftsmen who lived on diseased potatoes'; nor did he believe that he was striving out of the goodness of his heart to save Donegal from the fate that had overtaken London. Whatever his motives, he welcomed his interest. Now they would both have a goal in common. As conspirators against the Canon, they would spend more time together, which might provide him with the desired opportunity.

There were other advantages. Involvement in something impersonal like committee work was what he needed to take his mind off McGing. He would find himself immersed in lively discussion, with less time on his hands to brood over his dreadful secret. He would be engaged with other men in a common pursuit, which would knit his life to theirs and alleviate the loneliness he had come increasingly to feel.

The murder investigation had reinforced his sense of isolation. It was a drawn-out ordeal he would not willingly re-endure. First came question after question, and then the reiteration of questions he had already answered, while McGing took down his every word in a book he ominously called 'my little black book'. The detectives dusted the bar for fingerprints and scoured every room for blood prints, egged on by McGing who kept reminding them that 'all we need is a milligram of dried blood and we're there'. He could tell that he was under suspicion, though the chief detective had assured him that their questioning was pure routine. There was nothing routine about the way they let loose their Alsatians in his garden, nor in McGing's pompous talk about trace elements, somatic and molecular death, and the effects of refrigeration on hypostasis (whatever that was).

The homicide squad stayed in the glen for four days, interviewing everyone Eales had known, poking about in back gardens, dredging loughs and rivers, examining fridges and freezers, and scouring the wild places in the mountains. Wherever they went, McGing travelled with them, ostensibly as their guide over unfamiliar terrain but in reality to pester them with unnecessary and frequently bizarre suggestions. When they left defeated, he took it as a personal affront. He told Roarty over his morning black-and-tan that he believed the murder had been committed out of a desire to tantalise and provoke him.

'Why else should the murderer send me his victim's foot?' he asked. 'Not content with having committed the perfect murder on my patch, he had to let me know he committed it. Well, he's making a mistake. I have two years to go before retirement, and I intend devoting every single day of them to solving a crime that has defeated the experts.' Roarty believed him; there would be no peace, no let up, while McGing was on duty.

All was not ill-luck, however. It was fortunate, for example, that the letter for Eales had not arrived while the homicide squad was on the premises. As the envelope was typewritten, he was tempted to take it straight to McGing, but curiosity prevailed. He steamed it open to discover that it was from Cecily, asking Eales what had happened, demanding to know when he was coming to London. It was just as well that he had opened it. If McGing had seen it, the motive for the murder would have been laid bare. He burnt Cecily's letter but not the envelope, knowing as he did that the postman might well tell McGing that there had been mail for Eales. Ingeniously, he took a brochure for cat meat which Eales had had some months before and stuffed it in the envelope, then resealed it and gave it to McGing.

'Would you care for a nightcap, Susan?' he asked when they had cleaned the last of the fish. Feeling lonely and deflated after the excitement of the evening, he thought it might be soothing to put his feet up and talk to her before going to bed.

'I'll have a gin and tonic,' she said brightly. 'It will be nice to have a drink in peace and quiet.'

He went to the bar humming a tune from Schumann's Piano Quintet and came back with a tray of drinks and a bowl of salted peanuts. Susan was sitting on the old horsehair sofa, examining her fingernails. He put the tray on the low coffee table in front of her and sat down wearily beside her. She was cheap to run; she did not drink much, not as much as Eales, just a bottle of beer before lunch, which made her burp, and one or two gin-and-tonics in the evening, which made her giggly and giddy. She was an innocent sort of girl who never asked awkward questions. She was always affable, always willing to help, with always a calming word for tricky customers. She was barely twenty, and though you wouldn't call her plain, you wouldn't call her pretty either. Solidly built with big, well-rounded breasts, he found her oddly attractive, and as far as he knew she had no steady boyfriend. Looking now at her full lips as she smiled, he wondered what she'd say if he kissed her. Maybe she'd never been kissed. Except possibly on bonfire night or on the way home from a winter ramble in the wildness of the mountains, and then by a silent sheep farmer with the rain making runnels in his stubble.

Sitting beside her on the sofa had an effect on him that he hadn't experienced since he was a young man. She had a sturdy body with a round belly that protruded slightly beneath her belt, breasts that threatened to overflow, and strong, muscular legs, all of which lured him into that pleasantly seductive penumbra between the known and the unknown. They were sharing a house in which they were alone together. She had her own room; she was as free as a bird, and she seemed happy doing whatever needed to be done in the kitchen and the bar. Was it possible that in time she might come to accept him as an occasional visitor to her bed? He would benefit from a good tumble; it would take his mind off his troubles and have a rejuvenating effect on his thickening body. And it might help dispel morning low spirits, a condition that often persisted until he'd had at least three quick shots of what Potter called 'the amber elixir'. He put his arm round her shoulders. She turned and smiled, which he took to be a sign of genial fellowship.

And fifteen arms went round her waist
(And then men ask, Are barmaids chaste?)

It was no good. He couldn't remember the name of the poet. His memory was like a sieve these days.

'You prefer gin-and-tonic to whiskey?' he said.

'Yes, I do. Gin-and-tonic makes me think I'm by the sea on a warm day with a breeze coming over the water.'

'But you always have a glass of beer around lunchtime.'

'Beer makes me burp, which is fine in the morning. In the evenings I like to think of the sea.' Again she smiled, as if she was making fun of him.

'I'm the same,' he said. 'In the morning after a breakfast I don't really fancy, I often enjoy a beer and a good burp—what Dr McGarrigle, God save us all from his attentions, calls a "therapeutic eructation".'

'But you drink whiskey most of the time.'

'That's just to maintain the correct alcohol level in the blood.'

'Potter drinks nothing but Glenmorangie,' she said reflectively.

'He's a good customer. Do you like him?'

'He's very deep. He always says less than he means. I often wonder what Nora Hession makes of him.'

'I often wonder what he makes of her.'

She looked at him quizzically and laughed. Her breasts rose for a moment, stretching the fabric of her bodice. 'They're both deep,' she said. 'Deep people are hard to fathom.'

He longed to lay his head on her breasts and close his eyes on the world. She was wearing a low-cut cotton dress, and as she moved on the sofa the light and shadows played delicate games along the curves of her breasts with the darkest shadow in the valley between. He tried to think of a joke that would make her laugh so that he could watch her breasts heave again like two great jellies and re-experience that helpless longing he used to feel as a young man with out-of-reach girls he fancied. He told her how Budgeen Rua got his name and he mimicked Potter saying 'Cor Mogaill', but she only smiled with the whitest of teeth and never heaved a breast at all.

'Are you right handed or left handed?' he asked as a last resort.

'Left handed.'

He took her right hand, her destiny hand, and ran the nail of his forefinger along the line of life at the base of her thumb.

'Good news. You'll live to be a great age, but I can't tell you where.'

'What are you up to now?' she asked.

'I'm feeling your mounts. You've got seven of them and the most interesting is the Mount of Venus. It's very fleshy, a sign that you have love and music in abundance.'

'Where is my Mount of Venus?'

'There.' He pointed to the base of her thumb, inviting her to feel it for herself.

'It is very fleshy. I hope you're right.'

'Believe me, it's true.'

'You gipsy!'

As she laughed, her breasts like a cornucopia of fruit threatened to spill from her dress. Unable stand the tension any longer, he drew her head onto his shoulder and put his free hand on her breast. It was not in the least jelly-like to the touch but round and full like a grapefruit, with a strong nipple rising inside her dress. No wonder Potter had begun calling his pub 'The Bristols Bar'.

'Tell me about the mountain,' he said, caressing her breasts, his fingers now inside the cotton.

'It's very lonely. All you can see is one hill behind another and white roads running over them and maybe a house here and there and six or seven sheep grazing on a slope with their backs to the wind. And all you can hear is the wind whistling in the heather.'

'So you like living here in the village?

'There are more sounds to hear and there's more going on, but I prefer mountain people. The village people think they're a cut above everyone else.'

'You're right,' he said. 'Put six houses together in a row and you change the nature of the people who live in them.'

Pressing the tip of her nipple as if it were a doorbell, he kissed her slippery lips, inhaling the smell of fried liver, bacon, onions, and gin-and-tonic from her breath. It was an intoxicating smell that reinforced his tipsy feeling of sheer recklessness.

'It's the first time I've been kissed by a man with a beard. It's nice and soft, not at all as rough as stubble.'

He placed a kiss in the valley between her breasts and she seemed to wriggle inside her dress, perhaps because of the tickling of his beard. He unbuttoned her dress at the back and slipped her arms out of the sleeves, revealing two white breasts with brown nipples inviting the maddest of kissing.

'You don't wear a bra?'

'I like to let the air cool them in summer.' He could tell that she was every bit as proud of them as he once was of his penis. She wriggled again, this time surely with pleasure, he told himself.

He put her lying on her back on the sofa, and he lay between her legs and kissed one breast after the other, licking the erect nipples and going from one to the other like a man who cannot make up his mind where the greater pleasure lies. Meanwhile she caressed the back of his neck with strong fingers and scratched his head behind the ears as she might do to a cow to get her in a mood for milking. And he thought she was nothing if not sweet-natured, so different from his late wife with her willpower and sticklike figure and deter-mination never to be cajoled. If Florence had been in the garden with Adam, humanity would still be in its prelapsarian state. What excited Adam was not the rosiness of the apple but the longing of Everyman for pneumatic bliss. The adrenaline was running in his stomach as it always did at the thought of Florence's unyielding flesh. To regain his grip on sanity, he ran an exploring hand up Susan's leg. No bra. No knickers. Susan, bless her, was a latter-day Eve, and, like Eve, a fresh air fiend. She was moistly inviting, juicy as a peach. He unzipped his trousers, sharply aware of the great quiet in his crotch. Hoping that the furnace heat below would induce an immediate awakening, he tried and tried with a penis as limp as a lugworm, good for nothing but bait. Regretting his overhasty disposal of Eales's lust-finger, he fondled her clitoris with what he could only describe as regretful reverence. She clung to him like a waif in a storm, her *mons veneris* firm against his thigh while she wriggled with a low moan that betokened as much pain as pleasure.

'That was hard work?' she said.

'I'm dog tired.' He allowed his head to sink onto her arm, too embarrassed to meet her eye.

She held his head to her bosom and he began breathing heavily, pretending to be asleep, reluctant to confront her obvious puzzlement. As he emitted a long 'snore', she put her hand down inside his trousers and felt his sleeping penis all along its length which, he was still pleased to think, was quite considerable. She retracted the foreskin once or twice, slowly at first and then more quickly, squeezing gently, almost lovingly, each time, while he groaned like a dreaming dog and buried his head more deeply in her breasts. Susan, he told himself, was no stranger to these parts. Unlike Florence, she was a skilled resurrectionist, but sadly on this occasion the patient was proof against all known ministration. Finally acknowledging defeat, she slid out from under him but still he kept on breathing heavily. After a while she came back with a bedspread, which she laid lightly over his shoulders and kissed his cheek. His eyes still closed, he heard the click of a closing door and her heavy tread on the stairs.

On the verge of sleep, real sleep, he tried to hold a picture in his mind: fishing cod in the Sound on a windy evening in March, a leaden sea sploshing against the bows, the sky a blue-black cupola of low cloud and an opening in the west above the horizon where an invisible sun shot feathery cloud with golden light. It was such a contrast, the blue-black above like grim night descending and the window of gold over the water providing what light there was in the evening. Somehow it seemed to him then like an image of his desperate life, and he bent stoically over the gunwale to haul in a cod. When he raised his head again, the strip of light had gone. All was blue-black, the very image of premature night.

He woke with a shiver though the night was warm. It was almost three by his watch. He realised that he must have slept, that the weariness he had been at pains to feign was real. He picked up the bottle of whiskey and his empty glass, and quietly climbed the stairs so as not to disturb Susan. Without switching on the light in his bedroom, he went to the window to pull the curtains. As he raised his hand, a movement on the other side of the street caught his eye. Someone was lurking in the shadow of the gable opposite, looking across directly at the house. Wondering who it might be, he moved to the corner of the window without taking his eyes off the figure in the shadow. He did not have long to wait. As the church clock struck three, McGing emerged into the light of the street lamp and headed for the barracks.

Roarty was shaken. He already knew that McGing had vowed to catch the murderer but he had not realised that he himself was to be the quarry. He wasn't imagining things; there was no other reason why McGing should keep his house under surveillance. Regrettably, there was only one thing to be done: take McGing's mind off the murder by giving him something more urgent to think about. He would allow him half an hour to get back home to his bed. Then he would strike.

He put the Rhenish symphony on the gramophone and poured himself a drink, half-aware of an unresolved crux in the music and in his life. His hands shook as he poured but they usually shook first thing in the morning, and it was now only two hours from sunrise. He sat on the bed with a pillow between his head and the wall, consciously striving to expunge McGing from his thoughts. He visualised Potter peeing on Carraig a' Dúlamáin, a trusted friend compared with the wayward McGing. And he thought of Cecily playing *Papillons* with a lightness of touch that promised invincible innocence, now a grown woman writing in desperation to a debauched bugger from Kerry, her purity of heart overcome by the primacy of the clitoris. And finally he thought of the woman who had brought her into the world, and asked himself why he should marvel at the transformation that had overtaken her daughter. If he had knowingly chosen Florence for wife, if he himself had been the guilty author of his misfortune, he might conceivably forgive her. Instead he had been put upon, sat upon, and shat upon by that Innominate Agent unthinking men call Fate.

Superficially, he owed his wife to the dextrous student of Dante and Rimbaud, Dusty Miller. If Miller had not disappeared with the contents of the till, a nondescript girl called

Florence Kissane would not have entered his life. Admittedly, it had been a difficult time for him. He had left the seminary only a year before, and he was still trying to convince himself that in leaving he had done what was right for him. He could have taken a job in an office, of course, but he was driven towards the pub life because he saw it as a crossroads where good and bad meet and in the encounter get to know something of themselves and each other. After six enclosed years in a seminary subjecting himself daily to a masochistic scrutiny of his conscience, he felt he needed to rub shoulders with both the rough and the smooth in order to rid himself of the suspicion that he was a calf with two heads, a prize exhibit in a seaside circus. He needed to lose himself in a field full of folk, and he reckoned that a London pub was the twentieth-century equivalent.

For his first year outside the walls he lived without women, having rejected the possibility of seeking out a prostitute to rid himself once and for all of the virginity that had come to symbolise six fruitless years of incarceration. He went even further, taking a decision not to surrender to the urge of the flesh except for beauty, because it seemed to him at the time that to give up the priestly life for anything less would have been unworthy. He waited and waited but no beautiful woman came his way. At first he wondered about the effect of the kiss of a truly beautiful woman (healing or searing?). After a while he began wondering if there were any beautiful women in London. If there were, they did not seem to live in Fitzrovia. His mind was so fixed on his idea of beauty, that he barely noticed Florence who had replaced his friend Dusty in the pub.

She had come from Tipperary, from the Golden Vale as she called it, still smelling of milk and buttercups, a rare enough achievement in the fug of a public house. As the weeks went by, he spoke to her now and again, noting the efficiency and determination the landlord must have already spotted when he took her on. She was quick on her feet, quick to pull pints, quick to give change, and more quick-witted than necessary with any bohemian litterateur who thought he could make fun of her. Unlike Florence, the landlord was a slow thinker. His response to a jibe or a dig was to laugh and move out of earshot. One evening when an uncharacteristically sober journalist said in his hearing that his pub was the worst-run in London, he laughed even louder than usual. Hearing him, Florence looked over her shoulder from the till, and in her glance Roarty saw a girl for whom life held no terrors. She looked so confirmed in her self-confidence that he wondered if she must lack some feminine quality—some insight or intuition, some spiritual dimension—that other women take for granted. As his old professor of moral theology used to say, 'No one has all the gifts, and the presence of one gift necessitates the absence of another'. It occurred to him that here was something he must investigate, if only to satisfy his curiosity about women. She was far from beautiful but somehow without his knowing it beauty had lost its pre-eminence. Within a few weeks they had become friends, going places together on their day off and comparing their dreams and ideas of what the future might have in store for them. He was delighted to have found her because she came with a woman's mysterious aura as well as the kind of conversation he had thought only men could make.

They were both bent on going back to Ireland. They began at once to save for a place of their own. When a small pub in Roarty's home village came on the market, they bought it with all the confidence of a couple with 'London experience' setting up shop in Donegal. It was only a run-down shebeen but soon they had made it into a well-stocked, comfortable inn, a natural meeting-place for village wiseacres as well as a retreat for any intrepid traveller who found himself on holiday in Glenkeel. His sense of wonder at having discovered Florence so fortuitously remained with him throughout the early years of their marriage, until it occurred to him one morning that, quite possibly, it was she who had discovered him.

Still, he did not allow the thought to come between them. They were both thrifty without being niggardly, both capable of enjoying what pleasures country living afforded. Those early years of their life together were only a little less than heavenly. He looked after the bar and Florence looked after the financial side of the business. She kept the books and paid the bills, while he entertained his regulars with lively repartee and enjoyed an occasional glass of Jameson along the way. Meanwhile they were doing their level best to start a family. Neither of them wished for a large family. They were agreed that a son and daughter would do, but after four years of unremitting endeavour they still had nothing to show for their diligence. Roarty, unlike Florence, wasn't unduly worried; it seemed to him that this *vie en rose* could well continue into old age or even death itself. Then one night, as they were trying yet again for a baby, misfortune struck. He had been worried for months about the slow ebbing of his sexual urge like a tide retreating from an estuary, conscious that he no longer looked at Maggie Hession's breasts during Mass with a feeling of unutterable tenderness in his chest. Now things had taken a serious turn. For the first time in five years of married life he had failed.

Paralysed by the frightening quiet below, he lay facing his wife, the penis on his thigh as limp as Adam's in Michelangelo's depiction of the Creation. Florence, always a girl to take the initiative, tried to give him a helping hand out of his difficulty, but His Lordship was proof against any tricks of resuscitation in her repertory.

'Not my night,' she said, turning her back to him with a final shrug of the shoulders.

They tried in vain again the following night and the night after that as well. By now he was worried and so was Florence. Her diagnosis, however, was simple and unanswerable. 'You've got brewer's droop,' she said, 'and the cure is total abstinence.' Disingenuously, he told her that he was drinking only half a bottle a day, chicken feed for a man of his physique. Nevertheless, he went on the wagon because he did not wish to give her more leverage than she already enjoyed. He was old enough to know that moral blackmail is a woman's most common weapon in the war of attrition that is marriage, and also the deadliest. The cure, however, failed to match the simplicity of the diagnosis. After a week without drink he began getting the occasional tremor of desire, followed by a beguiling show of the flag at half mast. He would begin making love to Florence, knowing how badly she needed a rub of the relic, and when she was all shipshape and ready for action, his erection would collapse with a feeble trickle on his thigh.

The irony was that now as a teetotaller he was showing the classic symptoms of brewer's droop as enunciated by the Porter in *Macbeth*: 'Much drink may be said to be an equivocator with lechery; it makes and mars him; it sets him on, and it takes him off; it persuades him, and disheartens him; makes him stand to and not stand to...' And far from being amused by this most common of male jokes, he was so worried that a normal, self-confident approach to his wife was now impossible. At the best of times sex caught him, as it does all self-aware men, at his most vulnerable and ridiculous. Now the complications of failure were so disconcerting that it was simpler and more sensible not to begin. Florence agreed almost too readily, saying that it was cruel to set her on only to leave her high and dry with a sleepless night to follow. And she would not countenance any known alternative to full penile penetration. When he tried to explain to her that there was more than one way to skin a cat, she told him succinctly that there was only one way to make babies.

Soon her earlier mood of sympathetic resignation curdled into the sour whey of longsuffering. They took to sleeping in separate bedrooms and to eating breakfast in sullen silence. At times he was at a loss to understand how the shortest and least significant limb in his anatomy could loom so large in his thoughts and in effect determine his internal weather, not to mention his behaviour towards his customers.

Previously, all business decisions were taken by him alone. Now he found that she had begun to order extra barrels of stout without consulting him. Just because he had failed to trigger the ritual spasm in her vagina, he had dwindled within a month from a landlord to a cipher. As he had expected, there was method in her audacity. She was taking the opportunity to chat up draymen, excise men, weights and measures men, commercial travellers, and every stranger in trousers who came to the pub on business. She was no oil painting, not the type of woman who imbued men with the conviction that to make a pass was a matter of male honour. Florence was a sensible plain Jane who could not afford the luxury of coyness but must advertise immediate availability.

She must have done precisely that because one day, about six months after his first failure, she said over dinner:

'I can stand this no longer. I need a poke, and a good one at that, to keep what's left of my sanity. I won't shame you with one of the locals. Instead I'll have a sly one with MacSwilley's drayman on Thursday. I'm telling you in advance because I don't want you to think I'm being unfaithful.'

He was taken aback by her brutal logic. He couldn't help wondering why there were no great women philosophers. 'I appreciate being told,' he smiled with unobtrusive irony.

'Don't think of it as love-making, Tim. My biological clock is coming up to the fateful hour. I want to make a baby before the bells begin to chime.'

'I won't stand in your way. I'll go shooting on the appointed day.'

'And who will look after the bar?'

'I didn't think the bar was on your mind.'

'You'll stay here. It must be business as usual, so that customers don't suspect a rift.'

'You have a nice sense of decorum,' he said, almost choking over some gristle in the scrag-end of neck she had just overcooked him.

As was her wont, she got her way. He stayed in the bar making uneasy conversation with Old Crubog while a drayman in wide shoes drank tea in the kitchen and plunged on her bed upstairs. The incident had given him an insight into women which was almost blinding in its simplicity. Man's relationship with them, when all the talk of Michelangelo was done, could be reduced to a simple formula:

$$H = E + P + S$$
where $H = Happiness$; $E = Erection$; $P = Penetration$; *and* $S = Spasm$

If only he had tumbled to this truth before! What fun it would have been in the days when he used to give her two spasms on a single stalk. It was typical of the School of Life that it taught everything too late, when the knowledge was no longer of any use to the pupil.

'There's a run about the rocks today,' he had said to Crubog in an effort to regain his grip on commonplace perceptions.

'The sea can only do one of two things, rise or fall,' said Crubog sagely.

'Yet it's full of surprises.' Roarty looked out on Rannyweal.

'The sea is a woman,' Crubog said. 'A wise man never takes her for granted.'

The drayman came and went and a commercial traveller in cigarettes took his place. Florence became more civil as she became more unfaithful. She would make small talk about the regulars and jokingly promise to give him oysters to cure his droop. Sadly, he could not respond in like spirit. The joy of self-forgetfulness had vanished from his life. How could she turn her back on five rare years of marital happiness and treat the man who helped make them like a discarded dildo? If he had been morally culpable, he would have understood. He was no more to blame for the failure of his erection than for the fact that the axis of the earth is inclined about 66°33′ to the orbital plane. Wasn't it just typical that such an elementary truth should remain beyond the grasp of a woman, even an intelligent woman like Florence!

He went through the motions of living, noting her sprightly return from Donegal Town once a fortnight, wondering why the hell he did not wring her neck. Still, he did nothing, and one day when she told him that she was pregnant, he said that there was nothing more satisfying than success after unremitting application, and that now she could wait for the chimes with a clear conscience. To his surprise, she took her pregnancy seriously. She no longer saw the man or men who had sown her, and she spent the days of turgescence on the sofa in the sitting-room reading light novels and eating Turkish delight. Dr McGarrigle came and felt her belly, and told Roarty that there was some danger of a premature birth. A week later, when she was rushed to Donegal Hospital, Roarty experienced a sense of alarm that surprised him. He went to visit her, and was told that there had been complications because of her age. A healthy baby girl had been born by caesarean and the mother was in intensive care. She had opened two sunken eyes and taken his hand, and he knew that she would never take it again.

'We've had some good times, Tim,' she whispered. 'We've come a long way together. You'll never know how much you shortened the first hundred miles.'

What could he say? Her words bore the full gravity of life's tragedy, and no response of his could cheapen them. In dying, as in living, she had defeated him.

He looked after the child as best he could, somewhat grudgingly at first; then tenderly as she smiled whenever he stooped over her cot; and finally joyously as the first miraculous words brought new life the house. She was a lovely little girl, dark haired and dark eyed, her oval face bright with innocent intelligence. Within a year she had transformed his life. She was not only his daughter but was his little woman, too. He taught her to read and write before she went to school; he took her for walks and told her all he knew about the flowers and small animals of the glen; he drove her seventeen miles to Garron twice a week for piano lessons with the best teacher in the area; and when she was thirteen he sent her to the best convent school in the county. She was not of his flesh; instead she was the apple of his eye. And perhaps because she was not of his flesh, he was driven to mould her to an extent that no ordinary father would attempt. Forever at pains to provide a rich tilth of experience in which her young personality could grow, he was rewarded by the sweetness of her nature evident even in the delicacy of her piano playing.

Her holidays from school were heaven. The house would flow with music, and he would eat whatever she cooked and ask for more. He could see that she was already in possession of a young woman's grace of movement, but still he was reluctant to instruct her in the questionable designs of would-be boyfriends. He reasoned that there was no need. She was head of her class at the convent school. Surely she was capable of seeing through the wiles of unlettered bumpkins.

Then Eales came with his cats and transplanted her to a putrefactive tilth, the very midden of life where nothing grew but black-gilled toadstools. A fortnight ago he had written to tell her that she had won a university scholarship, imagining her joy and eagerness to come home at once. Sadly, he was still waiting for her reply. Instead he'd had her pathetic letter to Eales. He wondered if he himself was to blame. A caring mother would have warned her against the ungovernable tides of life.

The symphony ended, leaving him with a sense of life's, and perhaps Schumann's, unsettling ambiguity. His thoughts now hung on that iniquitous trinity of Eales, Potter and McGing. They had woven themselves into the warp and weft of his life, as if by some theological sleight of hand they had become one and the same person, the creation of his own insatiable demon. Day after day they tortured and oppressed him in their ubiquity, until he longed for some cleansing purgative to rid his mind and body of all trace of them. Yet in his heart he knew that without them he would no longer be himself. Was it not the obsessive nature of his imagination that coloured his every experience and formed the very core of his personality? We are all victims of our self-love, he thought. Even if we could be reconstituted and streamlined at a stroke, we would no more desire it than a lover of Schumann would wish to see his music rescored by a composer with a finer sense of orchestration, for the simple reason that it would no longer be Schumann.

He tiptoed down the dark stairs and let himself out by the back door. He took a pair of gardening gloves, a cold chisel, and a hammer from the garage and followed the west road out of the village. Turning north at the crossroads, he doubled back through the fields until he found himself fornent the high-walled churchyard. The sudden soss of a salmon rolling in the river gave him a start. He squatted on his hams and looked all around. He held up his finger before his nose, but the night was so dark that he could barely see it. An opaque sky pressed down like a black cope on the shoulders of the hills, ideal for the business in hand.

Having climbed over the drystone churchyard wall, he lurked for a moment in the shadow of the belfry. Satisfied that all was quiet, he stole forward to the sacristy window, put on his gloves and raised the bottom sash with a heave, thankful that some thoughtless altar boy had not put the catch back in place. Within minutes he had climbed inside. As a former altar boy himself, he had no trouble finding his way in the dark. Soon he was standing in the sacristy doorway, mesmerised for a moment by the flickering of the red sanctuary lamp. Eerie shadows darted along the walls at each upward leap of the flame, revealing aspects of holy pictures and objects he had never noticed before.

With an unnerving feeling that he was being watched by an eye that never closed, he tiptoed down the nave. The poor-box was inside the porch door. He prised it open and stuffed a fistful of coins in his pocket. Within twenty minutes he was back once more in his bedroom, grateful that the night's work was done. The Canon would order an investigation that should keep McGing busy for a week or two. It would be a baffling case, if only because of the difficulty of imagining who in a god-fearing community would sacrilegiously steal ninety-four pence from the poor. He couldn't help feeling a twinge of guilt, which was more than he had felt after the deletion of Eales. Luckily, he could make amends for his sin tomorrow by sending £2.00 anonymously to the St Vincent de Paul Society in Dublin. After all it was common knowledge that the urban poor were more deserving than their country cousins.

As his thoughts lost their way on the verge of sleep, McGing receded into the shadows while Potter loomed large with his extraordinary view that the Famine represented 'more austere and truer times'.

TWELVE

Has everyone got a drink?' Roarty asked.

He had locked the street door and taken the till from the bar so that if McGing knocked it would appear that he was having a social drink with a few close friends.

'Let the meeting begin,' said Cor Mogaill from the depth of the armchair by the fireplace. His sharp face glowed with eagerness, the face of a man who had long dreamt of revolution and could hardly believe that he had lived to see its dawn. He kicked his knapsack away from him and, resting his feet on it, inhaled the smoke of his cigarette so deeply that Roarty wondered if the effects might reach to his toes. Cor Mogaill was an innocent, he told himself; a Marxist perhaps but the salt of the earth, nonetheless. Not a man to cut through a dead man's tibia with a hacksaw, and far too serious to make schoolboy jokes in bad taste.

Roarty sat next to Potter on the sofa, while Gillespie with notebook and pencil sat at the table, and Rory Rua, accompanied by Setanta, his red setter, sat hunched on a stool in the corner. Potter, in a well-cut corduroy jacket, open-necked shirt and cavalry twills, looked the picture of suave urbanity at ease in the country. Suntanned and fine-featured, athletic and self-confident, he stared with handsome eyes that betrayed icy coldness for all their beguiling blueness. A thoroughbred, thought Roarty, compared with whom Rory Rua is a Clydesdale. Potter offered his tobacco pouch to Rory Rua who took it with the awkwardness of a man who had no sense of ceremony. He must have washed his hair; it looked redder than usual, almost as red as that of his dog, and the large freckles on his face and hands could have been blotches from some rare skin disease. He tamped his pipe, exposing the raw-red saltwater boils on both wrists. Rory Rua could have been some half-formed amphibious creature, less than human, a prosaic version of Caliban. I'm becoming far too sensitive, Roarty told himself, taking a therapeutic swig from his glass.

'We all know why we're here,' he began. 'Until we have formed an executive committee, I'll take the chair. The first thing we must do is elect officers. I propose Kenneth Potter for president and chairman.'

'I second that and I think Setanta here would agree.' Rory Rua patted his dog on the head.

'I appreciate your faith in me,' Potter said with a smile. 'However, I feel I must decline. I'm a stranger here, suspect in the Canon's eyes and therefore a liability in any negotiations with him that may ensue. Members of the executive committee should be above criticism. While I'm willing to give all the help I can behind the scenes, I must not be seen to hold elective office. I therefore propose Mr Roarty for president. He is a respected figure in the glen and, I feel sure, broadly acceptable to the Canon.'

'I second that,' said Gillespie.

It was put to the vote and Roarty was elected.

'Thank you,' Roarty said. 'Is it the wish of the meeting that I should remain in the chair?'

Everyone murmured yes, except Cor Mogaill.

'Can't we have an informal meeting over a few jars without making pompous asses of ourselves like a drove of schoolteachers at their AGM?' he asked. 'Is all this fiddle-faddle about proposing and seconding necessary among boon companions?'

'We must now elect a secretary,' said Roarty, ignoring him.

'If we must have a secretary, I propose myself for the job,' said Cor Mogaill.

There was a long silence while they glanced at one another and at the self-promoting Cor Mogaill, who was reclining in his chair with a challenging look in his eye.

'I don't think it would be a good idea to have a self-declared Marxist as secretary,' said Rory Rua. 'We must elect men who go to Mass on Sunday and receive the sacraments regularly. I propose Gimp Gillespie because he fulfils those two conditions and because he's used to the pen and in a position to give us valuable publicity in the *Dispatch*.'

'I second that,' said Potter.

A vote was taken and Gillespie was elected with Cor Mogaill abstaining.

'Now for the treasurer. May I have a nomination?' Roarty asked.

'I'm certain that Gimp will make a good secretary,' Cor Mogaill conceded. 'But I think I'd make an equally good treasurer. I don't mind going to Mass while this project of ours is in motion, so will someone nominate me, then?'

'Where are your Marxist principles?' Rory Rua demanded.

'I'll define my position but, like most politicians, only after I'm elected. As an upright citizen, I refuse to be interrogated.'

'No reflection on your honesty, Cor Mogaill, but I think that a man who has admitted to having robbed the poor box should not be in charge of the finances of what may well become an epoch-making society in the history of the church.' Rory Rua spoke with an unaccustomed twinkle in his eye.

'I didn't rob the poor box.'

'Then why did you tell the Canon and McGing that you did?'

'I did it to show McGing up for a jackass by later denying it all. And when the Canon asked me if it were Marxist doctrine to rob the poor of their coppers, I saw it as an opportunity to confuse him with Scripture by reminding him that the New Testament says quite clearly that gold and silver are infected. I told him that I threw the money into the sea in order to cleanse it before the poor received it. Do I make myself clear?'

'Cor Mogaill, you're quite mad,' Roarty said. 'Everyone in the glen now believes that it was you who robbed the poor box. Why did you blacken your name by admitting to a crime you didn't commit?'

'You're all sunk in embourgeoisement. What does the opinion of capitalists, even tuppence-ha'penny capitalists like you, matter to a Marxist revolutionary? I've already promised to repair the poor box and "return" the money—a master-stroke in my war against Church and State. Loftus and McGing are happy in their ignorance, while the real culprit may well be encouraged to commit a more serious crime in the hope that I'll take the rap again. In this I'm a true revolutionary, undermining society by seeming to take its sins on myself!'

'It's a Christ-like rather than a Marx-like gesture,' Potter smiled.

'Anyway we can't have you as treasurer,' Rory Rua declared. 'You're too confused in your thinking to seek high elective office.'

'Shit and piss and cock and balls,' said Cor Mogaill.

'I nominate Rory Rua for treasurer,' said Gillespie.

Potter seconded the proposal and Rory Rua was duly elected.

'And what about Potter and me?' demanded Cor Mogaill.

'We'll make you both honorary officers,' said Roarty, going to the bar for another round of drinks.

He was both angry and irritated. How could he keep McGing busy if Cor Mogaill was going to put a spanner in the works every time? He would have to think of something serious, something more indictable than robbing the poor box, something that even Cor Mogaill would not 'confess' to. Now, thanks to Cor Mogaill, McGing was free to devote himself to the murder again. He was running out of time, and he still hadn't devised a way of dispatching Potter. He was enjoying the meeting, however. It was a fresh venture, and with any luck it would obliterate the insistent pattern of thought that dogged him night and day.

'Next we must think of a name for our society,' he announced, returning with a full tray.

'Surely, you're putting the cart before the horse,' Cor Mogaill advised. 'First we should discuss what we aim to do.'

'I propose a self-explanatory name,' said Roarty. 'The Society for the Preservation of the Wooden Altar.'

'Too prosaic,' said Gillespie. 'We need a name that will lull the ear and linger in the public memory. We need a pronounceable acronym like Unesco. We must think in terms of public relations. And let me tell you, there is nothing subeditors like better than a snappy title. The column width of the *Dispatch* is only twelve picas, in layman's language two inches. Therefore we need a short name for headlines, which is why I propose the Wooden Altar Society, which will collapse into the catchy acronym WAS.'

Cor Mogaill, flinging his head back, collapsed in laughter. 'Why don't we call it the SFB?' he hooted. 'The Society for Bullshit because it's what you're all talking.'

'I agree with Gillespie,' said Potter. 'What we need here is the x-factor.'

'And what the fuck is the x-factor?' Cor Mogaill enquired. 'More bullshit, or I'm a giraffe.'

'It's the unquantifiable, the unpredictable. It's what made Wellington, Nelson and Churchill great leaders against the odds. With it, we could be the instigators of a revolution, a liturgical counter-revolution that will put the clocks back to pre-tridentine times and light a thousand candles under the cassock of every priest and bishop in the country.'

'Will you just imagine the heat!' said Cor Mogaill. 'It will burn the hair off their bollocks within seconds, if they've got any.'

Roarty could see that Potter was enjoying himself. He had the knack of bringing out the worst in Cor Mogaill, and he knew it. 'Our primary aim is to preserve the wooden altar,' Roarty said, calling the meeting to order.

'And possibly to remove Canon Loftus,' said Cor Mogaill. 'Let's not pretend to an innocence we as children of the dark don't possess. If we raise enough stink over the altar, the Bishop of Raphoe will want to know why Loftus isn't keeping his parishioners in line. There will be questions over the brandy and possibly a change of scene for our Canon.'

'We mustn't be led into cheap Marxist anticlericalism,' said Rory Rua. 'We must not show the slightest hint of personal animus. We must all appear upright and honourable, occupying the front seats at Mass on Sunday. We must reform from within, not without.'

'Rory Rua, you scoundrel and hypocrite!' roared Cor Mogaill. 'Tell the truth: you don't give a fiddler's fuck for religion. All you care about is lobsters.'

'If we keep sniping at one another like this, we'll deserve to be called the Altercation Society,' Gillespie smiled.

'And the perpetrator of such a feeble pun deserves to be strung up by the privities and shot with a ball of his own inspissated stool,' Cor Mogaill hooted.

'We may talk lightly,' said Gillespie, 'but this meeting could be a turning point in the history of the Church. We're not merely saying "no" to a limestone altar; we're saying "no" to a table altar, the centre-piece of the new liturgy. Our "no", if we say it loudly enough, could be the genesis of a counter-revolution, as Kenneth has reminded us.'

'You've mentioned the x-factor, but you haven't told us the title that's got it.' Roarty turned to Potter.

'It's quite simple,' Potter replied. 'The Anti-Limestone Society.'

'Sounds like a society for cranks, a geological variant of the Flat Earth Society.' Cor Mogaill shook his head.

'Precisely,' said Potter. 'We need a title that isn't too solemn, something to show people that we have a sense of humour as well as a nodding acquaintance with theology.'

'I do believe you're right,' said Roarty, putting it to the vote. On a show of hands, Potter's title was adopted. 'Now we must discuss tactics,' Roarty continued.

'Wouldn't it be more sensible to discuss strategy?' Cor Mogaill suggested.

'We'll discuss both,' said Potter.

'We need to hold a public meeting to which everyone in the parish is invited. But first we must show we mean business. We must do something to make us a topic of conversation in every chimney corner.'

'I suggest we do something at once painless and outrageous,' said Cor Mogaill. 'Like threatening to stop paying in collections and withholding our voluntary labour. That's what would hurt the Canon most, and show the bishop that he has lost all control of his flock.'

'No,' said Rory Rua, holding up a freckled hand. 'We must be seen to be reasonable. The farthest I'd go is to paint slogans on walls and hang banners across the village street. Once we've organised public support, we'll present a signed petition to the Canon with a carbon copy to the bishop.'

'A picture of banners with slogans is certain of publication in the *Dispatch,*' said Gillespie. 'I propose the slogan "We Want Wood" because in headlines it could be abbreviated to "WWW" or "W3".'

'You're obsessed with what you call subbing,' said Cor Mogaill.

'I suggest "Wood *v.* Limestone: Where Do You Stand?"' said Rory Rua.

'A slogan is a splendid idea,' said Potter. 'But it must be more than a slogan! It must be a battle-cry, which thanks to our friend Gillespie will soon be known from one end of the county to the other. We'll paint it on walls and display it on stickers in the rear windows of our cars. We'll even place a prominent ad in the *Dispatch.*'

'It all sounds highly promising but you haven't told us the battle-cry,' said Cor Mogaill.

'HOOA! HOOA! HOOA!' said Potter, raising a clenched fist.

'And what does it mean?'

'Hands Off Our Altar!'

'I don't like the sound of it,' said Cor Mogaill. 'It's neither Irish nor English. It's like a battle-cry from one of the emergent countries of Africa.'

'Get stuffed or stewed, whichever is the less convenient,' Potter said urbanely.

'I think Potter's idea an excellent one,' said Roarty. 'We'll make banners and stickers. HOOA! I can see it becoming a national watchword.'

'I know something of lettering,' said Potter. 'I'll set to work at the weekend.'

'We'll put up the banners in the middle of the night,' Roarty said. 'That way they'll have the maximum effect on Loftus when he sees them on the way to say Mass in the morning.'

'No,' Potter advised. 'We must not come like a thief in the night. We must act in the blaze of noon and let everyone know who we are.'

They talked for another hour until Cor Mogaill, assuming the role of chairman, rebuked them for repeating themselves. As the clock struck two, Roarty went outside to make sure the coast was clear, and one after the other they left by the back door, Potter last.

'What about a wee *deoch a' dorais?*' Roarty asked, gripping him by the elbow.

'A what?'

'One for the Strasse.'

'If it were any other night, I would. I've had three late nights in a row, and I'm absolutely knackered. I really must get my head down.'

'I think we can be pleased with the night's work,' Roarty said, still hoping to detain him.

'It was a very Irish night, no offence.'

'And you were the most Irish of all.' Roarty smiled encouragingly.

'*Hibernicis ipsis Hibernior.* Is that what you're hinting at?'

'You're not the first, and you won't be the last. I think I should tell you the precedents have not been all that happy.'

'Thank you for the thought. It's something I'll bear in mind.'

Potter vanished into the night, an elusive, chameleon-like figure, yet undeniably effective among men. He had declined to be president but he influenced the discussion more than anyone else by appearing so detached that his opinion unfailingly commanded attention. It was a pity that he did not stay for a drink because a chat when the mind is weary might cast a shaft of light on so much that was dark.

'A difficult man to corner,' he thought, climbing the stairs. 'I'll just have to run him out into the open, I suppose.'

His mind was too active for sleep. Still, he went to bed and lay on his back with his eyes closed. After half an hour he put *Fünf Stücke im Volkston* on the gramophone and looked up the article on Aqueducts in *Britannica*. Pablo Casals's cello playing and the drily technical language of the encyclopedist brought him a sense of comfort that was new. It seemed to him that the most subtle luxuries of life were his, that his greatest temptations were intellectual.

THIRTEEN

Roarty could see the parochial house from the west window of his bedroom. Nora Hession closed the front door behind her and tripped lightly down the avenue between the trees. She had a sprightly walk, so light-stepping that you felt she might at any moment take wing. She was tall and slender, the kind of girl with whom the young Yeats might have lingered in the Salley Gardens. Potter didn't know his luck. It was such a pity that she was only a baby when he himself was young.

Canon Loftus, who was on retreat in Letterkenny, wouldn't be back until Saturday, and in his absence Nora slept at her sister's or possibly with the smitten Potter. The parochial house would now be empty till morning, leaving him ample time to do what must be done. He bore the Canon no personal ill-will. Tonight conditions would be perfect. He knew what to do, and how to do it.

His only objective was to give McGing something to think about other than the murder, which he now talked about tediously every day. For some inexplicable reason he had become obsessed with Allegro, as if Eales's cat were the guilty party. He kept tickling him behind the ears to make him purr, but Allegro remained indifferent to all his attempts at blandishment.

'It's unnatural for a cat not to purr,' McGing said. 'He looks depressed, as if there was something terrible on his mind. Either that or he's seen something evil that's preying on his mind.'

Roarty stroked Allegro's head with his palm and ran his forefinger down the back of his neck. Allegro closed his eyes and began to purr.

'It's the smell of stout from your hand that does it,' McGing said. 'If you don't mind, I'll take him back with me to the barracks. I'd like to conduct a little experiment.'

'He's yours as long as he'll stay with you. I must warn you, though. He's very particular. With me he's had nothing but the best.'

He smiled as McGing vanished out the door with the cat. His sense of relief lasted only until he began wondering about the nature of McGing's 'little experiment'. All through September he'd felt harried as a hare, as if every wisp of his every thought was known to McGing. His discomfiting sense of self-exposure was accompanied by a psychological impotence that paralysed his will and kept him from doing anything to the purpose. Though Cecily had written to say that she wished to remain with her aunt in London, and that she would not be taking up her scholarship, he was so self-absorbed that he scarcely gave her future a thought. Far from going to London to bring her back, he pondered with indifference how he could have strayed so far from his former self. There seemed to be no escape from the tangle of his anguished preoccupations.

He was the rope in a tug o' war between two equal forces, pulled this way and that without hope of resolution. Thoughts of Potter and McGing pinioned him on an altar of stone, as if he were a victim to be sacrificed in a ritual he could not begin to understand. His health had deteriorated; he had begun to fear for his sanity. Even with the help of a bottle of whiskey a day, he could hardly get one hour's untroubled sleep at night. He would toss between dreams of criminal investigation, complex cross-questioning, and ghoulish meals with Potter where the entrée was a thick brawn made from a severed head that bore no resemblance to Eales's. So whose was it then? That was the conundrum that kept him from sleeping. In the grey of early morning he would stagger wearily to the bathroom while black memories of the night clung to him like suffocating cobwebs. Awake or asleep, there was no respite. He would drink three hot toddies before the tremor left his hand and it was safe to shave with a razor. Going to the loo was another nightmare, as he noted with hypochondriac horror that his stool was streaked with blood, conjuring up visions of vulturine surgeons in white bent on a colostomy. Again and again he would recite to himself lines he had once found amusing:

I noticed I was passing blood
(Only a few drops, not a flood)
So pausing on my homeward way
From Tallahassee to Bombay
I asked a doctor, now my friend,
To peer into my hinder end,
To prove or to disprove the rumour
That I had a malignant tumour.

How anyone could make fun of cancer surpassed understanding. His mind had become a kaleidoscope of revolting images. He was so worried that he made an appointment with Dr McGarrigle, who lived in Glenroe and held a clinic in Glenkeel on Wednesdays.

McGarrigle was a large, likable man, an indefatigable womaniser who fancied his chances with young and old, provided they washed regularly and appreciated the needs of a man of his social standing. His fine sense of discrimination was the secret of his success with women. None of them ever complained of an unwanted advance, for to be the object of a pass from him was seen as a cachet of respectability, and to be 'cured' by him was a pleasure not unknown to several widows in the Glen whose complaints had been proof against the ministrations of more orthodox doctors.

In spite of his readiness to indulge the fantasies of his more imaginative patients on occasion, he took his duties as a doctor seriously. A dedicated drinker in the evenings, he would often go up to one of his patients in a pub and advise him to think carefully before finishing his whiskey. 'If you drink it, you may be shortening your life by as much as a year,' he would say. 'I'm not telling you to put it down. I am merely ensuring that you'll enjoy it all the more by drinking it in the full knowledge of the consequences.' Not surprisingly, he was well liked, even by husbands whose wives had been cured of what he called menopausal melancholia by one or two visits to his clinic.

Curiously, the quality that endeared him most of all to his regular patients was his tendency to treat many of them for the same condition no matter what their symptoms, which encouraged a general sense of fellowship in the chaotic shipwreck that is old age. A few winters ago, when he was treating most of those who came to see him for septicaemia of the foot, Old Crubog went to him about rheumatism in the left shoulder only to be told that it was a referred pain originating in his big toe, simply a question of 'metastasis', or metathesis as Crubog reported. This year by all accounts he was treating most people for gout, yet no one seemed to mind. In fact, patients suffering from 'septicaemia of the foot', 'gout', or whatever disease was most prevalent in his clinic that winter were rather proud of their status, convinced as they were that they need not worry. It had long ago been observed that only patients who were treated for more prosaic conditions actually died.

Gimp Gillespie, who liked to think he had taken Dr McGarrigle's measure, evolved the theory that McGarrigle had what few doctors can be accused of—a professional sense of humour. Quite simply, he treated all patients suffering from imaginary ailments for the same condition on the principle that a placebo for septicaemia of the foot was as good as a placebo for rheumatism. Roarty could not help wondering if one of the good doctor's placebos might cure him of all his ills.

'Now what can be ailing a fine big fellow like you?' McGarrigle asked. He did not smile, which Roarty took to be significant.

'Blood in the rectum,' he said, pleased that unlike most of the doctor's patients he knew the word 'rectum'.

'Rectal bleeding,' said McGarrigle. 'Not as uncommon as you might think. Let's have a quick look at the seat of the trouble, no pun intended.'

'You're not going to poke something up my arse?' Roarty enquired, so alarmed that he forgot the word 'anus'.

'Unfortunately, that may be necessary.'

'Would you mind warming it in your hand first. I'm rather sensitive behind.'

'It isn't what you think,' the doctor said, pulling on a light rubber sheath over his index finger, which for some obscure reason reminded Roary of Eales's fabled lust finger.

'Now try to touch your toes with your fingertips.'

Roarty bent forward with his trousers round his ankles, and thought of Edward II, King of England from 1307 to 1327.

'Mm!' said McGarrigle.

'What?'

'I just said "Mm!" a sound that doctors make to assist diagnosis.'

'Well, what can it be? Gout?' Roarty asked hopefully.

'Why do you think it may be gout?'

'I eat a lot and drink a lot. I burn the candle at both ends.'

'It isn't gout,' McGarrigle said firmly.

'You think it may be a prostate problem?' Roarty ventured in desperation.

'Hold out both hands in front of you.'

Roarty watched his hands tremble though he tried to keep them still.

'How much do you drink in a day?'

'No more than a bottle.'

'Stout or whiskey?' McGarrigle asked humourlessly.

'Whiskey.'

'A bottle is probably enough.'

McGarrigle gave him such a thorough going-over that at the end Roarty felt as bruised and pummelled as a lump of plasticene. The doctor sat down at his desk as if suddenly weary of life and death.

'What's the verdict?' asked Roarty. 'Haemorrhoids?'

'No, it isn't piles. It's something more shadowy, lurking in the no man's land between the psyche and the soma.'

'And what does that mean?'

'I think it's a symptom of stress, mental stress.'

Roary laughed out of sheer relief. 'You're sure it isn't the Bucko?' he asked.

'The Bucko?' McGarrigle gave him the kind of look that one condemned man might give another.

'I don't like saying it because I'm a bit superstitious. It's the Latin for crab.'

'I can't be sure, and I don't want to alarm you unnecessarily. All I'll say is that we must leave no stone unturned. I'm going to have you admitted to Sligo Hospital for tests. It's probably nothing to worry about, but the modern GP is usually tempted to leave the verdict to a higher court. Could you drink less without putting yourself out?'

'I don't think so.'

'You could try.'

'If I tried, I wouldn't be myself.'

McGarrigle wrote a prescription for sleeping tablets, while Roarty wondered if it was a psychiatrist he needed, not a doctor. What would McGarrigle say if he had told him of his more alarming symptoms: the enfeebling dreams of macabre feasts with Potter or Sisyphean struggles with an eagle in red knickers? In many ways the latter was the more harrowing because he invariably woke up from it limp from exhaustion. Helplessly, he would watch a downy eaglet in an eyrie grow before his eyes into a golden eagle of fearsome strength and majesty that stared at him with predatory curiosity. He would fling a spear at the great bird's breast, which the bird would catch with its wing in mid-air and fling it back at him. The single combat between man and bird would go on through the small hours until Roarty in desperation would make straight for the bird and drive the spear through its furcula. Undeterred, the eagle would pluck it from its breast and drive it back in again with a laugh of aquiline contempt. Finally it would turn double somersault, revealing a pair of red knickers under its thigh feathers.

'I'm wearing red knickers, can't you see?' the great bird would crow. 'I'm utterly impregnable, you impotent half-wit.'

He would wake up sweating with exertion, as if he had undergone a real struggle with a real eagle. Though the red knickers probably referred to Florence's preference in night wear, he reasoned that the dream must symbolise his daily torture by Potter and McGing, which was nothing short of Promethean in its inexorable continuity. Perhaps McGarrigle had unwittingly stumbled on the root of his troubles, of which rectal bleeding was only a symptom. Quite possibly, the doctor had special insight into that mental fragility affecting seasoned drinkers, and the darkness within that threatens to overcome the light of reason.

He took McGarrigle's sleeping tablets for a week, and concluded that bad dreams were preferable to a thick head in the morning. The rectal bleeding concentrated his mind with every visit to the lavatory, after which the only relief was a walk in the garden for a moment's communion with the withered conifer. No longer dying, it was now dead. Still, he continued to feed the roots before facing breakfast in the morning. He would carry bucket after bucket of water to the bottom of the garden and feel the dust-dry needles crumble between his fingers, brown as snuff. Yet in the deepening twilights of September the conical silhouette of the dead tree gave it the very outline of life. 'What seems alive is alive, but only to an eye that is dead,' he told himself. 'I hope I'm not going mad. With every day that passes I make less and less sense, even to myself. Perhaps I should talk more to Susan. She's a big, healthy girl who thinks only healthy thoughts. She is fond of me, and generous of her time and body, if only I could avail more frequently of her generosity.'

He thought of Cecily in a foreign country, naïve and vulnerable, a prey to a kind of soft talk for which her sheltered upbringing and education had not prepared her. Life as he used to know it had come to an end. All that was now left was the outline, days of going through the motions for the benefit of onlookers, while his inner life lay frozen in paralysis. He had undergone a form of lignification; he had become an article of furniture in other men's worlds. They came to him for a drink, shook his hand, and whispered the latest joke in his ear; and he smiled, pulled pints, and took their money with as much conviction as a puppet in a sideshow. Where would it end? Imprisonment? Suicide? Further murder and a life not worth living? In destroying Eales, he had destroyed himself. Yet his instinct was still for life, and it burgeoned within him as he watched Nora Hession's carefree step on the fenceless road that led to her sister's cottage, or possibly Potter's.

He went downstairs to help Susan in the bar, noting with interest that Potter was missing. As he had decided to limit himself to six whiskies, the evening dragged; every twenty minutes had become an hour. He felt pleased when the last of the locals had gone and he and Susan could begin the washing up. He said good night to her at half-past twelve and slowly climbed the stairs to his room. Since it was too early to begin the night's work, he lay over the bedclothes listening to Schumann's piano quintet and reading the article on Alchemy in *Britannica*. Sadly, the transmutation he desired was such wishful thinking that he put down the volume and closed his eyes, suddenly alive to the spontaneous clarity of a young man's music.

He had first heard the quintet on his honeymoon in London and knew at once that it was the music of a young man in love. Years later he discovered that Schumann had written it in the first blissful weeks of his marriage to Clara Wieck; and though his own marriage had turned to bitter aloes, he felt grateful to Schumann for confirming his perception of a reality he himself had found all too fleeting. Also grateful for these few stolen moments of transparency in a world that had become so opaque, he reached for a tattered biography of the composer and opened a page at random near the end:

Suddenly on the night of February 10 the final dissolution of personality began. Previously Schumann had been distressed by aural illusions. Now what had formerly been a noise became a persistent note. As sleepless night followed sleepless night, the sound grew into music, 'a music more wonderful and played by more exquisite instruments than ever sounded on earth'. In the disordered mind whole compositions appeared to compose themselves.

   After Dietrich left the house Schumann quietly collected a few effects and asked Clara to send for Dr Böger in order that he might be taken into an asylum. He feared the night. 'It will not be for long,' he said. 'I shall soon come back, cured.'

Unlike the egomania of Nietzsche, the madness of Schumann flowed from an oversensitive nature that was capable of the most exquisite self-knowledge. There was mental instability in his family, and Schumann himself had experienced symptoms of mental disorder by the time he was twenty-three. After such knowledge he must have lived from one year to the next with the fear of insanity pressing darkly like a storm cloud on his head, until the hammer blows of experience finally put him down. Suffering, he had read somewhere, was the surest way to self-knowledge. Now he knew that suffering was not enough. One needed nerves of steel to survive long enough to profit from it, for what was the use of suffering that snuffed out the sufferer?

Who suffered more, Beethoven or Schumann? The answer, if suffering could be measured in a unit like ergs, might conceivably be Beethoven, yet he had the will and stamina to survive to compose the Choral Symphony, the Missa Solemnis, the Diabelli Variations, and the last five string quartets, while poor old Schumann had already succumbed to the stress of living by the time he was forty-four. There was no doubt in Roarty's mind which of the two he found the more congenial.

He recalled a spring day when he was barely eight, a day of fleecy clouds that made him think of open fields and sheep grazing. Parked in the village was a big, white ambulance with mad Lanty Duggan sitting in the back clutching a spray of bluebells to his chest, shaking his big empty head while sparse ringlets of grey hair swept his shoulders. On the way home from school he and some other boys peered in through the open door to find Lanty crooning the word 'Kruger' over and over again. With dismay in his big, red eyes he gazed at them uncomprehendingly and flung the bluebells in their innocent faces. An old-timer called Dúlamán from the village came up behind Roarty and croaked:

'Say goodbye to Lanty. You'll never see him again.'

Roarty looked at him as if he had a screw lose himself.

'Go on, Tim. Lanty is your uncle, though you may not want to know.'

Lanty Duggan's ringlets swung like cowbells as he grabbed Roarty by the elbow.

'Ask your good-for-nothing father if his fingers smell in the morning,' he neighed.

'Is Lanty Duggan my uncle?' he asked his mother when he got home.

'Who told you that?'

'Dúlamán.'

'Dúlamán should be on his knees saying his prayers.'

'Is Lanty Duggan your brother, Mammy?'

'He was my brother when we were children.'

'He told me to ask Daddy if his fingers smell in the morning.'

'He doesn't know the meaning of what he says. But don't mention it to your father; he might not like it.'

Roarty knew little of Lanty Duggan except what he had gleaned from overheard gossip and in later years from his mother, who told him that Lanty had been a black sheep from the beginning. At seventeen he tried to rape her, after which he took a religious turn that manifested itself in an extreme distaste for women. Since no woman would look twice at him, he was determined to make life impossible for lovers. He would lie in wait for courting couples and belabour them with his ashplant. On one occasion, having put the man to flight, he tore off the girl's knickers before letting her off with a warning. In fairness it must be said that he was no common or garden fetishist; instead of storing his trophies to help while away a winter night, he would climb up a telegraph pole and nail them to the crossbar as a reminder to passersby that Lanty Duggan had been there.

His father was so horrified by his exploits that he paid his passage to Glasgow and promised to send him three pounds a week on condition that he stayed there. The life of a remittance man was not for Lanty, however. After four months he arrived back in the glen with a new-found knowledge of Scottish poetry and a crooked staff which, he claimed, had once belonged to the Ettrick Shepherd. It would seem that the Scots had cured him of his misogyny, for now he began leading the life of a quiet vagrant who knows every cranny and nook of his hinterland. In summer he lived in a tent which he carried everywhere on his back and pitched in a roadside field wherever night overtook him; and in winter he would take up residence in an empty barn or hayloft and emerge during the hours of light to warm himself over a fire of turf and brushwood in the shelter of a rock or hedge.

He saw himself as the last of the ancient Fianna, leading the life of Oisín after all the comrades of his imagination had departed. It was a romantic image that was not borne out by the reality. He would spend the day begging for milk, eggs, fish, potatoes, turnips and cabbage as well as turf to make a fire on which to cook them. In his way he was something of a gourmet. He would never eat baker's bread from the shop. He insisted on having soda bread and homemade butter, and not every housewife in the glen could make those very special commodities to his liking. It was little wonder then that he was made welcome in those houses where the housewife took his begging as a compliment and accolade. On such occasions he was in the habit of saying that there were two things not every woman could make—soda bread and butter—and that half the secret was to know how much soda to put in the former and how much salt in the latter.

Though regarded by some as a halfwit, he was generally seen as a prince of beggars because he never accepted money. Drunken farmers in pubs on fair days would thrust pound notes under his nose just to tempt him. Though he would accept as much whiskey and stout as he could hold, he was never known to sully his hands with cash. Not surprisingly, many of the glen folk saw him as a saint, albeit a saint who neither washed nor shaved and who allowed his hair to grow in greasy ringlets down to his shoulders. His sainthood might have received formal recognition from the Church if the grand climacteric had not unbalanced him. In his sixty-third year all sense of shame, as the locals put it, deserted him. He would sit by the roadside with his flies undone, sunning his cock and scrotum while reminding passersby that his was the only suntanned cock in Christendom. Worse was to come. He began taking an interest in little girls. He would wait for them as they came home from school and offer them butterscotch in return for what the schoolmaster called 'intimate personal services'. Predictably, that ended the exploits of Oisín. The parish priest had a word with the sergeant who had a word with the doctor, and before Lanty Duggan could say 'Christendom' the ambulance had whisked him off to the asylum.

Dúlamán was right. Lanty Duggan never came back. He died in a straitjacket a year later, shouting his head off for beautiful women. Roarty had a vision of a smelly old man in the back of an ambulance clutching a bunch of bluebells, and suddenly he feared for himself. It seemed to him that far from being too short, life was longer than he cared to contemplate. Day upon day reached into the distance, a dusty plain that the traveller must traverse unaided and alone. Each day was a lifetime in itself, full of pitfalls, encounters, and unwanted conversations that smothered the yearning spirit and exhausted the body's vim. If only he had not been blessed with such a vivid memory! Though it afforded him the pleasure of learning by heart whole articles in *Britannica*, it was a curse in that it preserved old hurts and sores best forgotten.

His consciousness was largely the product of his experience, and the force of his experience flowed from his unusual memory. If only he could control it as a rider controls a horse, suppressing what he wished to forget and remembering only those things that came with a warm glow. His active imagination, which in normal times enriched his life, now led him into a search for endless meanings where none might have been intended. His life had become a book that clamoured for close textual analysis. Now he could not hear even one of Potter's mellifluous sentences without repeating it to himself, changing the inflexions and recasting it in the hope that by some arcane linguistic alchemy the Englishman's dread secret might be exposed. Likewise, he could no longer pass the time of day with McGing without dwelling on the dedicated single-mindedness of a hunter who was half in love with his quarry simply because it was his quarry and no one else's. If only he could anaesthetise himself against the sting of these encounters; if only he could enjoy one day of self-forgetfulness without having to pour a bottle of whiskey down his neck to achieve oblivion by the evening.

He put Schumann's piano concerto on the gramophone and imagined that he detected a foreshadowing of madness in the evanescent darkness of the first movement. It was only a moment's intimation, shattered by flashes of heavenly light, and try as he might he could not discern the lack of mental robustness he so eagerly sought.

At half-past two, when the moon had set, he crept downstairs, took a hold-all from the kitchen, and stuffed into it a pair of thick woollen socks, a pair of gloves, a torch, a cold chisel, a club hammer, and a box of cigarettes, cigarette ash and charred matches from the waste paper basket in the bar, what Potter referred to as the WPB. Finally, he took a small bag of blue till or boulder clay from his hiding place under the sink and let himself out by the back door, taking the side-road behind the Ard Rua where he was less likely to meet a car or pedestrian.

He lurked briefly under the trees by the parochial house gate, alert for any unusual sound but all he heard was the fluttering of a roosting bird he had disturbed and a groan from a spancelled donkey in the next field. He looked at the stars through a threadbare roof of branches overhead, noting that the wind was due west and that clouds were coming in over the sea. With a tremor of anticipation, he opened the hold-all, pulled on the woollen socks over his shoes, and put on the gloves. Keeping to the shadows under the trees, he sidled up to the house and nimbly crossed the lawn to the back.

With a tap of the hammer he broke a pane in the kitchen window and, retreating quickly to the garden, he stood listening. He waited ten minutes, ready for the slightest stir on the road or in the house, but all was silence. Again he stole forward, and in a matter of minutes he had opened the window and climbed through. As a prominent member of the parish council who had business with the Canon from time to time, he knew the house so well that he went straight to the little door beneath the stairs, where the Canon kept his vintage claret and the guns he was in the habit of showing to visitors of social consequence.

He took out the Canon's two shotguns and put them standing against the wall in the hallway where Nora Hession would see them in the morning, and he put two bottles of claret in his hold-all for his own enjoyment and Susan's. He and Susan always had a late Sunday lunch together, and after a bottle each it was anyone's guess what might be achieved. Rummaging in the Canon's glory hole, he found a leather leg-of-mutton bag which he knew contained a .22 Remington rifle belonging to Dr Loftus, the Canon's brother, who came to Glenkeel to shoot from time to time.

He opened the bag, balancing the rifle on his hands in the dark. A fine weapon, a pleasure to handle, and he knew it to be in beautiful condition. He gripped the small of the butt with his right hand and felt for the trigger with his trigger finger. Having pushed the safety catch over, he took aim at the centre of the fanlight above the front door. He pulled the trigger, listening appreciatively to the decisive click of the striker pin. Very satisfying, provided the right man was at the far end of the barrel. It would have to be a heart shot because he did not believe in causing a fellow sufferer unnecessary pain. A professional job, cold and impersonal, sharp and sure as the death of the seal on Carraig a' Dúlamáin.

He put the rifle back in its case and went into the sitting-room, scattering blue till and trampling it into the Canon's new carpet. He filled an ashtray with cigarette butts, cigarette ash and seven burnt matches, not forgetting to spill some of the ash on the Canon's mahogany table. Finally, he went to the sideboard and shone his torch on the bottles. His eye passed over the Bushmills and Jameson and rested on an unopened bottle of Glenlivet. He poured out half a glass of the whisky and, without tasting it, poured half of what was left down the kitchen sink, praying God to forgive the unforgivable waste. Then he placed the bottle beside the glass on the table and placed a chair and the Canon's leather footstool alongside. As an afterthought he poured a little blue till on the footstool, which gave him a dart of pleasure far in excess of the action.

For a moment he stood by the door and shone the torch on the table. It would make a perplexing sight for McGing when called out to investigate in the morning. He would take it as a personal affront that anyone should have the cheek to break into a house within half a mile of the barracks, steal a rifle, smoke eight or nine cigarettes, muddy the carpet, and drink half a bottle of the Canon's best Scotch before leaving. It was not the kind of thing that happened in the best policed parishes. He could not keep himself from laughing as he climbed out through the window with the hold-all and rifle. For the first time since receiving Potter's bogmail letter, he felt in full possession of his life again.

He made his way down the fields to the river, crossed the Minister's Bridge, and found a secluded culvert he remembered from boyhood. Pushing back the rushes at the entrance, he crawled inside and hid the rifle in the uppermost and driest part. Backing out, he pulled the woollen socks off his shoes, filled them with stones, and flung them into the deepest part of the river.

He felt quite elated. His head had cleared and the black anxiety that had been gnawing at his gizzard for weeks had vanished. He had missed his vocation. Essentially, he was a man of action who had been born into the wrong age. Instead of enjoying the camaraderie of the officers' mess or the explorer's campfire, he was living the life of an idle publican, condemned to mete and dole unappreciated pints unto a savage race.

Reaching home at four, he scraped the labels off the two claret bottles with his penknife and slept soundly until morning. He got up at ten to find Susan in the kitchen serving a breakfast of rashers and black pudding to a ravenous Allegro.

'That McGing has no cat sense,' she said seriously. 'He should have known better than to give Allegro cheap Whiskas from a tin.'

'He's neither a cat-man nor a dog-man,' Roarty said, putting an appreciative arm round her waist. 'Never trust a man no animal will trust.'

FOURTEEN

Potter was reading a book about bogs, sent to him by Margaret. It was, he felt, typical of her childish sense of humour to find the idea of bogs amusing. 'Think of it,' she wrote. 'The announcement "I'm going to the bog" will have a new and refreshing meaning for you. What a pity I am unable to share in the experience.' Though she might be surprised to hear it, he was reading the book with interest and in the knowledge that he was adding to his fund of arcane and, to him, completely useless information.

He now knew that the bogs on the west coast of Ireland, unlike those on the central plain, were classified as blanket bogs. He had a good mind to write her a boring letter explaining at great length the difference between bogs of the ombrogenous and soligenous varieties, not to mention *Hochmoore*, *Niedermoore*, and *Übergangsmoore*. If nothing else, it would teach her not to send him presents tongue in cheek. If only she'd leave him alone to forget the past and allow him to live with a clean slate. Not content with walking out on him, she was bent on reminding him at least one a week of how much she was enjoying herself. 'We share past versions of ourselves, you and I,' she'd written. 'They may be versions we've outlived but they're precious. We must never forget them. We must always remain friends.' Margaret was a mystery. He would never understand her, nor could he begin to imagine what she was up to. Compared with her, Nora Hession, though enigmatic in her Irish way, was an open book. Women, he thought, were a total mystery, and that of course was half their fascination.

He went to the kitchen window. It was the last week of October and most of the garden trees were bare. Day after day over the past month he had watched them change colour, seemingly at random, to olive green here and light yellow or brown there; and he had watched them falling in twos and threes, floating soundlessly to the earth through still air. He would get up in the morning expecting to find that a wind in the night had blown them all away but the nights remained untypically calm and most of the leaves remained on the trees. Then at the weekend the weather turned cold, bringing a still, dry chill that pierced the stone walls of the cottage, and he woke on Sunday morning to find that most of the leaves had fallen, as if the cold of the night had nipped their attenuated stems.

A big thrush lit on the mountain ash whose red berries had gone, apart from an out-of-reach cluster at the tip of a drooping branch. Recalling summer mornings and birds breakfasting, he noted how the fernlike leaves, some a sickly yellow and some a faded green, looked as if they belonged to different trees. His eye travelled to the weeping willow by the stream, whose drooping branches waved to and fro like ribbons sweeping a circle of black, sticky earth on which nothing grew. A single leaf fell from a sycamore and stuck in the wet clay beneath, a cheerless sight that made him think again of Margaret. She had left him of her own free will but he would never be rid of her entirely. He was stuck with her; at least until she found another man capable of occupying whatever vacuum he had left in her life. There were several niches in every woman's Pantheon and only one man could occupy each of them because no man had all the gifts. If he married Nora Hession, what would she make of Margaret's letters? And if Margaret married, what would her husband make of her obsession with 'an old flame', who, in Margaret's phrase, was little better than 'an old soak'? He was crossing bridges before coming to them. He would live in the present and deal with the future when it came.

Day was fading from the sky. Ink-black clouds pressed together over the north mountain while in a corner of the west a single shaft of crimson light pierced the heavy cumulus over the sea. It was a picture of his own disappointing life, so far from the high ideal with which he had set out. Still, he was grateful for the single shaft of light that was Nora Hession. It was beginning to rain, and with the rain came sadness. Nothing was perfect, least of all the weather. He found himself humming an adagio from an early Mozart symphony that Margaret loved to listen to on Sunday afternoons.

In spite of his memories, he had much to be thankful for. He had enjoyed the past two months. As he predicted, Nora had flowered. In the space of a few weeks she had brightened into a laughing, happy girl who had only rare moments of doubt about the reality of what was happening to them both. She came to the cottage and cooked him meals on the open peat fire, simple meals with flavours as fine as her own sense of humour. At first she came to his bed with a semblance of diffidence and longing that reminded him of his adolescence and made him feel closer to her than he really was. Later she was open and loving, meeting him as an equal partner with a gift of jogging him into moments of self-mockery and happy self-discovery. Never before had he such a sense of sharing in something so unexpected, so different from anything in his previous experience. He took her to the local hotel for drinks, to Donegal Town for dinner, and for walks on the mountains and along the sea cliffs where she shared his field-glasses and soon came to recognise the rarer species in which he was interested. They talked about everything except their relationship, which was a welcome change from Margaret's recently acquired passion for the kind of dissection that kills all spontaneity and creates a feeling that life is no more than a puppet-show to be ridiculed.

When he was not at work on the mountain or with Nora Hession, he was immersed in the erratic affairs of the Anti-Limestone Society. He was devoting far too much time to it, simply because without his constant urging it would have died a natural death. The so-called executive committee, provided it had enough to drink, would talk the hind leg off a donkey without giving a thought to action. Roarty seemed willing enough at their evening meetings, only to appear absent-minded and preoccupied the following day. At times it was difficult to know what precisely was on his mind. Rory Rua, though sensible and sharp-witted, was too unwilling to offend the Canon while Gimp Gillespie was a man of words rather than deeds, and his words followed a formula that never varied. His anodyne report of one of their most obstreperous meetings read like a mischievous parody of the affairs of the Irish Countrywomen's Association.

Cor Mogaill alone was willing to match words with deeds. He and Potter hung banners across the village street and distributed stickers to every car owner in the glen. They organised a well-attended meeting in the local hall and visited every house in the parish, collecting signatures for a petition to Canon Loftus with a copy to the bishop, but still the Canon sat tight. They had expected fulminations from the pulpit and at least a letter of acknowledgement from the bishop only to be met with a wall of ecclesiastical silence.

Potter did not believe for a moment that Loftus would give up without a fight, and he was determined to show at all costs that he and his friends had not run out of ideas. After much toing and froing, he prevailed on Roarty, against the counsel of Rory Rua, to call a public meeting to discuss the possibility of withholding financial support from the new church, unless the Canon gave in. In addition he urged Gimp Gillespie to write a lively piece for one of the Dublin dailies in view of the bishop's known sensitivity to adverse publicity. Gillespie, however, had his own ideas about his proper role. 'I'm a Donegal man writing for Donegal men, not an unprincipled hack writing for Dublin jackeens who wouldn't know what to do with a square meal if they saw one.'

Gillespie's refusal to put himself out was an all-too-frequent manifestation of the cussedness of the Irish character. From what he'd seen of them since his arrival, he liked the Irish. They were distinctly more attractive at home than abroad—like their national drink, they did not travel well. What he could not understand was their readiness to be taken in by conversation. They seemed to believe that if you talked about something for long enough, it would come to pass without raising a hand or foot. As an attitude, it might be excusable if the conversation itself was ingenious. On the contrary, he had come to the conclusion that the so-called inventiveness of Irish conversation was a myth put about by reticent Englishmen.

The Irish in his view were not great conversationalists in the manner of Dr Johnson; they were great talkers content to brogue away over pints of stout, constructing verbal castles in the air without a thought for matter or meaning. If the essence of conversation was communication, then the Irish failed the test, dealing as they did in the embroidery of obfuscation. Irish conversation was like one of those Celtic designs in the Book of Kells made up of a simple form like a serpent that tied itself into a thousand ornamental knots before finally eating its own tail. He wasn't sufficiently small minded to wish to teach the Irish how to converse but he had already shown one or two of them how things were done. Now he would have another word with Gillespie, in the hope that he might finally see the folly of his ways.

He drove to the village in the gathering dusk with great raindrops splashing against the windscreen and drumming on the metal of the roof. He had promised to take Nora to the hotel for a quiet drink at eight, after she had served the Canon his dinner. They would sit by the big peat fire with the long-legged tongs and exchange simple stories of the day. This evening he would tell her about his hopes, and perhaps she would tell him about hers. He had told her more about his past than she had told him about hers. She was a private person, placid on the surface but deep; a sensitive girl who'd been hurt in love more than once. He could see that she liked being with him, but more than that he could not say. Perhaps he'd never get to know her, and perhaps it did not matter. He'd felt he knew Margaret, only to have her tell him that he was one of those men who'd never get to know any woman because he lacked the insight that makes the crossing of boundaries possible. He must not think of Margaret because thinking of her reminded him of so many things he wished to forget.

Gillespie lived at the top end of the village in a low, thatch-roofed cottage with great eaves that had deepened over two centuries. Potter opened the door without knocking as was the local custom, and found Gillespie at his desk with two long index fingers poised over an antiquated typewriter. On the shelf above him were the tools of his humble trade—Brewer, Bartlett, Chambers and Fowler—and along the wall were great stacks of dusty newspapers, back copies of the *Donegal Dispatch* which he plagiarised unashamedly whenever news was scarce. He peered at Potter through a pair of steel-rimmed glasses that gave him the look of a wise old owl in a book of nursery rhymes.

'What are you writing?' Potter asked.

'Next week's notes for the *Dispatch*.'

'Don't you even wait for the news to happen?'

'I know it already,' said Gillespie, handing him a typewritten sheet.

Potter sat at the table and read with the sense of utter disbelief he always experienced when confronted with a sample of Gillespie's prefabricated prose:

A gentle, kind and charitable member of the Baltimore community has passed to her eternal reward in the person of Miss Detta Cunningham. News of her death cast a shadow of gloom over Glenkeel last week though the deceased had not returned to her native Tork since emigrating to America towards the close of the last century. She had just celebrated her ninety-sixth birthday and was for many years head cook to General Eisenhower before he became President.

The potato crop in mountainy townlands is the best in living memory. The moist, boggy soil coupled with the long, hot summer and no blight accounts, farmers are agreed, for the prolific crop. It has been a vintage year for Aran banners in particular.

Glenkeel shopkeepers are reporting an early demand for Christmas cards this year with stronger emphasis than usual on religious themes. This early demand is regarded as highly significant. One surprised shopkeeper told your correspondent that customers are either disregarding rising prices and high postage or have decided that their decision not to send cards last year was too Scrooge-like to be worthy of a people who walk in the footsteps of Saint Patrick.

'But there isn't a word of truth in what you've written!' Potter laughed. 'There is no gloom over Glenkeel. There are no queues for Christmas cards. Dammit, man, it's only October. So why have you written this pack of lies when you could have tossed off a column of the truth about the business of the Anti-Limestone Society? Or are these seemingly idiotic notes a clever allegory for something else?'

'You fail to realise that there is a received style for the "Donegal Notes and News" which must be adhered to at all costs. When someone dies, a shadow of gloom invariably falls over the area. A dead man is always described as being of sterling character and having come from a highly esteemed family, and a deceased woman as kind, gentle and charitable. If ever those time-honoured epithets were omitted, the relatives of the deceased would want to know why. I've heard of a correspondent from Garron who got two black eyes for misspelling the word "sterling".'

'I'm not complaining about the style. I'm complaining about the subject. Why not write what everyone is talking about in the pubs: bestiality in Ballinamuck; the threat to stop paying in church collections; the theft of the Canon's rifle and claret? If you were on a Fleet Street paper, you'd be sacked on the spot. Why, they wouldn't even have you on *The Times!*'

'I write what people expect to read. They don't expect to read about bestiality in a Christian country.'

'This is not a society of self-publicists, Gillespie. Its only voice is you, and your notes are the only reflection of themselves that people see from one week to the next. They don't read books and they don't watch television. All they read is your notes, and this is what you give them!'

'You don't understand, Potter. They read my notes simply because they already know what they will find in them. What they seek is not the new or the sensational, but sanction and reassurance in repetition. They enjoy the stories of the shanachie over and over again for the very same reason. They don't want to hear about your Anti-Limestone Society; they wish to read about shoals of mackerel off the coast in summer, bumper crops in the autumn, and impassable roads in winter—things that assure them all is right with the world. If you wish to know how this society represents itself to itself, don't read my notes but go down to Roarty's and listen to the conversation in the bar. It's the nearest thing to art that this society creates.'

'No, Gillespie. You go down to Roarty's and listen. Then come back and write your notes.'

'Have a drink, Potter. You're taking all this far too seriously.'

'I don't want a drink, thank you. I came to ask again if you are going to write a few wise words for the Dublin dailies about the Anti-Limestone Society. I can let you have some photos of the church and our banners to add weight to your fulminations.'

Gillespie went to the dresser and came back with two bumpers of whiskey.

'Sorry, I don't rise to Glenmorangie. All I have is Irish, I'm afraid.'

'You'd better give me plenty of water. Neat Irish gives me the most vicious heartburn.'

Gillespie vanished into the kitchen and returned with an impressively large ewer, which he placed on the table by Potter's elbow.

'I'm still waiting for your answer,' Potter said.

'Why the hurry? Can't you sit back, stretch your legs, enjoy your drink, and let your mind hover over pleasantries?'

'If you won't do it, I will.'

'Well, what's stopping you?'

'Can I borrow your typewriter?'

'Yes, provided you return it in time for next week's notes.'

'If you like, I'll write them, and I promise not to make them up.'

'You're a changed man, Potter. When you came here first, I thought you had a sense of humour. This anti-limestone business has taken you over lock, stock and barrel. Where is your philosophy, man?'

'Talking of lock, stock and barrel, you must do an exposé of McGing. The man is mad. He practically accused me the other day of stealing the Canon's rifle and claret.'

'As Roarty says, the law as personified in McGing is not merely an ass but an egregious ass. I can't imagine why he picked on you?'

'He said the burglar must have known his way around the parochial house, and that I could have been briefed by Nora. He also said that the burglar drank half a bottle of Glenlivet and left a full bottle of Bushmills untouched, something apparently that no self-respecting Irishman would do.'

'You should have told him that no self-respecting Catholic would drink a Protestant whiskey from the North if he could get Scotch.'

'I'll never get the hang of all this Irish tribalism. I told him that Glenmorangie not Glenlivet is my tipple, and that I have a perfectly good Winchester of my own.'

'McGing sees himself as the new Holmes. Believe it or not, I once heard him say in all seriousness, "My methods are based on the observation of trifles".'

'So what are you going to do about it?'

'Me?'

'Are you going to expose him in the local press for a dangerous lunatic or are you going to write about potatoes?'

'You'd like me to write about the flower of a single summer. I take the long view. I write about the hidden rhizome in the soil that puts forth again and again.'

'Gillespie, you're impossible,' Potter said, rising to go.

'Where's your hurry? Stay until we've emptied the bottle and fulfilled ourselves in philosophical conversation.'

'I'm afraid I must go. I'm taking Nora to the hotel for her brand of philosophical conversation.'

'As a bachelor, what can I say? The way of an eagle in the air; the way of a serpent upon a rock; the way of a ship in the midst of the sea; and the way of a man with a maid. They are four things which I know not.' Gillespie gave him one of his lopsided smiles.

'Come up to my place for a drink tomorrow evening. I've got a full bottle of Glenmorangie and I'll get in some Guinness to help out.'

'Potter, you're a gentleman. And we'll continue our discussion of the flower and the rhizome.'

Potter pulled up outside Roarty's, hoping that a large Glenmorangie might cool his throat after the fire of the Irish whiskey. Roarty was at his most affable. 'I've got news for you,' he smiled. 'The Canon has invited all of us on the executive committee to the parochial house for a meeting on Friday at eight. He's bitten at last, the devil.'

'I wonder what's on his mind,' said Potter.

'Devilment! What else?' said Roarty.

Potter drank his whiskey with lingering appreciation and discussed with Crubog whether snipe should be drawn before roasting. As he turned to go, Roarty, who was collecting glasses, caught his arm.

'I heard you on about snipe. Are you game for a snipe shoot the morning after the next full moon? If the night before is clear and calm, they'll be sitting close, just right for a shot.'

'There's nothing I'd like better,' said Potter, determined to get the bigger bag.

FIFTEEN

An evening without whiskey was a trial to Roarty. For that reason he usually avoided places without a ready supply of the amber elixir. Needless to say, he was not looking forward to an evening of near abstinence in Canon Loftus's parlour. He was confident that the Canon would be sufficiently civilised to offer them a drink, but it would be 'a drink', not drinks, certainly not enough to wet a drinking man's gullet. As it had now gone seven, only an hour remained to top up the alcohol already in the bloodstream and ensure a glow of physical comfort that would last for at least a further two hours. Though he'd just poured his sixth double of the evening, he was still on edge, still aware of that contraction of the muscles or nerves or whatever caused this pervasive sense of discomfort. He could relax neither standing nor sitting. Everything but everything impinged on him with aching immediacy.

The only exception, the only oasis of pleasure in his life, was Susan. She came to his bed quite frequently now, often when he least expected her. Unlike Florence, she didn't seem to mind his *outré* lovemaking technique. She was one of those women who took pleasure in the exploration of obscure byways. Last night she'd said to him with a smile, 'You and I have a secret we can't share with anyone. We're members of a club of two, and that makes us special.' She could see the funny side of his predicament, and it seemed to him that she valued him all the more for it. She would brush slowly against him in doorways and stand close to him in the bar when there was no one else around, allowing her breasts to rub against his chest. After closing time she'd sit in his lap and stroke his beard and allow him to kiss her breasts. 'You're the best lover any girl could wish for,' she once said to him, putting her hand down inside his underpants. 'All pleasure and no risk.'

Still, he had his regrets. He'd become so fond of having her around that he couldn't help worrying that she might get restless and leave for a better-paid job. Now more than ever he needed Eales's lust finger, and he deeply regretted having interred it with its owner. But had he interred it? He really could not recall. His memory had gone to pot. So where was it now? Still in the bog or under Potter's pillow? If only he knew the right address, he could order one for himself. The address was given in Eales's sex magazine, which was also with Potter, at least according to his first bogmailing letter. He would have to think of a way of getting his hands on one. It was the kind of novelty that Susan would appreciate. Besides, the name would appeal to her sense of fun.

Strangely, in spite of his best efforts, he never dreamt of her. The pattern of his preoccupations condemned him to dream only of Florence. Night after night she exhausted him by her insatiability, treating him as an unreliable dildo, humiliating him whenever his battery ran flat. One night he went in uncircumcised and came out without his foreskin. He looked for it between the sheets but it was nowhere to be found. The horror of it dismasted him on the spot. 'I want my foreskin back,' he shouted. 'And I won't rest till I've found it.'

'You'll find it where you left it,' she scoffed. 'All you need is a key to the chamber.'

His dreams had convinced him that he owed his impotence to Florence. If she had been a normal, healthy woman like Susan, he would never have been gripped with this fear of uncharted recesses. Perhaps he should have read medicine. All that clinical dissection of cadavers, both male and female, would have demystified the whole horrifying business. He would have had a scientific name for everything. He would know the function of every cog, lever and sprocket, and the knowledge of both name and function would have made him invulnerable. The famed Dr Johnson had once said that the sole end of writing was 'to enable the readers better to enjoy life, or better to endure it.' As with writing, so with knowledge. His impotence was nothing more than the impotence of ignorance, which would account for his sense of the world being a place of nameless fears. The most prevalent male fear, as he well knew, was vaginal fear. Dr Eustace Chesser must have realised that when he called his book *Love without Fear*. He'd overheard Potter mention it in a literary discussion with Gimp. Perhaps he should arm himself with a copy. Judging by what he'd heard, it would make for comparatively light reading after the avoirdupois of *Britannica*.

This morning, as he was standing outside the pub, he had a visitation from fear of a different sort. He's been looking idly at a red van coming up over the Minister's Bridge, when suddenly an apprehending hand on his shoulder sent a tremor down his spine. He looked round and there was Flanagan, the principal light-keeper in full uniform. He must have seen him with the tail of his eye, and had associated the uniform with the law. The incident was an eye-opener, living proof of the enervating sense of insecurity with which he had been living for the past two months, a feeling that Potter's latest letter had done nothing to mitigate. It read:

Dearest Roarty:
Knowing why you stole the Canon's Remington puts me one move ahead in the end game. I've left a sealed envelope with my solicitor which is to be handed over unopened to the police should anything unusual or unexpected happen to me. Nuff said?
Bogmailer.

He had read the note five or six times, seeking every conceivable nuance of meaning, but still he was not impressed. It was a clumsy attempt at bluff, clumsy because dead men don't tell tales. Potter could set down in black and white how he had witnessed the murder; he could give the location of the body and the name of the murderer; but he could not ensure conviction. There would be suspicions and questions, admittedly, but he would arrange to have satisfactory answers. And since he was paying the blackmail in cash rather than by cheque, there was nothing that might connect him with the blackmailer. Potter was in for a rude awakening though. Come to think of it, 'awakening' was hardly the word. A possible solution was within his grasp, yet his questing mind refused to rest. He was glad of one thing, however. The burglary was keeping McGing fully occupied. He had practically forgotten about the murder; he talked of nothing but the stolen rifle.

'If only I had the tools of the trade, I could solve this crime in a day,' he'd said over his morning black-and-tan. 'There are ways and means,' he nodded knowingly. 'The thief, careful though he was, left a trail of electrostatic footprints on the carpet. All I need do is sprinkle polystyrene beads on the floor. They will stick because of the electrical charge left by the feet, and the magnetised beads will show the size and shape of his shoes.'

'So why don't you do it?' Roarty asked.

'No cooperation either from Sligo or Dublin. Where are the polystyrene beads to come from, if not from them? And the cigarette butts I sent off for analysis probably ended up in the dustbin. No one wants to know about a stolen rifle. Only murder makes them sit up and take notice.'

'Surely, you're not saying we need another murder?' Roarty said seriously.

'Well, of course not. But speaking purely as a detective, I'm inclined to say it would help. Murder, like its concomitant hanging, concentrates the mind wonderfully.'

'There must be clues you haven't noticed,' Roarty reasoned. 'Fingerprints, for example?'

'There aren't any. I've dusted every inch of the room. The only fingerprints I found belonged to the Canon and Nora Hession. We're dealing with a cunning intelligence here, a veritable Moriarty. He probably had the foresight to wear gloves.'

'If you catch him, your name will be made.'

'I'm convinced that when I catch him, I'll have caught the murderer. Oh, he's a cool one, drinking half a bottle of malt Scotch and smoking seven cigarettes before leaving the scene of the crime.'

'He must be very self-confident to be so contemptuous of the law,' Roarty mused.

'My policeman's instinct tells me there's worse to come. But what really worries me is the amount of time I'm devoting to him.'

'Isn't that your job?'

'I read recently in an American book on criminology that detectives spend less time on the cases they solve than on those they don't.'

'You mean that the more time you spend on a case the less chance you have of solving it?'

'I mean that a case that's capable of solution will be solved quickly.'

'In other words only easy cases are solved?'

'But what is an easy case?' asked McGing, beginning to enjoy the interest of his interlocutor.

'An easy case must surely be one where the identity of the criminal is obvious.'

'An easy case for one policeman may well stump another. Horses for courses, policemen for criminals… that's the secret. A criminal may go scot free for years until he happens to run up against the right—or for him, the wrong—policeman.' McGing looked at Roarty as if he'd said more than he should.

'I don't understand?'

'A policeman with the right affinity, a man who can peer into the dark convolutions of the lawless mind and even anticipate its next move. The great Sherlock Holmes solved his cases by logical deduction, but in my view reason without intuition is not enough. In the perfect detective what we criminologists call the cognitive and the intuitive are perfectly balanced. Both are necessary because one nourishes the other. A man who is deficient in one is therefore deficient in the other. I don't think I'm being immodest when I say that I've got more intuition than Holmes.'

'By the look of things, you need every ounce of it in this parish,' Roarty said encouragingly.

'Isn't that why I've been discussing it with you? You've just given me a new line of enquiry.'

'How come?'

'I mustn't tell you, not yet,' said McGing, straightening his cap and leaving with a wave of the hand.

At five minutes to eight Roarty and Potter left the pub for the parochial house. The Canon himself in sombre canonicals opened the door and ushered them into the parlour where Cor Mogaill, Rory Rua and Gimp Gillespie were deeply ensconced in one of the two sofas on either side of the fire. The Canon, tall, craggy and red-faced, with a noticeable economy of phrase and gesture, offered them a choice of beer or whiskey. They made small talk about the weather while he poured the drinks and showed the seriousness of the occasion by his silence. Occupying the armchair directly in front of the big turf fire, he stretched two long legs, exposing white woollen socks beneath the turn-ups of his black trousers, and put the fingers of both hands together as if he were about to deliver himself of a prayer. Cor Mogaill looked at Roarty, who in turn looked at Potter. For a moment the silence held them all in the paralysis of uncertain expectation.

'Will you open the proceedings, Canon, or shall I?' Potter enquired, breaking the Canon's spell in smithereens.

The Canon stared at him and then at the others before clearing his throat, as he usually did in the pulpit before a sermon. Roarty sipped his whiskey and wished he had brought his hipflask. After all, it might be possible later to nip out to the lavatory for fortification as opposed to evacuation.

'As your spiritual director, I didn't ask you here to preach to you,' he began. 'I invited you here to share some of my thoughts on the new church so that as reasonable men of God we might part in agreement. When I first came to Glenkeel, the roof of the old church was leaking, the seats worm-eaten, the floor uneven, the windows rotting, and the altar a disgrace to its exalted purpose. What must I do, I asked myself. Renovate or rebuild? I knew that either way the burden of the cost would weigh heavily. Then one evening, as I was walking by the sea, I looked into the clouds above the sunset and saw a modern church, a simple structure, a cone on a cube, and I knew I had my heaven-sent answer.'

'It's a vision that only a very holy man could have,' Rory Rua said. 'I've spent my life on the sea and I never once saw a cone on a cube in the sunset. It just goes to show.'

'What does it show?' Cor Mogaill asked.

'Divine intention,' the Canon offered. 'We must acknowledge the possibility. As a man of the cloth in a sinful world, I knew there would be difficulties. I knew I would have to face those who cannot envisage a church without a steeple. I knew I'd be vilified, just as Pope Julius II was vilified for introducing Michelangelo's *terribilità* into the Sistine chapel.'

'I hope you're not comparing a mathematical cone on a cube with the ornate ceiling of the Sistine Chapel,' Cor Mogaill asked.

'What I saw in the clouds was a simple church, built from simple materials, a church that conveys something of the austerity of the lives of our saintliest coenobites. A church that in its outline reflects the simplicity of the life we live here.'

'Then why have you put a big expensive window in the west transept reaching almost to the floor?' Cor Mogaill demanded. 'I find it distracting, to say the least.'

'If you came to Mass more often, Cor Mogaill, you might get used to it. I will only add that it has a divine purpose. If you look out, what do you see? Nothing but the tombstones of the graveyard, reminding you of the imminence of your end.'

'You're right there, Canon. The very same thought came to me last Sunday at Mass,' Rory Rua enthused. 'I thought the tombstones had invaded the church.'

'But it isn't enough to remember death. You must fear death, feeling the force of *timor et tremor* and of William Dunbar's best-known poem:

> *Our pleasance here is all vane glory,*
> *This fals world is bot transitory,*
> *The flesche is bruckle, the Fend is sle:*
> *Timor mortis conturbat me.*

I needn't translate, because the English of Dunbar, thanks to the Ulster Plantation, is near enough the dialect you all speak—excepting Mr Potter, of course.'

'We've heard all that before,' Cor Mogaill said. 'We're here to discuss the limestone altar and the ideals of the Anti-Limestone Society.'

'I'm coming to that.' The Canon held up his hand but not in blessing. 'The old wooden altar was beautifully carved and lovely to look at, but it is now worm-eaten beyond repair. The dust it sheds falls into the chalice whenever I uncover it during Mass. The new altar is one of stern austerity, in keeping with the bare brickwork of the screen and the naked concrete blocks of the walls. Can anything be simpler and more pleasing to our Creator than stone created by His own hand?'

The Canon looked at each of them in turn, as if challenging them to disagree. Potter looked at Roarty, who was looking into his empty glass.

'You have made an eloquent case for your new church and altar, Canon,' he said, having realised that he was to be the spokesman for the opposition. 'I don't question the sincerity of your motives, but your arguments fail to meet the fears and doubts that drove your parishioners to found the Anti-Limestone Society.'

'A handful of my parishioners.'

'Like me, Canon, you're a stranger in the glen, a "blow-in", to use the local phrase. A bird of passage, here today and possibly in another parish tomorrow. You may be well-meaning, but you do not have to live a lifetime with the mistakes you'll leave behind. That, unfortunately, is the lot of your parishioners. Those who have been born in the glen and will spend their lives here are better qualified than I to remind you of what the old altar means to them. I think Tim Roarty, who was born and bred here, unlike either of us, can do that better than any of us.'

Roarty had been observing with fascination how the Canon's face turned a deep crimson on hearing Potter's mellifluously stinging tones. The blood rose into his cheeks, spreading down through his jowls and neck to disappear beneath the tight, white collar. It was the face of a man who was accustomed to being addressed in tones of servility, and who saw in Potter an injurious threat to his undisputed autarchy.

'The wooden altar is not a priceless treasure like the Chalice of Ardagh or the Book of Kells,' Roarty began. 'It is rather a piece of local history, carved by local craftsmen whose direct descendants are still coming to Mass on Sunday. It has seen four or five generations of glen people come and go; it has seen their baptisms and marriages, and finally their funerals. It has become an intrinsic part of the experience of every man and woman in this parish. Now this icon of local history is to be put on the fire and replaced by a nondescript "table-top" altar of the kind you see in every nondescript town in Ireland. We founded the Anti-Limestone Society to ensure that we are not shorn of a vital part of our history. We are not anti-clerical, Canon, but we will not be led like lambs to the shearing pen.'

Potter listened with head bent as Roarty said his piece. It was well said, yet in a curious way it missed the mark. His delivery sounded so much like the Canon's that he wondered if Roarty would have made a better canon than the real one. Roarty was an enigma. No one knew what he truly believed. And he suspected he didn't believe in the Anti-Limestone Society either. Was he one of those unfortunate men who were born to believe in nothing? He liked Roarty but he would never understand him.

'The table-top altar is not my invention,' the Canon said. 'It is a feature of the new Roman liturgy that has emerged from the great debates of the Second Vatican Council.'

'Codology, not theology,' said Cor Mogaill, rising to his feet and addressing them all as if he were speaking from the back of a lorry at the hustings. 'Ask any theologian, Canon. The Last Supper, and therefore the first Mass, was celebrated at a wooden, not a limestone, table.'

'Will you pipe down, Cor Mogaill, and give your arse a chance,' Rory Rua shouted, pulling at Cor Mogaill's sleeve. 'We can discuss our differences without insulting the Canon.'

'The Canon can look after himself,' said Loftus severely. 'You are both at fault. You, Cor Mogaill, for your intemperate language and you, Rory Rua, for referring to a part of our anatomy that is foreign to the subject we are discussing. Your reference to the Last Supper, Cor Mogaill, might have come more appropriately from a man who came to Mass every Sunday and received the Sacraments regularly!'

'HOOA! HOOA! HOOA!' said Cor Mogaill, with upraised fist.

'I didn't invite you here for an unseemly quarrel, but to put to you what I shall describe as a modest proposal,' the Canon said. 'For some time now I've been observing with interest the operations of Mr Potter's firm Pluto Explorations Inc. But first I must recount a piece of local history, which some of you in your enthusiasm for your Anti-Limestone Society may have overlooked. From the seventeenth century the mineral rights and the surface rights of the south mountain have been held by the Church of Ireland, which for Mr Potter's benefit can be translated as the Tory Party at prayer in Ireland.'

Roarty observed a twinkle of delight in the Canon's eye which he construed as nothing less than a twinkle of mischief. He had rested his taurine head against the back of his chair and folded his arms over his capacious stomach, as if confident that the tenor of the discussion was his to manipulate. Roarty leaned forward in case he might miss something, and he noticed that Rory Rua and Gimp Gillespie were doing likewise. The Canon cleared his throat and continued:

'For three hundred years local farmers paid a rent to the Church of Ireland for grazing rights on the mountain, which for a reason I haven't been able to establish was discontinued in 1926. On taking legal advice I discovered that you local farmers have acquired at least what may be called "squatters' rights" to the grazing in the fifty years that have elapsed since 1926. The more complex question, and therefore the more costly to determine, is whether you have also acquired other rights in the mountain. Now Mr Potter's firm has secured a five-year option on the disused mine with the right to take up a 25-year lease at £5,000 plus a modest royalty if mining of barytes should restart. We all know which party has the best deal: it is Mr Potter's firm. There is no doubt about the party with the worst deal: it is you local farmers whose rights have not been consulted.'

'Utter nonsense!' said Potter, 'plus a dollop of codswallop for good measure.' He looked at the other members of the executive committee but they were not listening to him; they were looking expectantly at the Canon.

'It may seem far-fetched now, but will it seem so in ten years' time? As a result of my enquiries, I've learned that the south mountain deposit may contain as much as 700,000 tons of ore. At a modest £25 a ton for the untreated rock, the total deposit might be valued at £17.5 million, most of which will line the coffers of Mr Potter's American firm. The Americans will pay a pittance to the Church of Ireland, which is no better at business than theology. They will ship out the unmilled rock, leaving this country with the minimum economic advantage and the farmers whose rights they have usurped without a brass farthing.'

'All this is a fictive confection of your extravagant imagination,' Potter interjected.

'Now, no swearing in front of the Canon!' Rory Rua admonished.

'I didn't swear!' Potter snapped.

'I heard you say "fick",' Rory Rua insisted. 'We all know what that means.'

'Let Mr Potter finish,' the Canon smiled. 'I think he said "fictive", which means something that isn't literally true… But you were saying, Mr Potter?'

'I have bad news for you, I'm afraid. In the samples that have so far been analysed, the percentage of barytes is too small to make for economic mining. I've been told by the London office that, barring miracles, my team will be recalled before the end of the year.'

The Canon held up a hand and smiled. 'It is in Pluto's interest to conceal the size of the deposit and stress the operational difficulties. They think they'll get their way by saying one thing and doing another, but they haven't reckoned with a certain canon in the Diocese of Raphoe. I propose to organise the local farmers into a vociferous and single-minded group since they all, you included, have a claim to some rights in the mountain. I'll find out what those rights are and insist that they be acknowledged. I think you will agree that the time has come to disband the Anti-Limestone Society and raise the flag of the Anti-Exploitation Society.'

'We're sufficiently ambidextrous to manage both,' said Cor Mogaill.

'It is not an option. If you want me to lead the Anti-Exploitation Society, you will have to bury the other. I am not being immodest when I say I have friends in high places (I refer to this world, not the next), and friends among the legal fraternity on whose services we shall have to call. You know I'm not a loser. In this venture, and in the words of Christ himself, he who is not with me is against me. Are you with me, Roarty?'

Roarty studied the challenging thrust of the Canon's chin. He was a blunt man with none of Potter's polish, and in his crafty way he had found the answer to the Anti-Limestone Society. There was 'gold' in the south mountain, some of which might help pay the blackmail.

'Well, Roarty?' asked the Canon.

'I'm with you,' Roarty mumbled, not daring to look at Potter.

'Rory Rua?'

'You can count on me, Canon.'

'Gillespie?'

'I have my reservations but still I'm with you.'

'Cor Mogaill?'

'Go to now, ye rich men, weep and howl for your miseries that shall come upon you. Your riches are corrupted... your barytes is cankered; and the rust of it shall be a witness against you, and shall eat your flesh as it were fire.'

The Canon held up a fatherly hand again and laughed.

'Even a Marxist can misquote Scripture for his purpose. May I give you a greater authority than James? Christ himself said: "The labourer is worthy of his hire." Here, my dear Cor Mogaill, we're on the side of the angels.'

'The fallen angels?' Cor Mogaill enquired. 'I think, Canon, you must have been reading Machiavelli.'

'There is nothing devious or self-seeking in my methods. I shall be perfectly frank. You all will get a share of any profits arising, and a portion of your share will find its way into the collection plate on Sunday, I hope. In short, this is one of those rare and satisfying occasions when it is possible to serve God and Mammon simultaneously.'

Cor Mogaill gave a high-pitched squeak and delved madly into his rucksack. He pulled out a bundle of tattered newspapers and held up one of them before the company. 'I'll only say this, he shouted, finding his place:

'"Let us always be truly poor. If we have nothing, no one can take it from us. If we own nothing, nothing can own us. Only an absolutely poor man is absolutely free."'

'A fine Marxist, you are!' the Canon jeered.

'I'm a Marxist with a difference. I don't merely seek a redistribution of wealth. I seek a redistribution of suffering as well. And we all know the distributor of that!'

'A true Marxist would say that you can't redistribute one without redistributing the other... But my dear Potter, you are curiously silent.' The Canon gave one of his self-satisfied smiles.

'I'm flabbergasted at the speed with which my friends have turned Turk. Only the other evening they were quoting the penny catechism and papal bulls in support of their anti-limestone ideals.'

'The vagaries of the human mind and heart are what make human life so fascinating. We live and sometimes learn. But now we have business to do, business that may embarrass you, Mr Potter. As a servant of Pluto, you can hardly be expected to join in a plot to deprive them of their profits. We shall, therefore, understand if you should wish to withdraw.'

'I have no desire to stay.' Potter glanced around at the sheepish ex-officers of the disbanded Anti-Limestone Society.

'Neither have I,' said Cor Mogaill, joining him.

As the Canon accompanied them both to the door, Roarty wondered what on earth he should say to Potter the following evening. The Canon returned, rubbing his hands, pleased with the outcome of his tactics.

'Now we can put our heads together,' he said, pouring them another drink, much to the surprise of Roarty.

SIXTEEN

Potter was sitting by the window of the cottage with an oil can and a wad of tow on the chair beside him. He was cleaning his shotgun, having spent the morning shooting. It was almost three o'clock, about forty-five minutes before sunset, and already the November light was fading. The sun, shyly hiding somewhere in the west, had permeated with deep evening reds the feathery clouds that hung like threadbare curtains in the high heavens. Below them, long streaks of blue-black cloud were piling in from the sea in dark contrast to the quiet, heavenly light in the upper reaches of the sky.

Were these frayed, reddish clouds really becalmed or did they just seem becalmed by comparison with the furious activity below? Thinking of a tondo by Tiepolo, he closed one eye and observed the clouds through the branches of the mountain ash. They were moving eastwards very slowly, almost imperceptibly, and he wondered what a meteorologist would make of the varying speeds of the wind at different altitudes. Would he expect a change in the weather or would he say that it was yet another instance of how easily the uninformed eye may be deluded? So much in life was a matter of illusion.

There was nothing illusory about the November weather over the past week or so. It was hard and cold, so cold that he was obliged to move from the bedroom and sleep in the alcove bed next to the kitchen hearth fire, which he never allowed to go out. Now for the first time in a fortnight the sky promised rain. He had enjoyed the first weeks of November, which again and again brought home to him the beauty of the countryside in early winter. As the sunrise was late, he saw it every morning on the way to his work on the mountain.

Frosty mornings made him shiver, not just with cold but in wonder at the scores of objects to which the frost had given a quality of graphic simplicity: fallen leaves in the laneway with their veins and serrated edges picked out in grey; twigs that looked as if they'd been furred by an unseen hand in the night; the worn gatepost with a grey fungus of hoar frost on its top; and the bare, black trees of the garden with thrushes like birds of ill omen in their branches. Frost had transformed everything into stark and simple forms as in a painting by an artist with no eye for detail.

One morning in particular lingered in the memory. He had risen early to go bird-watching on the Ross Mór. The sun, hidden in cloud, did not shine on the grey rime that lay everywhere except on the black earth beneath the weeping willow. It lay on the tiled roofs of houses; on the zinc roofs of byres and barns; on the coping stones of walls; on hard-as-rock cabbage heads in the gardens; and on the paving flags of the laneway from the cottage

By the time he'd prepared and eaten breakfast, the sun had burnt its way through the cloud, and the hoar frost had melted. The upper side of the branches of the apple tree, previously grey, were now a shiny black, and clear droplets hung like pearls from their undersides, dripping luminously as the sun rose higher. For one precious moment it seemed to him that this melting and dripping would never end—until he realised that his time in the glen was coming to an end, that he was living out the final weeks of his stay. The sense of something ending came as a shock, as if he had discovered too late in life that he was mortal.

He had been lucky that morning on the Ross Mór. He spotted a male merlin flying down a meadow pipit, and later a hen harrier, which according to his bird book, was rarely seen in Donegal. He hadn't made a note of it that day, so he opened his diary at Saturday, 27 November, and wrote:

Ross Mór 9.00 -11.00 a.m—Saw one male merlin decapitating a meadow pipit. One hen harrier flying uncharacteristically low.

Troubled by the cheerless vacuity at the centre of things, he looked out of the window, hoping perhaps for a ray of meaning or even reassurance. Which? He did not know. Rory Rua's donkey was rolling in the road, his hind legs reaching heavenwards, his forelegs bent. As he struggled to his feet, he was joined by another donkey that began scratching his comrade's neck in playful camaraderie, which soon took on the guise of unhurried homoeroticism. He watched them with voyeuristic contentment, two male donkeys unself-consciously sniffing each other's groins, while their black pintles lengthened slowly like hanging concertinas. He could not help wondering about the nature of what he had seen. Sex was not the only reality, but it was perhaps the only reality potent enough to blot out, at least temporarily, the consciousness of death and the memory of a male merlin decapitating an unsuspecting pipit.

Rory Rua's red setter came up the lane with a bone. Carefully, he scooped out a shallow grave in his master's field, covered the bone, and examined his footwork with a sniff before putting the donkeys off their lovemaking with a furious fit of barking. The dog was obviously a policeman, and the donkeys, errant humanity following its instinct in its customary pursuit of pleasure. For all he knew, he could have been in Soho, watching from a window the motley press below. But why go to Soho when all human life, at its most primitive and uninhibited, was to be enjoyed here free of charge? He felt like going to bed and pulling the blankets up over his head. Ever since that bruising evening with the Canon, he had been suffering from a malaise of the will; a kind of Oblomovism that rendered him incapable of even the simplest decision.

As he turned away from the window, a movement caught the tail of his eye. A grey rat with a hairless tail vanished into a hole in the garden wall. In one continuous movement, he took two cartridges from his pocket, loaded the gun, raised the bottom sash, and rested the barrels on the sill. As he waited with the safety catch cocked, he recalled a bright Saturday morning in October when Rory Rua was threshing and he had stood back from the corn stack and blasted each rat up the Khyber as it fled. It was an expensive method of extermination but it pleased Rory Rua and provided mild entertainment on a morning when he had nothing better to do.

The rat emerged with its pointed nose to the ground, looked to and fro, and made for a half-eaten potato by an upturned creel. Potter took aim and pulled the trigger as the rat, turning, looked up from its meal. Unnecessarily, he held the gun for a moment with the heel of the stock firmly against his shoulder, but the rat was already dead. Struck by a disabling sense of the ridiculous, he did his best to ignore the memory of a Victorian photographer taking a picture. It was the way the rat had looked up at him in the moment of death that brought the image to mind. Again, he was taking a photo of Margaret, and as usual she was bent on absurdity, repeating the word 'Cheese!' over and over again whenever he pointed the camera in her direction. He dismissed the thought as irrelevant. After all, he had managed to shoot the rat. That was something Oblomov would never have had the strength of will to do.

Satisfied, he took the tongs from its place by the fire, lifted the flabby grey body, and flung it over the garden wall for the dog to enjoy. Returning to the house, he sat down to clean his gun once more.

He would not go to Roarty's tonight. He would stay at home, read a book, and have a swig or two from the bottle of Glenmorangie he kept in the dresser for emergencies. Ever since Roarty and Gillespie had shown the white feather in their discussion with the Canon, he had not been going to the pub as regularly as before. He should have known that the Irish, in spite of a handful of anti-clerical writers, were by nature priest-servers. They might poke fun at the arrogance of their ignorant clergy when their back was turned, but confronted by a cassock and surplice they tugged the forelock and said, 'Yes, Father,' with an alacrity that had as much to do with superstition as religion. If it were merely a survival of attitudes from penal times when the priest was thought to bear the future of the race with the housel in his pyx, he would have understood; but as far as he could discover, there were no satirical portraits of randy friars or venal pardoners in classical Irish literature. There was no fourteenth-century Irish Chaucer, no Irish Wycliffe, only the earlier excesses of ascetic monasticism. However, the undertow of racial inclination did not excuse Roarty, Gimp Gillespie, and Rory Rua in their treachery. All three were men of intelligence. They knew what they were doing, and they did it not merely to please the Canon but in the vain hope of lining their own pockets.

The experience, however disagreeable, had opened his eyes. He had been too sympathetic, overeager to enjoy what he had seen as the genius of the country. He had become more detached, less ready to applaud because of a picturesque phrase in a pub; and he was prepared to believe that his new-found ambivalence was an emotional and perhaps an intellectual enrichment. Thankfully, he still could rely on Nora Hession. She had a way of making light of obstacles that at first glance seemed insurmountable, and she had the knack of making him laugh at his own excesses. Whereas Margaret had become an agent of aggro and a creator of absurd situations, Nora could bring order out of muddle and laugh him out of his ill-humour. She was so sensible, so committed to looking at everything with a practical eye, that he sometimes wondered if she saw right through him—a thought that troubled him more than he cared to admit.

He put away the cleaning rod, oil and tow, and placed the gun on its rest above the kitchen door. He switched on the light, pulled down the window blinds against the descending night, and poured himself a long drink to provide company for an hour. As he leaned back in his fireside armchair, the intimate comforts of the cottage leaped to his eye. It was a genuine peasant cottage with a low thatch roof, flagged floor, whitewashed walls, hearth fire, a curtained kitchen bed in an outshot, a garret for storage above the kitchen, and a loft above the lower bedroom. Both outside and inside it looked the very antithesis of the modern bungalows now being slapped up for tourists by profit-hungry contractors who put asbestos sheeting under the thatch and introduced such anachronisms as tiled floors, wooden ceilings, central heating, and piped water. This cottage had brown scraws and smoke-blackened rafters beneath the thatch, an open fireplace with a sooty crane, and barnacle-eaten beams which spanned the width of the house and had obviously been cast ashore as flotsam in the days of sail.

What he liked most about the cottage was the open turf fire. Admittedly, there was a cooker run on Calor gas by the dresser but he never used it except to make a quick cup of tea in the morning. He did most of his cooking over the peat fire because of the subtle flavour it gave the food, a tang he liked best in lamb stew made from mountain 'mutton'.

He took Gimp Gillespie's book from the only shelf, an account of Ireland during the Famine by a visiting English philanthropist: *Narrative of a Recent Journey of Six Weeks in Ireland in Connexion with the Subject of Supplying Small Seeds to Some of the Remoter Districts with Current Observations on the Depressed Circumstances of the People, and the Means Presented for the Improvement of their Social Condition.* He stretched his legs across the hearth and, as he began the first chapter, wondered vaguely if he could interest a London publisher in a similar composition concerning the depressive influence of the Catholic Church today on the circumstances of the Irish people with suggestions for the improvement of their intellectual condition.

As he began the third chapter, he looked up, wondering if a mouse had stirred in the wall. Again he heard the noise, a soft tap like that of a forefinger on a hand drum, followed a second later by a metallic ping. Looking at his watch, he worked out that the pings were occurring at four-second intervals. Rain, he thought, though he could not hear anything between the taps and the pings. He opened the door to find that the night was full of the sound of falling water. It was dripping from the eaves, whispering in the trees, and gurgling in the runnel by the gable; but try as he might, he could not identify the source of the tapping. The ping, however, was coming from the edge of the outshot roof onto the side of an overturned bucket. Curiosity satisfied, he returned to the fire and his book. The warmth inside and the rain outside filled him with an unexpected sense of well-being; the sense of security of a man of forty who is in good health and has long since solved life's economic problems.

'I'll go my way and let Roarty, Gimp Gillespie and Rory Rua go theirs,' he muttered. 'Life is too short and the world too wide to devote thinking time to trifles. In the immortal words of Gimp Gillespie in his cups, "Hast any philosophy in thee, shepherd?"'

Suddenly the door opened and Nora Hession came in out of the night, water from her grey raincoat forming a circle on the floor flags.

'Am I glad to get in out of that waterspout!' she said, pushing the door closed.

'Am I glad you've come! I was nodding over a book, trying to stay awake.'

He took her coat and hung it on the back of the door. Kissing her on the cheek, he carried her to the corner seat and put her sitting by the fire.

'The Canon's gone out to Glenroe to hear confessions,' she said. 'He won't be back till after nine.'

'It's just as well he performs a few of his duties. Otherwise I should never see you.'

He took off her wet shoes and placed them by her chair, out of the direct heat. In a moment she had transformed the small kitchen with the mystery and excitement of the night. Sitting by the blazing fire with her stockinged feet on the cobbled hearth, she took the glass of wine he offered her as if it were a queen's ransom, her face alight with the pleasure of talk that made no demands on either of them. That was one of the things he liked about her, the fact that, unlike Margaret, she was possible to please. She was intelligent without being an intellectual, and now and again she was original in a way that had nothing to do with what she'd read in the women's pages of the newspapers. She didn't play conversational games to prove that she was different; she believed in whatever she said, at least while she was saying it. Best of all, no one would ever accuse her of being shrill; her voice was soft and even as she smiled her eyes in their dark depths bore a disturbing intimation of the ultimate loneliness of the night.

'Before you came in, I was thinking that my time here is coming to an end.'

'If only you'd found enough barytes… ,' she smiled.

'In a way I'm glad we didn't. At least it will teach those two arch-toadies, Roarty and Gillespie, a lesson.'

'I don't share your opinion of the Canon, Ken. It's one of the things we'll never agree on.'

He got up and sat on the arm of her chair. 'Come away with me, Nora. Come to London, to a new and wider life. We can always come back here for a month in the summer. We'll rent a cottage, and spend the time exploring places we haven't explored before.'

'Why don't you stay here with me?'

'I'm only here on secondment. When this job ends, there's nothing left for me to do.'

'You could get a job with the county council.'

'I can imagine the pittance they'd pay me, nothing like enough to keep you in the style to which you should be accustomed.' He grasped her hand and placed it against his cheek. 'Think about it, Nora. Come to London.'

'I went to London two years ago and came back.'

'I know. You went to London and came back, and it was a very cold day.'

'It wasn't cold,' she said humourlessly. 'It was the middle of summer, so hot that I fainted in the Underground for want of fresh air. When I think of London, I think of being lonely in public parks on Sunday afternoons, feeling empty from having nothing better to do.'

'It will be different with me. We'll have lots of friends, a nice house and a big garden. You could grow onions and tomatoes. If you like, you could grow potatoes.'

'I'm not going to London,' she said firmly.

'Then come to bed, you impossible girl.'

He bolted the door, switched off the light, and heaped his clothes on the back of a chair while leaping flames from the fire cast grotesque shadows that chased each other around the walls. As she undressed, the firelight caught her white thighs and the low droop of her bottom, prompting him to think that Velàzquez should have seen her before painting the *Rokeby Venus*. He caught her elbow and spun her into his arms. They stood locked together on the hearth, the heat from the fire pleasurably probing their exposed legs and thighs. He carried her to the outshot bed behind the curtains, and they lay between the warm blankets with the firelight glowing through light fabric, reddening the wall in contrast with the dark rafters under the thatch.

They lay quietly in each other's arms because any movement, even the simple act of kissing, would have been superfluous, so perfect was their pleasure in the touch of each other's skin.

'What's happened to your sheets?' she asked after a while.

'They're in the wash. They're the only ones I've got.'

'It's nice lying between blankets. You're more conscious of them on your skin.'

'To those of us who are not sheiks, they are more erotic than silks.'

He kissed her tenderly on the lips, eyelids, neck and breasts. They lay still again, their legs entwined and his erect penis pressing against her flat belly. There was strange comfort in the firmness of her body, bringing him closer to the living centre of her, awakening an avatar within that the false promise of pneumatic bliss could never have recalled to life. He kissed her breasts again, small and firm as a Cox apple, and suddenly and unexpectedly, she was ready to receive him. He had to move carefully because of his tight foreskin and Nora's anatomical peculiarities. He used to worry about his foreskin when he first began going out with girls. The Harley Street consultant whose advice he sought had said, 'Not quite phimosis, not sufficiently serious to warrant surgery, just a nuisance you'll have to put up with.' Then he met Margaret whose capacious accommodation introduced him to a new kind of love life that put him in mind of the dreamy atmosphere of Debussy's prelude about the sensations of a faun on a hot afternoon. Now Nora Hession had woken him from his reverie with a warm ache in the tip of his penis that both protracted and intensified his pleasure. The Harley Street consultant must have been married to another Margaret. Only that would account for his failure to appreciate the poetry of this ineffable fusion of pain and pleasure. Quite possibly, a tight foreskin was the beginning of both poetry and philosophy; he wondered if there was any mention of the condition in classical literature. Without such an advantage, how could any man have a sensitive appreciation of the magic and terror of sex? Perhaps Napoleon's foreskin was giving him trouble when he said, 'Not tonight, Josephine,' and then set out for Moscow the following morning to get on with what he thought he was best at. And, of course, if Henry VIII had had a tight foreskin, the history of England would have been different.

'That was a quiet one,' she said when he had exhausted himself. 'It's curious that it's never the same twice. Is it different for you each time as well?'

'Sex is a kind of sunset. No two are ever the same.'

'Is it really different for you, tell the truth.'

'Men don't weigh things up as carefully as women.'

'Men are too insensitive to appreciate sex to the full.' She gave his shrunken penis a little squeeze. Holding it in her fist, she rubbed the tip against her labia and, kissing him, gave him a taste of her tongue. He thought he'd already experienced everything, but her unexpected kiss proved him mistaken.

'Are men really less sensitive than women?' she asked, letting his penis rest between her thighs.

'We just see the sunset differently, that's all.'

'If sex is the sunset, what is the sunrise?' she giggled.

'The sunrise was when I first clapped eyes on you, courtesy of Gimp Gillespie.'

'If that's true, then men must spend most of their day thinking about every woman they meet?'

'I can't speak for all men. I spend most of my day thinking about you.'

'You say the nicest things, Ken. If only they were true.' She put her forefinger to his lips and whispered, 'Don't go away. Stay like this. I'd like to be quiet for a while.'

She went limp in his arms and within minutes she was asleep. He felt deliriously happy, telling himself that she would never have fallen asleep with a man she did not trust. He had fallen in love with her because she was different from any other woman he'd ever met. She was simple in her tastes, yet not simpleminded. She knew her own heart in all its vagaries and she was capable of pointing out what she called his 'fegaries' as well. Though slender in figure, she was a fully rounded woman with insights that often surprised him into self-discovery, and now and again, self-criticism. At times it occurred to him that she had become a complementary extension of his personality, an insight he'd never had with any other woman. Now he began wondering if he'd imagined it all, because most of the women he'd known in London saw him as a confirmed misogynist or what they called a 'male chauvinist pig'.

Such thoughts were beside the point, though. In her wisdom she had confronted him with a simple choice. Stay in the glen and live in love and in straitened circumstances or go back to London without her and possibly live to regret it. She was right, of course. She was born here and belonged here in this small, self-contained community. She was a flower of great beauty but a flower of one clime. She would wilt and wither in the rough winds of the anonymous and amorphous world he himself called home. He wondered if he were genuinely trying to find a way out of an impossible situation or seeking to excuse himself from facing up to what must be done. There was no painless exit. If Margaret in her omniscience knew of his predicament, she would say that he had brought it on himself; that she could have predicted the outcome if only he had consulted her in time.

So what was the future? The impossible English rose of his imagination? Another Margaret? Or even another Diana

Duryea? Diana was a huntress. He'd met her at a press reception to drum up publicity for 'a new and superior make of soil pipe'. In the crowded room she had approached him confidently, glass in hand.

'I hope you won't think me stupid,' she smiled. 'What on earth are soil pipes?'

He bent over her abundantly flowing mane and whispered an answer in her ear.

'Oh, you are a one, I can tell,' she smiled. Then she asked him to bend down again, and when he did, she whispered that she was assistant editor of the magazine *Lift*.

'So what do you lift?' he asked, as if in puzzlement.

'I meant lifts that go up and down, elevators, you know. Now I've given myself away. Now you must know I'm American.'

'And what might you be doing with soil pipes in an elevator?'

'I always find that a fool question is the best conversational gambit. You see, already we're on the same wave length. Neither you nor I spend our evenings thinking about soil pipes. Life at its best is to do with passing the time pleasantly.'

They had several drinks together, and after the junket they had more drinks in a pub in Chelsea and finally in his flat in Fulham. By this time she was Brahms and Liszt, as she kept saying in imitation of her Cockney flatmate. While he made black coffee, she lay on his bed with her long legs apart and her arms shading her eyes from the light. And while the coffee was percolating, he made love to her with a french letter protecting his vulnerable foreskin. The coffee had gone cold by the time they'd finished, but she said that she loved iced coffee and that she'd drink cold coffee since it was already halfway to being iced. She had dressed with quick efficiency and combed her hair in front of his mirror while he thought of her blue-veined breasts and how far apart they were, not quite right for intermammary ecstasy.

'That was a clitoral,' she said, letting the hairs from her comb fall on his newly shampooed carpet. The word 'clitoral' pierced his eardrum with a triple-jab, because he had never heard it said in an American accent before. It was not a word he himself used every day. And this was the first time he'd heard the adjective used as a noun.

'That was a clitoral,' she said again. 'I thought you might be pleased to know.'

'And what is a clitoral? Not a term I've come across in engineering, as far as I'm aware.'

'A clitoral as opposed to a vaginal orgasm.'

'It's all news to me. I suppose I've lived a sheltered life. Or perhaps it's just that English women like to keep their men folk in ignorance of these little refinements,' he said in an effort to divert her thoughts from the possibility of further clitoral stimulation.

'You do surprise me, honey. It's a fundamental distinction that any self-confessed member of the technologico-Benthamite society should be capable of making. Most American men know all about it, but unfortunately there's a world of difference between the theory and the practice.'

'Personally, I don't buy all this feminist theory. As a straight up and down sort of bloke, I feel more at home with the practicalities. If you ask me, the two-orgasm theory of sex will have as many proponents in a hundred years' time as the four-humour theory of medicine has today.'

She put both her arms round him and gave him a bear hug of such horsepower that he felt helpless as worked-over putty in her hands.

'What I like about you is not so much your wit as your small ass. We American women love men with neat asses. In a recent poll thirty-nine per cent of women in Greenwich Village thought a small ass the most attractive thing in a man whereas only two per cent yearned for a large penis. So you see, you needn't be afraid of us women. We're not the vultures you think we are. I'm on your side. I like the cut of your jib, as my flatmate says.'

Feeling quite exhausted, he followed her down the stairs into the night and put her on a taxi home. He never saw her again but he would not forget her combative style of conversation, nor her readiness to devour his most sensitive part in the hope of what she called a second bite of the cherry.

Nora nudged him. He could hardly believe he'd been asleep.

'We both must have dropped off,' she said. 'It's half-past eight. I'd better get back before the Canon does.'

They dressed in the dark, shivering after the warmth of the blankets and because the fire had died down while they slept.

'You talk in your sleep, Ken,' she said.

'I never knew that. What was I saying?'

'Something to do with mining, I think. Barytes, or coal maybe. All I could make out was the word "clinker".'

He switched on the light and kissed her in grateful wonderment at the stroke of luck by which he'd found her.

SEVENTEEN

He drove her back to the parochial house gate in the rain and, in spite of his earlier resolve, went straight to Roarty's, that smoky den of male fantasy where the heartache of life's disappointments and dishonourable compacts could be forgotten for at least an hour. As it was Saturday night, the bar was crowded. He made straight for the corner by the window, where Gimp Gillespie, Crubog and Cor Mogaill had established a bridgehead while debating without benefit of science whether lugworms were hermaphrodites. Cor Mogaill was saying that lugworms were really earthworms and therefore must surely share the sexual characteristics of the earthworm. As they were all keen observers of the antics of earthworms, the conversation became quite spirited for a while.

He bought a round and tried to interest himself in the intricacies of Cor Mogaill's reasoning, but his mind was on Nora and a dilemma that would not let go of him. Now in retrospect he thought her wilful, even wrongheaded, yet while he was with her, he could not find words to counter the inescapable logic of her argument. Argument, of course, was the wrong term. It was really a matter of deeply ingrained feelings. The outcome he desired ran counter to her whole way of looking at things. He wondered if he was being selfish in putting his own happiness before hers, and then he told himself that most men in his position would do precisely that. If only he could share his thoughts with a friend. Gillespie was hardly a disinterested party, and Roarty, his only other friend, was rarely stone cold sober. He looked round the bar and told himself that his sense of isolation was really one of enrichment, a vital part of life's chequered experience. The great Victorian explorers had been here before him. He did not need to swaddle himself in the comforts and familiarities of childhood friends.

He arrived home at midnight and, reluctant to go to bed just then, he put more peat on the fire, made himself a cup of coffee, and opened Gimp Gillespie's book at chapter three. It was an interesting little book, but in his present mood a thriller might have had a better chance of lifting the deep, deep gloom in his mind. Ever since his arrival he had been busy savouring what delights the local life had to offer. Now he had withdrawn to take stock and in the unwonted quiet, there was time for light reading. He was not a habitual reader of thrillers. In London he simply did not have time and besides, he felt that they lacked that imponderable ingredient that makes fiction truer than fact. Understandably, those of them that sported an intrusive infrastructure of fact lacked the ingredient all the more conspicuously. In spite of all that, he could enjoy a good thriller just now with the wind and the rain outside and the sea rising in the air and spilling onto the rocks below the cottage.

He finished the book at two, covered the dying coals with ash, and undressed. The kitchen had lost its warmth; he could feel on his bare ankles the draught that came in under the door. The bed curtains shivered in the draught but it did not matter. In a moment he would be lying snugly behind them under warm blankets that bore the memory of Nora Hession's sexuality. He pulled the blankets up beneath his chin and closed his eyes. Outside, the night was wild. The door strained at the latch, the mountain ash scratched the window pane, the rain beat on the stone threshold, and the sapless rafters of the roof creaked under the force of the racing wind. All were distinct sounds which he identified one by one but they merged in a Wagnerian flow that dulled his brain to the verge of sleep.

He woke to what seemed like a dull thud and a splintering of glass, then realised that he'd heard a rifle shot at close quarters. Rolling out of bed, he lay flat on the cold flag-floor, waiting for either a second shot or the sound of retreating footsteps, but he heard nothing except the confused noises of the wind and the rain. With his head down, he crawled across the floor and came on a shard of broken glass with his hand. Someone had fired a shot through the window, and whoever it was might well try again. He groped in the dark for his socks and, unable to find them, put his shoes on his bare feet and laced them. Crouching, he went to the back door and pulled on his overcoat over his pyjamas, took his shotgun from the wall, put two cartridges in the breech, and stuffed four more in his pocket.

As the shot had come from the front of the house, his best bet, he felt, was to surprise the intruder from behind. Gently, he unbolted the back door and slipped outside without a sound. He stood with his back to the barn wall, peering into the darkness on either side, alert for a telltale sound or movement. It was still raining; the water running off the eaves trickled coldly down his neck. He edged forward towards the garden wall, and keeping his head below the level of the coping, made his way stealthily behind the hedge at the front corner of the cottage.

He raised his head, inch by inch, but in the darkness not even the whitewashed cottage was visible. The sky seemed only three feet above his head. He was finding breathing difficult; he was afraid he might cough at any moment. Picking up a stone, he flung it over the hedge so that it landed with a thud on the flagstones by the front door. He listened but no sound followed. There was no point in remaining outside with the wind whipping his ankles and the rain making runnels down his neck and chest. Carefully and soundlessly, he retraced his steps to the back door. He still felt shaken. It was a relief to be inside again out of the rain.

His watch said half-past three; he would have to wait for almost five hours before he could investigate further in the relative safety of daylight. He towelled his hair and neck, poured a stiff whisky, and crouching over the dying fire in his dressing gown, warmed his feet on the hearth. His sense of incredulity was so strong that he could barely put one thought after another. What had he done to arouse such animosity? And in a place at the world's end, where plain living and plain thinking had made the inhabitants so philosophical that they always put off until tomorrow what they need not do today. Surely it must be the work of some prankster, Cor Mogaill perhaps or someone trying to get Cor Mogaill into trouble.

Whoever fired the shot obviously knew something of his habits. It would have been natural to assume that he slept in the bedroom, as he had done during the summer. It was only since the weather turned cold at the end of October that he began sleeping in the kitchen bed, next to the hearth fire. The people who had access to this piece of intelligence were very few indeed—Nora Hession, Gillespie, Roarty, and Rory Rua—and none of them seemed a likely suspect. He stayed pondering by the fire until well after four. When finally he turned in, he lay with his head at the foot of the bed as a precaution. Though he did not expect to sleep, he dropped off immediately. When he woke around nine, daylight was visible through a round hole in the window blind.

As he expected, one of the panes in the lower sash was broken. There was a hole in the bed curtain and a bullet buried in the wall of the outshot, no more than six inches above the pillow where his head had rested. He opened the front door on which was pinned a sheet from a jotter with a simple warning in red block letters: 'Hands Off My Maid'.

Surely, he reasoned, this must be the work of a practical joker. Then he asked himself if a joker would have fired a shot of such uncanny accuracy. The only course open to him was to report the incident to McGing.

He sat at the table, lingering over a breakfast he was not enjoying. Everyone, including the practical joker, would now be at nine o'clock Mass, wondering more than likely if the sermon would ever end. On the other side of the window, glimmering light was trying to break through grey mist as in a late Turner. In the garden, droplets were falling from the slender branches of the mountain ash, not the pearly droplets of a bright summer morning but the cloudy droplets of sunless winter. He counted four droplets hanging from the underside of a branch. A thrush lit on the end of the branch and three of the droplets fell, glancing off another branch on the way to the ground. On any other morning he would have delighted in the accuracy of his observation but today it all meant nothing to him. The force that propelled his interest in the minutiae of nature had spent itself like a wave on an upward-sloping shore. He felt angry with himself for having misjudged his 'friends'. In his enthusiasm for all that was unusual and amusing in the local culture, he probably had romanticised Glenkeel, but surely romanticism was not a crime. In any civilised country not even a desiccated classicist would shoot you for it.

He allowed McGing sufficient time to recover from the tedium of the Canon's preaching. He found him eating breakfast in his uniform with his cap on the table next to a heaped plate of fried liver, bacon, onions, black pudding, and a mountain of buttered toast.

'And what can I do for you so early on a Sunday morning?' he asked.

Potter sat opposite him at the table and accepted a cup of black coffee but declined the offer of buttered toast and marmalade.

'Someone took a pot shot at me in bed last night, and I should like to know who.'

As if in response to the seriousness of Potter's news, McGing put on his policeman's cap but continued eating without raising his eyes from his plate.

'Go on, I'm listening,' he said after a lapse of at least a minute.

'He broke my window, missed my head by inches, and pinned this note to my door.'

'Hands Off My Maid.' McGing read through a mouthful of streaky bacon.

'Do you think it might be Loftus?' Potter asked.

McGing looked up from his plate at Potter as if he were contemplating the prime suspect.

'Whatever may be said of Irish parish priests, they don't go about shooting their parishioners.'

'Loftus has a motive. He doesn't approve of my relationship with Nora Hession, and he has told me so in no uncertain terms.'

'You're right to mention it. We mustn't rule out a man because of his collar, but we mustn't rush into accusations either. Loftus comes from a sporting family. His brother is a doctor and the best shot in the county. Though the Canon might conceivably shoot you on the run, he'd never stoop low enough to shoot a sitting duck.'

Potter took a moment or so to ponder this piece of information. 'What do you make of it, then?' he finally asked.

McGing slowly munched a piece of gristle in the bacon and spat it out on the side of his plate.

'There are two possibilities. Someone did it for fun or someone meant business. There aren't many people who'd want you dead but there are lots who might want to take the wind out of your sails—just for fun, you understand. We Irish are noted for our sense of humour.'

'This shot was fired out of personal animus. There's no other adequate explanation.'

'I agree with your analysis, Mr Potter. And what is more I have a shrewd idea of the man who did it.'

'Who?'

McGing poured himself another cup of coffee and began picking at a back tooth with his fingernail.

'It wouldn't help you to know at this stage.'

'It might help me to guard against further attack.'

'All right then. The prime suspect is Gimp Gillespie.'

'But he's my friend!'

'I say Gimp rather than the Canon for a very good reason. As any psychologist will tell you, it's more dangerous to come between a man and his fantasy than between a man and his maid.'

'You speak in riddles, Sergeant.'

'Gimp may well be jealous. He's mad about Nora Hession, always has been, but she won't as much as look his way. Life, Mr Potter, is very unfair, as Nora herself has found out. She went through hell for the love of a good-for-nothing brat, and now she's giving Gillespie the same medicine—she's out to wreak revenge on the whole male sex. Take care, Mr Potter, you may be next. You think you're special, but she'll send you packing when it suits her purpose. In her eyes you're only so much cannon fodder. No pun intended.'

'I won't have my girlfriend traduced in this way, Sergeant.'

'Suit yourself. In our little republic here every man's opinion carries the same weight.'

'But not the same value, surely!'

'Have you ever heard of the Case of the Tumbled Trampcock?'

'Of course, I have. It's a classic of detection in these parts,' said Potter, realising that McGing was determined to go the long way home.

'Well, there's an even stranger case, the Case of the Priest's Maid's Knickers. They were stolen from the clothesline in the priest's garden, three pairs belonging to Nora Hession. Naturally, I went down to the parochial house to investigate but the Canon wanted everything swept under the carpet— he wasn't going to have a scandal about his maid's knickers in the local paper, he said. The whole thing was best forgotten, probably the work of a passing tinker with three bare-bottomed wives. The Church is not the Law, however, and McGing is nobody's fool. Unbeknown to Loftus, I began keeping an eye on his garden. Three weeks later, not far off midnight, I caught my bold Gimp jouking under a pear tree, not a hundred miles from a certain clothesline displaying two pairs of Nora Hession's pink drawers. So I marched him out of the garden and knocked up the Canon.

"What's all this?" he said, putting his head out of the bedroom window. "Is it a sick call?"

"It's the law," I said. "I've just caught Gimp Gillespie trying to steal two pairs of your maid's underpants,"—I couldn't say "knickers" to the priest. He came down in his overcoat, and I told him I'd found Gimp skulking under the pear tree.'

"And what do you think you were doing in my garden at this hour?" the Canon demanded.

"I came to steal a pear," said Gimp.

"A pair of what?" asked the Canon.

"I was reading St Augustine's *Confessions* before turning in and I came to the place where he steals pears. Well, I couldn't resist the temptation of the pear tree in your garden, father."

"I didn't know Augustine stole pears," said the Canon. 'I thought his offence had more to do with unholy loves."

"He stole pears, too," said Gimp.

"The *Confessions* are good Catholic reading. You should be ashamed of yourself to find them an occasion of sin. *Tolle lege, tolle lege.*"

"Shall I book him, Canon?" I asked.

"Release him," said the Canon. "Tell him to go his way and sin no more."

That's the Canon, no stomach for the law. But I know, as does everyone in the glen, what Gimp was up to in that garden. Now a man who could find a priest's maid's knickers so magnetic might well take a pot shot at a man he thinks may have put his hand up them.'

'I beg your pardon,' said Potter, suddenly very English in phrase and posture.

'Luckily, fetishists are notoriously ineffectual.'

'You wouldn't have called this one ineffectual if you'd heard the whistle of his bullet.'

'You can see the pattern that's emerging, can't you?'

'Which pattern?'

'Drawers!' said McGing, going to the window with a mug of coffee, just as detectives do in the movies.

'Drawers?' enquired Potter, convinced that McGing was raving.

'Knickers,' said McGing, eyeing him as if he were a simpleton.

'What about them?'

'First, Nora Hession's vanishing from the clothesline, then the torn knickers on the tumbled tramp-cock, now a shot at you in the dark. All three are connected, don't you see?'

'How?'

'I must ask you a very personal question, Mr Potter. Has Nora Hession left a pair of her pink knickers at your cottage? If so, or if Gimp Gillespie has reason to think so, we may be on to something.'

'I can assure you, Sergeant, that I have no knowledge of either the colour or the fabric of Miss Hession's undergarments.'

'Then something is rotten in the parish of Glenkeel. For years the only offences here were poaching, after-hours drinking, and the odd run of poteen at Christmas, all of them manly crimes, signs of a healthy community. In the last six months we've had robbery, murder, more robbery, and now attempted murder. It cannot be that the population has suddenly turned criminal; it is more likely to be the work of one man, a village Moriarty. Let me tell you one thing: in me he is destined to meet his Holmes, so help me.'

Potter scratched his head and wished for an unimaginative English constable who would make a few notes and draw sensible conclusions.

'If you know the identity of the criminal, what are we waiting for?'

'A little thing called evidence. All we have at the moment is hunches. Time is on our side, however. Gradually and unmistakably, I'm amassing the circumstantial details, all of which reminds me, we must hurry to the scene of the crime in case any evidence is overlooked or lost. What about the bullet, for example?'

'It's still in the wall, I'm sure.'

'Good. An amateur digging out a bullet with a penknife might well scratch it and obliterate the rifling marks, all valuable evidence. The bullet will tell us whether it was fired from the stolen rifle. Have you seen the cartridge case?'

'I'm afraid I didn't notice one.'

They both got into Potter's car, and on the way to the cottage McGing delivered a lecture on forensic ballistics of such cogency that for a moment Potter felt he could not be in better hands. McGing was two men in one. The first, who had a mind like a magpie, was a treasury of forensic knowledge. The second, who drew conclusions, was an inept imbecile.

EIGHTEEN

Potter dressed with greater care than usual, believing as he did that the success of a shoot depended to some extent on the suitability of the sportsman's gear. Shooting, like going to the opera, was something of an occasion; it behoved one to look and feel the part. Having put on his thornproof plus-fours, heavy roll-neck jersey, tweed hacking jacket, and balaclava, he looked in the mirror and pronounced the transformation in his appearance a distinct success.

He had done a lot of brooding over the past week, and he was taking the day off in the hope that a morning's shooting with Roarty would take his mind off his troubles for a few hours. Ever since the pot shot, he had been dogged by feelings of insecurity, troubled as much by a sense of incomprehension as physical fear. Though his friends, particularly Roarty and Gillespie, had shown genuine concern for his safety, he could not help feeling that somewhere in the glen was someone who wished him dead. At times he longed to be back in the London suburbs, commuting to Charing Cross every morning and complaining about the weather, late trains, and irresponsible trade unionists.

He stuffed several handfuls of cartridges into his pockets, hung his side-bag on his shoulder, took his shotgun from the wall, and locked the door behind him. The morning was dry and cold with a north-east wind sharp enough to skewer an arctic fox. A great red sun sat on the saddle of the hill, and as he drove to the village, he found that he could look it in the eye without discomfort, so thick was the haze on the higher hills. As the bar was not yet open, he entered Roarty's by the back door and found his friend reading a newspaper behind the counter with the shutters up and the lights on. What looked like a halo of tobacco smoke hung over his shiny pate.

'You're early,' Roarty remarked.

'You said we'd start out before nine.'

'There's a bit of a haze. We'll give it half an hour to clear. Here, have a drink on the house to warm you up. I'm having a quick one myself, just enough to take the tremble off my hand.'

'It's fresh out there,' Potter said.

'Did you notice the smell on the wind?'

'I can't say I did.'

'You only get it here in October, November and March when the wind is north-east. Crubog calls it a *gal phiútair.* He says it's the smell of coal from Derry.'

Roarty came out from behind the counter with the drinks and they sat by the fire and lit their pipes.

'It's a good morning for a snipe shoot,' Roarty said after a while. 'They'll be sitting close, and they should be in good condition after a whole week of thaw. They're always plump after a frosty spell—the worms come to the surface in a thaw, as you know.'

'They were probably feeding all last night in the full moon.'

'That's what I mean. They'll have full crops this morning, too sleepy to move till we're well within range. We'll make two good bags, wait and see.'

'As Rory Rua says, it isn't the bag that matters but the places you go to fill it. He reckons that the wild places in the hills leave their mark on a man's soul.'

'Rory Rua hasn't a penn'orth of interest in the ways of wildlife. He sees no farther than the end of his gun barrels and, worse, he eats his game straight from the gun.'

Roarty spat into the heart of the fire. Potter looked at him, surprised by such assertiveness so early in the day.

'Have you ever shot with him?' Roarty asked.

'Once or twice.'

'He has two rotten molars that stink when he laughs, which is why I always walk on the upwind side of him.'

'It's a sportsman's solution,' said Potter, noting the slight tremor on Roarty's hand as he raised his glass. Yet he would swing his gun so fast that it would not matter.

Ever since that unfortunate evening with the Canon, he had been aware of a muddy undercurrent in his relationship with Roarty, and at first he used to wonder if he imagined it all. Did Roarty have some grievous secret that he wished to share but could not find words to express? Or was it just a case of personal guilt at having failed a friend? He would begin sentences and leave them unfinished or perhaps forget what he was about to say. He would invite him to stay for a drink after closing time, as if about to reveal the root of all his sorrows, but nothing ever came of these after-hours heart-to-hearts except sportsmen's small talk about whether to walk snipe upwind or downwind or use number six or number nine shot. Potter would have liked to help him out of his difficulty but did not wish to appear inquisitive. He simply came to the conclusion that Roarty was unhappy over the way he had deserted the Anti-Limestone Society for the Devil's Party, or that he was lonely and sought the kind of friendship or meeting of minds he could not have with any local man.

At half-past nine they said goodbye to Susan and climbed the side of the hill above the village while Grouse, Roarty's springer spaniel, followed at heel. Roarty was wearing a buff donkey jacket over an Aran sweater and carrying a rucksack large enough for the most ambitious sportsman. They climbed slowly, pausing every so often to look back at the straggle of houses and the snakelike village street below. On reaching the plateau they loaded their guns, and at a signal from Roarty, Grouse went ahead, quartering the ground with eager thoroughness. He was an experienced gundog. No matter how fiendishly he worked, he kept his mind on Roarty, ready to obey his every command. Soon he turfed out a jack hare from a mound of rushes. Roarty swung his gun barrels over its ears. It cartwheeled in mid-leap and went down, shot cleanly in the head. In spite of his morning tremor, there was nothing the matter with Roarty's shot.

They decided to walk the snipe downwind to make for easier and quicker shooting. The snipe would rise facing them, against the wind, and as it paused for a second before turning, it would present a more stable target than in a going-away shot. Their downwind approach would be less silent, of course, but after a bright, calm night the birds would be sitting well in the early morning.

Potter's turn came next. With a loud 'scaap' a snipe rose out of a poached track before him. He snapped it as it hung momentarily in the air before turning on its zigzag retreat. He was not so lucky the second time. With a white-and-brown flicker another snipe rose close to him. Caught off guard, he decided to let it come out of its jinking flight before trying a going-away shot. He must have misjudged the distance or failed to make enough forward allowance; and Roarty, a hundred yards away, raised his hands in mock horror. Just then another snipe rose before Roarty who raised his gun in an effortless swing and snapped the bird in mid-jink as the very best snipe shots do.

By lunchtime they had traversed the hill and tried all the favoured spots, the pools and drains and the spongy patches that Roarty knew so well. Potter was pleased with the morning's sport. He had bagged a pair of hares and eight snipe, with a kill-to-cartridge ratio of four to five for the snipe. A piercing hail shower coming in from the north-east took their minds off sport for a while. They made for the shelter of a ruined cow house which had been turned into a makeshift sheep pen, Potter running with his side-bag bumping against his hip.

'How did you do?' asked Roarty as they found shelter in the lee of the drystone wall.

'A pair of hares and four couple. How about you?'

'A jack hare and seven couple. One of my better days. I only wasted one shot.'

They lit their pipes as the hailstones whitened the greenish-brown mountain and hopped off the rocks in front of them. Grouse came up with his snout to the ground and sought the warmth of Roarty's leg. Roarty chucked him under the chin and gave him a digestive biscuit.

'On a morning like this he's worth his weight in gold,' Potter said.

'A pedigree retriever would be wasted here. Grouse has a nose and brains, and kens how to use them. He's an all-rounder; he can do a bit of everything.'

'I was just thinking that. If everyone went about his work with such intelligence, we'd live in a better-run world.'

'I wish McGing was as efficient,' Roarty said. 'I don't suppose you've heard from him?'

'He knows the culprit, he says. All he needs now is the evidence.'

'Well, I hope for your sake he finds it. Being shot at can't be good for your peace of mind.'

'It pulls you up short, I can tell you. Makes you dare to think beyond the next drink.' With a sense of absurdity, he realised that he was describing his feelings from what he perceived must be Roarty's point of view.

'It's good to be confronted with evil now and again. It makes you aware of the residue of good within you.'

Wondering if Roarty might still be imprisoned in the theology he had imbibed in his seminary days and reluctant to get involved in such metaphysics, he took out his handkerchief and sneezed into it.

'"Evil" is a short word with a big, big meaning,' he said. 'I prefer to say "disorder", or maybe lawlessness or criminality.'

'If you'd sensed the physical presence of evil, you wouldn't think of it as just lawlessness. I know because I've sensed it. It's a smell that pervades the whole house and lingers in every room, and when you go outside you can still smell it on the wind.'

'Whatever it is you're talking about must be within. The mind that apprehends evil does so only because it's a vestigial presence in the mind itself.'

'Then how do you explain this? I've been aware of evil as a continuous presence for the past fortnight. Sometimes it smells like a field of rotting cabbage and sometimes like sweaty feet. I was glad of the smell on the wind this morning. It went some way towards smothering the other.'

'But there was no smell on the wind this morning,' Potter said, drawing on his pipe. 'At least none that I could detect.'

'There's something the matter with your sniffers, then. I saw Grouse from my bedroom window with his nose to the wind, and I wondered what could be troubling him. That was a good half hour before I got the smell myself.'

Dogs and men, we are all deluded thus, Potter quoted to himself, puzzling if he had got it right. Two months ago he had seen Roarty as a practical, no-nonsense man, the sort of man who has never been troubled by a thought or intimation contrary to his declared system of beliefs. Perhaps he had been taken in by his picturesque beard and slow but amusing turn of phrase. Now he wondered if Roarty, for a reason he could not begin to guess at, was troubled by some mildewed kernel within.

He listened indulgently as Roarty defined the two manifestations of evil: evil that has a physical embodiment and evil that is unrelated to anyone or anything—the most frightening form known to man. He and Roarty lived in two separate worlds, which in some ways seemed odd since they were such kindred spirits. Perhaps Roarty expected him to give a sign, to say something that would confirm the reality of those shadowy perceptions of his and free him forever from the burden of self-doubt. Knocking out his pipe against a stone, he asked himself if Roarty might be a latent homosexual who had missed a turning, a haunted man who turned to the contemplation of imponderables as a means of escape from his predicament.

'Were you afraid the night you were shot at?' he asked as if it followed logically from his discourse on evil.

'I was too angry to be afraid. I didn't enjoy having my sleep so rudely interrupted.'

'You're rather isolated up there in that cottage. Why don't you come down and stay with me? You'd have the pick of three spare bedrooms. You'd be living above the bar, an inestimable advantage for any drinking man.'

'It's very kind of you, I'm sure, but I think I'll stay put for now.'

'It was just a thought,' Roarty said, tickling Grouse behind the ears.

The hail shower was over. They headed downhill without a word while Potter wondered if Roarty had arranged their snipe shoot, less for the bag than the conversation.

NINETEEN

Sunday, 19 December
A 'large grebe' on the Lough of Silver turned out to be a goosander,
rare in these parts. Took off for the Lough of Gold with a 'kraah',
leaving me alone with a moorhen flashing white underparts. Failed
to see Roarty's black water bird. A manifestation of evil visible only
to himself?

Potter put away his diary and heaped more peat on the fire.
The weather had turned even colder. A damp, creeping
cold that seeped through your clothes, a cold that only whisky
could keep from freezing the very marrow of your bones.
Here the days were noticeably shorter than in London,
though Donegal was only three degrees farther north. The
mornings were the worst time as he drove to work with the
headlights on, the upturned collar of his overcoat rubbing
chill into the back of his head while his feet threatened to
freeze in his damp gumboots.

That morning he had awoken in confusion. It was so dark
that at first he thought the alarm had gone off too early.
Peering through the curtains, he discovered that a thick fog
had descended on the glen, delaying the coming of day. The

sky seemed to have swallowed the hilltops, and the cottages down by the shore loomed vague as ghosts through a heavy shroud of grey. He went to early Mass and ran into Nora Hession who told him that she would call up to see him that evening. He kept thinking of her throughout the morning and spent the afternoon by the loughs watching waterfowl through his field glasses. Nothing he did pleased him. He simply could not escape from the hell that was himself.

Surely, he reasoned, there must be a way out of this maze of imaginary obstacles, if only there was a thread they both could agree to follow. We all make our own difficulties, and to compound them other people then present us with a set of more ingenious difficulties. Everyone means well; everyone is acting in good faith; yet the result is a shambles that no one desires. Even if he could convince her to come away, she would only pine and lose her sweetness and the peace and wellbeing she was so good at conferring. Life, it seemed, was fraught with possibilities that did not beckon, bridges that loomed but led nowhere. As he poured himself a drink, he wondered if there was any point in drinking it. Absentmindedly, he turned the newly washed sheets he was airing on the back of two chairs before the fire.

It had been a disastrous week, beginning with Gimp Gillespie's sensational article in one of the Dublin Sunday papers. Under the cumbersome heading 'Exploitation, Reformation, and Attempted Murder in Donegal', Gimp told the story of an English engineer who was very nearly murdered in his bed as the representative of a foreign company trying to get its hands on the most valuable deposit of barytes in the country. At first the engineer, a certain Kenneth Potter, appeared to be well meaning, if a trifle naïve. Apparently, he had come to Donegal with the intention of converting the people to Lollardism, which for the benefit of his readers, Gimp described as pre-Lutheran Protestantism. In the pursuit of his programme he founded an Anti-Limestone Society and converted many of the innocent locals to his beliefs, only to be exposed by the vigilant parish priest who saw in the Lollardism and Anti-Limestone Society a smokescreen for surreptitious exploitation.

Potter could hardly believe that he was reading about himself. He had seen Gimp Gillespie as a friend, an amusing hack who found literary fulfilment in innocuous notes on bumper potato crops, marauding foxes, and shoals of mackerel off the coast in season. After enjoying his hospitality, drinking his Glenmorangie, and eating his roast snipe carefully skewered by their own beaks, how could he pen such libellous twaddle? The following morning a telegram from head office summoning him to Dublin took his mind off Gillespie, at least temporarily. As soon as he saw the look on his American boss's face, he realised that Gillespie had done even more damage than he'd imagined.

'I can explain everything,' he had assured Ben Shockley, a heavy man with a formidable crew cut that did nothing to reduce the size of his head. 'It's all in the imagination of a provincial journalist with no respect for the truth.'

'Did you or did you not found an Anti-Limestone Society?' asked Shockley with trans-Atlantic directness.

'Yes, but—'

'And did you say that you were bringing Lollardism to Donegal?

'That was a joke.'

'You're off your rocker, Potter, and I'm not joking. I'm surprised they didn't shoot you and have done with it.'

'The whole thing has been twisted and exaggerated out of all—'

'Don't you see you've set back the business of this company in Ireland by at least ten years? You've dragged the image of Pluto in the mud. This is a politically sensitive field we're in, where charges of exploitation come easily, and tub-thumping politicians are only too ready to get up on their high horses. My mission was to keep a low profile and maximise profits in peace. I don't want trouble. I don't want publicity. And what do you do? You go up to Donegal in plus-fours, 12-bore in hand, to preach Lollardism to the natives. You're a dangerous simpleton, Potter. You're not fit for the field. I'm recalling you to head office and a desk job, because that's all you're capable of doing.'

'Get stuffed,' said Potter.

'Take that back,' said Shockley.

'You can stick your low profiles and your maximisation of profits. I know when I'm not wanted. I'm going back to Donegal to pick up my things.'

'The sooner the better,' said Shockley. 'Please don't consider yourself under any obligation to give a month's notice.'

He discovered from Shockley's secretary on the way out that all operations in Donegal were being suspended and that the other engineers in the northern part of the county were also being recalled. He did not care. He was no longer under obligation to please anyone except himself and Nora. He would drive back to Glenkeel a free man, or at least a freer man.

Nora came at six and set about cooking a dinner of casseroled hare over the peat fire. The conditions were far from perfect. It was an old hare that had not been hung long enough, and he did not have all the necessary ingredients. He skinned and jointed the hare for her, while she busied herself with the vegetables. He drank a whisky and water, and she had a glass of wine. As they waited for dinner to cook, they lay behind the curtain over the bedclothes and he fondled her and told her how much he loved her. She seemed chirpy enough. She certainly didn't seem troubled or unhappy. At times it seemed that nothing had changed between them but he could not conceal from himself the niggling unease in his mind. They didn't make love because somehow lovemaking was not on the cards. This was not because of anything either of them had said but because of a haunting presence lying between them in the bed. It was all very strange, so strange that he kept asking himself if he was imagining it all.

'I've been meaning to tell you, Ken. I'm pregnant.'

'Are you sure?'

'Yes, I'm in my second month.'

'It's the best news I've heard.' He kissed her and, grasping her hand, put it to his cheek. 'It's the best thing that could have happened to us. You'll have to come to London with me now.'

'I can't,' she said. 'My life is here with people I know. Why don't you stay with me? Then we could both be happy.'

'What would we live on? I'd have to take up lobster fishing with Rory Rua.'

'You could get a job inspecting the roads or something.'

'They'd only pay me a pittance. I love you, Nora. I want you to live in comfort. We can't do that here.'

'I've told you before, I don't like cities. I like the country and the sting of the sea air.'

'What will become of you? What will you live on? And what will the Canon say?'

'He'll say, "God looks after his own".'

'You have a touching faith in the Irish clergy.'

'I've already told him.'

'You told him before you told me!'

'I had to. He heard me being sick in the bathroom this morning.'

'And what did he say?'

'He put his hand on my shoulder and said I must make my confession at once and ask for absolution, and that everything would be all right then. He got his stole and heard my confession in the parlour sitting by the empty fireplace.'

'And you were kneeling, I suppose?'

'Well, yes.'

'And you told him about us?'

'I had to tell him everything. If I didn't, I wouldn't get forgiveness. At the end of it all I felt weak. He helped me to my feet, and the power from his hand went right through my body like a dart of electricity.'

'Did he say anything while this transfer of power was going on?'

'He took my hand and told me not to worry, that my sin was forgiven, just as Mary Magdalene's was forgiven. He said she was the first person Christ appeared to after the Resurrection. Suddenly I got my strength back.'

'I call it cheek. I have a good mind to go down to the parochial house and thump him.'

'What's got into you, Ken?'

'So you don't mind being compared to Mary Magdalene? She was a prostitute for God's sake.'

'You don't understand, Ken. The Canon is a very holy man. He'll see I come to no harm.'

'You don't have to rely on the Canon. I'll make sure you have everything you need. The baby you're carrying is yours and mine. We made it together. It belongs to us both. And

I'm proud of what we've achieved. I'll support you and the baby. You won't have to rely on hand-outs.'

'Then stay here. We don't need riches. As the song says, "All you need is love."'

It was hopeless. They were going round in circles. Still, he made one last attempt. 'I love you, Nora. You've given me feelings I never had with any other girl. I'm determined to see my young son or daughter grow up. I promise you, I'll stay in touch. I'll be back.'

'The thing I need now is peace. Just to be left alone. My sister Maggie is a nurse. I'll be in good hands.'

'So which is more important, our feelings for each other or the baby?'

'It's a question I don't like to answer.'

'You mean it's the baby?'

'Well, after all she's mine in a way she can never be yours. I'm carrying her. Soon I'll feel her first kick, Maggie says.'

'Or his first kick!'

'His or hers, I'll be the one who'll feel it. I'd better have a look at the pot. I think I can get the smell of cooked meat.'

They didn't talk further about their predicament. Over dinner she told him about the local gossip, who said what about whom. She was as lively as ever. He smiled at her jokes while trying to conceal the hurt of rejection and the torn state of his feelings.

'It's a starry night. I'll walk back with you,' he said, thinking that at least a walk would take longer than a drive. Perhaps on the way she might pause between sentences and listen for the fluttering movement of a roosting bird in a hedge, or say, 'Stay for another week, Ken. It will give us time. Who knows, we may yet find a way.'

'I feel tired after all the excitement,' she replied. 'Maybe you should drive me back.'

He watched her retreating figure from the parochial house gate as she walked up the avenue to the heavy door which swallowed her up, closing with a thud behind her. He stood there feeling foolish, looking up at the tall house, thinking she had vanished out of his life into the darkness of the unknown.

He felt angry and confused. If the Canon were a holy man, he would not have been so troubled. The Canon was vain, shallow and overbearing, a tireless meddler in other people's lives. As neither an objective observer nor a disinterested adviser, he had no business interfering. Beneath the priestly façade, he was just a man with the same vanities and impulses that drive all men to distraction. How could Nora, an intelligent girl, be so naïve? If she was so desperate for confession, he would have driven her to Garron or even Donegal Town, where she could confess to a total stranger she'd never see again. Confessing to a self-admiring peacock like the Canon was granting him a position in her life that he himself did not have and would never aspire to have. The only thing that made an easy relationship between a man and a woman possible was that neither knew the true thoughts of the other.

He was surprised to find himself back at the cottage. The cheerlessness of the kitchen was so unbearable that he did not take off his coat. What the situation demanded was a strategy of desperation, the kind of strategy that overturns all predictions and expectations. With a keen sense of personal failure, he drove straight to Roarty's, desperate for the harmless deceptions of male companionship.

TWENTY

Gillespie had invited him to supper in the declared hope that he might remember the glen for the excellence of the cooking. Aware of the local gossip about Gillespie's heroic eating habits, Potter lunched lightly by way of preparation. Since he didn't expect Gillespie to dust down a bottle of the best wine, he wrapped a bottle of his own modest claret in a newspaper and laid it in readiness on the passenger seat of his car. When subsequently it occurred to him that his host would hardly go to the trouble of getting in some Glenmorangie, he reasoned that it might be a good idea to stop at Roarty's *en route* for his apéritif.

To his surprise he found Gillespie at the counter deep in conversation with Crubog and Cor Mogaill.

'I hope I haven't got the wrong evening?' he said in reply to Gillespie's greeting.

'There's no such thing as a wrong evening here,' Gillespie explained.

'Who's cooking dinner then?'

'The dinner's in the oven. Relax and have a welcoming drink on your host.'

Crubog laughed and Cor Mogaill winked at Potter. 'I hope you've brought your longest spoon,' he said. 'Gimp is noted for his lack of cutlery.'

It was all good-humoured joshing, and Gillespie didn't seem to mind. After one or two rounds Potter and Gillespie made their escape and faced up the street against a biting wind. Gillespie's kitchen was clean but untidy with a bunch of onions on the table, a crate of Guinness on the floor, a bottle of Irish whiskey and a big head of cabbage on the worktop, carrots in the sink, and pots and pans everywhere.

'Two is really the minimum for a dinner party,' Gillespie said.

'The rule we follow in London is no fewer than the Graces and no more than the Muses.'

'And how many would that be?'

'No less than three, no more than nine.'

'Now isn't a classical education the grand thing!' Gillespie exclaimed, peeling off his pullover and rolling up his sleeves. He handed Potter a glass and the bottle of Jameson and told him to pour himself a drink. He himself uncapped a bottle of stout, and watched the myriad-eyed froth rising up the side of the tilted glass as he poured.

'You scrub the potatoes and I'll chop the onions. Unfortunately, it's the wrong time of year for scallions. We'll boil the potatoes in their jackets and in sea water to give them the desired *je ne sais quoi*. And don't scrub them too clean; the clay in which they grew is part of the flavour.'

'Do you serve them in their jackets, clay and all?' Potter looked worried.

'No, I'll be making *brúitín*, what some people call champ or colcannon.'

'And what is this ... brooteen?'

'Potatoes mashed with onions or scallions and butter as well as a little sprinkling of milk.'

'I think I can get the smell of roasting meat? What is it?'

'We're having slow-cooked crubeens, a speciality of the house which I reserve for highly valued guests.'

'What are crubeens?'

'Pig's trotters, pettitoes to the squeamish, thought by the elect a delicacy. I always get the butcher to give me the hind ones; they're the meatiest.'

Potter was beginning to feel distinctly uneasy. He'd never been keen on pork. He'd loathed the weekly roast pork at his school, but even at school he'd never been given trotters. Next, Gillespie commissioned him to peel and chop some carrots while he himself split the head of cabbage down the middle and began cutting it up with a fearsome looking kitchen knife.

'I hope you're a cabbage man,' he said. 'If you are, I'll put on the whole head.'

'I'm not what you'd call a noted cabbage man but I've been known to eat it. My mother used to say it was good for the character.'

'Your mother was right, Potter. I boil my cabbage first and then toss it lightly on the pan in the fat of the crubeens. Is that how your mother used to do it?'

'No, she was not a noted crubeen person.' He glanced at Gillespie to see if it was all a leg-pull but his host was grimly intent on his chopping.

At last, when everything was in a doing way, they rested from their labours to enjoy what Gillespie called 'a well-earned apéritif'. Sitting at the bare pinewood table and listening to the bubbling and hissing of the potatoes in the big saucepan, they discussed Cor Mogaill's combative debating style without resorting to it.

'Sorry to be losing you, Potter,' Gillespie said eventually. 'You'll be taking Nora with you, I suppose.'

'I'd like to but she refuses point blank to come. She's been to London once, apparently. Nothing will make her go back.'

'It isn't London, it's the Canon,' Gillespie said firmly.

'The Canon has nothing to do with it. She doesn't like cities. She says she wouldn't even want to live in Dublin. For Nora it's what she calls "the sharp sting of sea air" or nothing.'

'You don't know her history, Potter. She's in love with the Canon. Everyone knows it. We were all surprised when you managed to deflect her thoughts for four whole months.'

'Don't be absurd. Nora and I love each other. For me there is no other girl. I've proposed to her twice, but she isn't as sure of herself as other girls are. I'm going to keep in touch. She needs time to discover what's in her heart.'

'You must face the facts, Potter. If she loved you, she'd marry you. I say that as a friend.'

'The child she's carrying has come between us. It has taken her over, and that's the long and the short of it.' He regretted having said it. Gillespie was a gossip. Not a man to keep his mouth shut.

'She's pregnant then?'

'Perhaps I shouldn't have told you. Keep it under your biretta at least for the moment.'

'I'm sorry, Potter. You must be worried stiff.'

'If only she'd come to London with me, all would be well. What's to become of her here? She can't stay on at the parochial house. And they won't give her back her old teaching job, I'm sure. Just think of the scandal.'

'You needn't worry. She'll come to no harm. Here we have a long tradition of looking after one another. It may be the best thing that's ever happened. She can come and live with me. I'll give her a place in my life any day.'

'I love Nora. I'm worried because I know that if the Canon should turn against her, not one of you would be man enough to stand up to him. It would be the craven Anti-Limestone business all over again.'

'You forget I'm in love with her, too, and I haven't given up hope. I earn enough to keep both of us in comfort, and I have two empty bedrooms. We could live in this very house like the king and queen of Sheba.'

'Those vegetables must be cooked now.' Potter sought a polite way to end a disconcerting exchange of views.

Gillespie drained the potatoes and invited Potter to peel them. They were lovely potatoes, even-sized and smooth-skinned, and so floury that Potter thought it a pity to mash them. That precisely was what Gillespie did with a big wooden pestle, which he called a beetle, claiming it had been given him by a gypsy woman who'd said it dated from prehistoric times. As he mashed, he added some hot milk, butter, and finely chopped onions and kept pounding until the mixture was as smooth as paste. Next, he drained the fat off the roast crubeens and fried a mountain of boiled cabbage in it to achieve what he called 'concurrence of flavour'.

Gillespie might not be a great chef, Potter told himself, but he was supremely efficient in the kitchen. Predictably, he looked at the carrots and pronounced them done to a tee. He was the kind of man who never failed to cook a meal to his own satisfaction. It was a gift not given to every bachelor. Potter could grill a chop or a steak; boil, fry and poach eggs; but he could never scramble an egg like his mother. It was one of the many things he should have learnt from her but didn't. For that reason alone, he considered the presence of a good woman in a man's life not a matter of choice but of necessity. Nora was such a woman. Her manifold talents would be lost on a do-it-yourself fanatic like Gillespie. Gillespie was nothing if not self-sufficient and therefore nothing if not self-satisfied. What Nora needed was a man like himself who would not feel complete without her.

At last everything was on the table. Potter poured the claret and Gillespie removed the lid from an impressively large bronze tureen, revealing eight trotters lying heads and thraws at the bottom. Potter's appetite vanished on the spot. He had never seen, never imagined, so many severed feet together in one place, each with its four sharp toes, two large and two small, but what finally administered the *coup de grâce* to his appetite was the thought of the farmyards in which they'd trodden up to the ankles—or was it fetlocks?—in slurry.

Gillespie put two of the largest crubeens on Potter's plate, picked up another for himself and began eaten it out of his hand. Gingerly examining one of the crubeens before him, Potter noted the rough pads under the big toes and the loose, anaemic skin covered in fine bristle. He rubbed the pad of his forefinger against the bristles, which were almost invisible but very much there. Not even at school had he been subjected to such a disconcerting culinary experience.

'They're lovely,' said Gillespie. 'Lovely to suck. I suggest we disregard the Talmudic injunction: fill a third of the stomach with food, a third with drink, and leave the rest empty.'

'I should be happier following the practice of the ancient Greeks if only I could remember it. Can you?'

'I'm afraid I can't help you there. The ancient classics were never my stomping ground.'

Potter put on a show of eating but his heart wasn't in the exercise. The fried cabbage was passable, more acceptable than boiled cabbage, but the thought that it had been tossed in the fat of the trotters ran counter to the judgement of his taste buds. He was glad of the brooteen, however. It was tastier than any mashed potato he'd ever eaten, but mashed potato on its own hardly made a meal. As Dr Johnson once said, 'this was a good dinner enough, to be sure; but it was not a dinner to ask a man to.' Observing Gillespie working his way steadily through the heap of trotters and vegetables on his plate, he sought to recall the moral of Aesop's fable about the stork that had been invited to dinner by a fox. Now he could sympathise with the stork in her predicament. Fittingly, her response was to invite the fox to an equally impossible dinner. From his schooldays and occasional travels abroad, he himself knew of several such dinners. If his time in the glen weren't coming to an end, he would pay his host back in his own coin.

When Gillespie had dispatched the last of the crubeens, he cleared the table and laid out a spread of cream crackers, cheese and grapes. As he approached the table with the drinks, he staggered and almost lost his balance. Recovering, he set the bottle of Jameson and a fresh glass before Potter, who realised that his host was quite drunk. He had been sober leaving the pub. The claret, which he'd pronounced very drinkable, had done for him. Gillespie returned to the table with four bottles of Guinness for himself, which he placed within easy reach of his hand.

'Now that the formalities are over, let the real business of the evening begin,' he said. 'Drink and conversation.'

The little kitchen had become quite warm. Potter loosened his tie and undid the top button of his shirt. Gillespie poured himself a Guinness and attacked the grapes and cheese.

'Do you ever suffer from doubts, Potter?' he asked through a mouthful of grapes.

'Religious doubts?'

'No, just doubts. There are two types of men: men who suffer from doubts and men who suffer from certainties.'

'Personally, I'd plump for the pleasures of certainty rather than live in the torture chamber of doubt.'

'The men who suffer from certainty are boring. Could anyone be more certain and more boring than Rory Rua?'

'I find Rory Rua quite engaging,' Potter said, beginning to wonder where Gillespie's conversation was leading them.

'I think you're a doubter yourself, Potter. That's why you're such good company. You have the type of mind that is always peering behind the back of the obvious. I know because I have that sort of mind myself. It never gives you a minute's peace. But it means you're always ahead of the game. You've foreseen it all, if only as a remote possibility. I see doubt as a gift from heaven. We should be grateful for all the insights it gives us.'

Potter could not begin to imagine what Gillespie was driving at. He looked passionately serious, as if about to lapse into one of his melancholy moods. Celts were like that, brooding on the darkness of winter nights one minute and the glory of a summer's day the next. Gillespie obviously felt that everyone thought and felt as he himself did.

'Are you certain about Nora, for example?' he asked. It was an odd question, and it had come at Potter out of the blue. He scrutinised Gillespie's shut-down face, and Gillespie returned the scrutiny.

'I'm not at all sure I get your drift, Gillespie.'

'Are you sure you're the father of the child?'

'You're not suggesting you are?' Potter laughed, though somewhat uneasily.

'Alas, I'm not. But don't get me wrong. I'm only trying to alert you to possibilities. As I see it, life is a river and we're all rowing against the flow. On one bank are the probabilities; on the other, the possibilities. It's up to us rowers to choose which bank to hug. The adventurous go after the possibilities; those who play safe go for the probabilities.'

'Gillespie, you're into deep water now, too deep for me.'

'What Englishman said, "Never patronise, never explain."'

'I think the saying is, "Never apologise, never explain." But to end all this futile speculation and to set your suspicious mind to rest, let me assure you that I know Nora in a way no other man has ever known her. She was a virgin when we first made love. Some things can't be faked, my dear Gillespie.'

'You and I are fellow victims, Potter. We've both suffered injury at the hands of the Canon. Like the devil himself, he never rests. Repulse him on one front, and before you have time to look round, he's advancing on you from another.'

Potter felt angry but it was not his way to show it. He had taken Gillespie's measure. As a failed lover, he must know the torments of jealousy; and there was no surer way to avenge an ancient hurt than to inspire jealousy in the man he saw as his rival. Gillespie was not the boon companion he'd taken him for.

'Look, Gillespie, the Canon is twice her age, old enough to be her father.'

'Or her father figure!'

'I'm her father figure. I'm ten years older than Nora. I love her and she loves me. And there's an end on't.'

'Spoken like John Bull himself. What I like about the English is their unshakable objectivity. We Irish are far too hot-headed.'

Potter felt uneasy. Any discussion about the English and the Irish was fraught with explosive possibilities, especially in conditions of high inebriation. He reached for the only subject guaranteed in Ireland to calm the stormiest of alcoholic seas. Poetry was something everyone could agree on because no one could be certain of what it was about.

'I admire the Irish above all for their poetry,' he said. 'It seems to me that the most profound question in all literature was asked by Captain Boyle in *Juno and the Paycock.*'

'And what question is that?' Gillespie asked.

'What is the stars?'

In quoting, Potter took care not to imitate a Dublin accent, in case he might give offence by getting it wrong. Gillespie's eyes lit up. Potter could have sworn he'd heard the click of points changing in the other man's mind.

'Haven't I often asked myself the very same question?' Gillespie mused nostalgically. He was off, and now there was no unseating him. Potter relaxed and poured himself another whiskey. Their discussion of poetry, or, more accurately, snatches of poems remembered from school continued past midnight, and throughout the discussion they were both in total agreement on the merits of every poet and poetaster in the history of Irish and English literature.

'Look at the time,' Potter said finally. 'Thank you for a most stimulating evening. I'll never eat a pig's trotter again without recalling the first time I tasted one.'

'The first time is what matters,' Gillespie stuttered. 'I enjoyed the evening, too. There's nothing to beat a good literary conversation.' He tried to rise from his chair and failed honourably in the attempt.

'No, don't get up. I'm sure I can find my way out.'

'I think I'll sleep *in situ*. There are times in any thinking man's life when the bedroom no longer beckons.'

It was almost one when Potter reached home. It had not been the most appetising of suppers nor the most rewarding of evenings. Was Gillespie an innocent or one of those Irish eccentrics who have no idea of the effect their conversation is having on other people? It wasn't easy knowing how to respond. Gillespie could say the most outrageous things and smile like a four-year-old while saying them. In the wrong company he would have earned himself a fist in the face and a bloodied nose.

He felt disappointed, not just in Gillespie but also in himself. Though he had got through half a bottle of claret and half a bottle of Jameson, he was still stone cold sober. This discomfiting lucidity of mind was unnatural at this hour of the morning. Besides, he was hungry, irritable, and in urgent need of animal comforts. He poached two eggs and ate them with buttered toast, after which his condition began to improve. He'd always been a breakfast man. It was encouraging to think that he would be having another breakfast in less than six hours. He got ready for bed though he knew he wouldn't sleep.

TWENTY-ONE

Roarty held up a glass beaker of his urine against the bathroom light, turning it slowly in his hand like a landlord testing the first glass from a fresh barrel. Though it wasn't cloudy, it didn't look like his urine. It rather resembled a malt whisky, and with justice, he thought somewhat ruefully. Noting the heavy sediment at the bottom of the beaker, he sniffed the contents and wished it was something as innocuous as hops or smegma. He emptied most of the contents into the lavatory bowl and transferred the remainder to an empty pill bottle for the attention of the sexually dextrous McGarrigle.

Soundlessly, he returned to his room, having satisfied himself that Susan Mooney had switched off her light. He locked his door without a click and took Dr Loftus's rifle from the bottom of the wardrobe. He had retrieved it from the culvert the previous night, and now he balanced it carefully and appreciatively on his hands. Though it was showing a fair amount of use, it must have had a careful owner. Only that would account for its beautiful condition, he thought, rubbing his forefinger along the slightly worn fore-end piece. It was one o'clock. He still had an hour to kill, long enough to take in Schumann's first and fourth symphonies. He put the first symphony on the gramophone and lay on the bed, looking through the article on 'Bridges', one of his favourite pieces in *Britannica*.

After memorising a few of the formulae, he laid the volume on the coverlet and closed his eyes. For the past few days he had been more than usually aware of the transience of human perceptions. Our insights come, give a moment's pleasure or even pain, and are gone like fading coals. Even in a man with a good memory the precise experience of one day never survives to the next, for those experiences that return to torture or delight undergo a sea change each time we recall them. Life, he told himself, is a palimpsest of expunged experiences. The Florence he summoned up daily was neither the carefree girl he once loved nor the efficient business woman she had become in middle age. Remembrance had transformed her into a fearful dragon. His memories of school were equally vivid, but did they represent the reality of school or were they fictional accretions of his own fabrication, suffering a renewed transmutation with each recalling?

Now as he looked back, he saw his schooldays overcast by a blighting sense of unreality. While other boys dreamed of becoming doctors, lawyers or engineers, he sat in the classroom wondering where all those words might lead, curious only to discover if they related to anything except one another. History, which should have enlivened his boyish imagination, died as it fell on his ear. The master droned on confusingly about the campaigns of Wallenstein, compounding the complexities of the Thirty Years' War, so that Wallenstein remained for him a name rather than a man, and the duchies of Friedland, Sagan and Mecklenburg places without substance that conjured up nothing but the sickly fear with which he beheld pink exam papers. And when the master told them that Wallenstein was murdered after a banquet by Scottish Protestants and Irish Catholics from his own army, Roarty was neither surprised nor saddened but rather overcome by the futility of a further nugget of information which would keep rising like flotsam to the surface of his mind for the rest of his life.

In his final year at school, when other boys were preparing for university, he could not imagine what he wanted to do because everything was happening at two removes away and there was nothing in the whole wide world that he truly desired. Tentatively, he concluded that the battle must be fought not in the world but within himself, an opinion which was confirmed for him by an overheard conversation between a Franciscan and a teacher who had left the order and applied for laicisation.

'And how are you finding the great world these days?' the Franciscan asked.

'Are you trying to find out if you were right to turn your back on it?' the lay teacher smiled.

'It's a thin world as I well know,' said the Franciscan. 'You could travel it from end to end and come back empty handed.'

That brief exchange left an impression on Roarty. When a Holy Ghost Father came to the school on a proselytising mission, he promised to join the order almost as a matter of course. He joined out of horror of the muddle that was humanity and to further a romantic attachment to asceticism, of which he found little evidence in the seminary.

The burden of empty experience weighed on him as heavily as might the burden of a thousand years. He had survived his unhappy schooldays. It was only now after a lifetime of reinvention, of heaping one false memory on another, that he had begun to wilt under the load. In recalling and recreating, he had pruned and refined, eaten away the fleshy fruit until only the bitter core remained. His memories no longer encompassed the length and breadth and depth of his experience; they were toxic distillations that had become lethal in their concentration. Florence was not dead. She had risen to wage war on him, to consume his masculinity, to threaten the very centre of his sanity. If only he could re-experience his life as lived, he would be healed. If only he could exchange his memories for those of Potter, say, he would find peace without having to wrestle daily with the venomous toad in his heart. But if he bartered his memories, would he not be surrendering the personality he was at such pains to preserve?

His memories of the seminary were more destructive than those of school because in the seminary he had been tortured by the knowledge of how his mad uncle had met his end. In his final year the president of the college called him to his study and handed him an anonymous letter he'd had from a so-called well-wisher, saying that Timothy Roarty's uncle had died in an asylum because of his predilection for sex with young girls, and asking if the nephew of such a degenerate could have the purity of heart indispensable in a consecrated priest.

'Is this a factual statement?' the kindly old president had asked.

'In essence, yes,' said Roarty.

'We are all subject to temptations, some sadly more than others, and we all must combat them with what weapons the Lord in His love and wisdom has given us. Look into your heart, my son, and see what you find there. Should you ever wish to talk to me, I shall be here at your disposal.'

Roarty did look into his heart only to find the stench of pent-up concupiscence and unfulfilled carnality. He recalled how on holiday he had watched young girls in their white first communion dresses returning from the altar rails and how in his heart he had desired them. He did not get up from his pew as Lanty Duggan might have done because he had not yet strayed that far from reality. But what if he should in years to come? Lanty Duggan lived within him, an evil-smelling old man, a corrupter of innocence. He had left the seminary to escape from that old Adam whom he knew would haunt him unrelentingly in a life of celibacy. Now in middle age the battle had begun to go in the old man's favour. As it happened, he was impotent but his impotence clothed his desires in the most lurid and fantastical shapes and colours, threatening to drive him off the highroad into hedges and ditches like a wild tramp of the hills. Lanty Duggan, like Florence, still lived. He was a maggot within his brain that daily consumed his reason.

He picked up the rifle, opened the bolt, and pressed five rounds down into the magazine.

'Victorian man feared the workhouse; modern man fears the madhouse,' he muttered.

He stole down the stairs, careful to avoid the loose tread that creaked. The night sky was low and starless. It was pitch dark between the houses and cold enough for snow. Pulling his woollen scarf up under his chin, he took the fenceless road that climbed the hill, leading to Rory Rua's cottage.

Crubog had come into the bar that morning crowing about the great bargain he had driven, and how he had sold his farm to Rory Rua for £4,250 and a hot dinner every day for as long as he lived.

'I didn't sell it for the money,' he explained in mollification, 'but for the hot dinners. At my age no sensible man would want to spend what little time he has left in the kitchen.'

'You could have chosen a better cook,' Roarty smiled. 'You could have sold it to a man with a wife. All the cooking Rory Rua ever does is to boil eggs and potatoes. You may find yourself on short rations in your old age.'

'I've taken care of that. He's to cook me something different every day, meat five days a week and fish on Wednesdays and Fridays. Leave it to Old Crubog. He's as good as any lawyer.'

'So it's all signed, sealed and delivered?' said Roarty nonchalantly, as if it was no business of his.

'No, we'll both be going to see our solicitors next fair day.'

Though incensed by the sale, Roarty had kept his cool. While planning the next move, he talked to Crubog about the ground frost and advised him to expect snow. Crubog wouldn't hear tell of it; he said the sky was all wrong for snow. 'Where is it going to come from?' he asked, putting down his whiskey glass with a rap, which was his way of ordering another.

As he turned to the optic, Roarty recalled the number of free whiskies he had poured down Crubog's neck in the hope that he would agree to sell him his 'mountain acreage'. Those whiskies cost good money and gave him a personal stake in Crubog's farm, which Rory Rua had now wrested from him by foul means, not fair. If he had known that Crubog fancied a hot meal every day, he could easily have provided it. Susan was a competent cook. Crubog could have had his meals as well as his drinks in the pub. It would have saved him shoe leather, and made excellent sense. Actually, he would have been doing Crubog a favour: the foxy old bugger would eat like a prince every day of the week rather than a pauper.

All was not lost. The conveyancing was not complete; and no money had yet changed hands. There was still time to frighten Rory Rua into backing out. He was not sure how best to frighten him but he suspected that the fizz of a bullet at his ear as he slept would make him sit up and think twice before clinching a deal. To clarify matters and to leave him in no doubt of the seriousness of his situation, he had prepared a little note to pin on his door. It was a cryptic note to start several hares in the mind of McGing, written in capitals and in a different script from the one he had left for Potter.

Smiling inwardly at his own ingenuity, he stepped onto the green verge to muffle his footfalls. Strangely enough, the farmyard gate had swung open. He paused by one of the piers and cocked the safety catch of the rifle. A cat squealed somewhere among the trees on his left. He squatted on his hunkers to see if he could make out the shape of the house and farm buildings against the sky. A muffled noise like the wheezing of a cow followed by the jingle of a chain came from behind the house. Feeling in his pocket for the biscuits he had brought for Setanta, he edged forward with his back to the hedge, suddenly aware of the beating of his heart. He sidled across the yard with one arm outstretched until he felt the pebbledash of the end-wall against his hand. Something soft brushed against his leg. He bent down and gave one of the biscuits to the dog, still alert for the faintest sound. He moved along the wall, placing one foot carefully in front of the other in case he should upset an empty pail or bottle. The byre door was open with a dim light shining inside. Rory Rua was evidently sitting up looking after a sick cow. It was too risky to advance any farther. He would go back and wait for a more auspicious night.

As he turned, two powerful arms gripped him from behind, pinning his elbows firmly against his ribs. Roarty swung round with all the strength of his huge body, lifting his assailant off his feet. His assailant temporarily lost his grip, and grasped the barrel of the rifle in an effort to regain his balance. Desperate to maintain his hold on the gun, Roarty swung round in the opposite direction. The other man lost his footing, pulling the gun down with his fall. There was a loud report as the rifle recoiled in Roarty's hands. The man clutched Roarty's leg with a groan. Roarty, reacting, freed himself with a kick and pressed the muzzle of the gun into the man's heaving chest. A single word came up out of the dark with a rattle.

'Bogmail.' The voice was laboured but he recognised it as the gruff voice of Rory Rua. Somehow he knew the word would be his last. Bending over the dark heap, he found the wrist, but there was no answering pulse. His hands were shaking badly and a cold sweat had broken out on his chest and forehead.

His initial impulse was to hoof it back home as quickly as he could but, first, he thought, he must make sure that his tormentor was dead. He dragged the deadweight into the house and switched on the light in the kitchen. Rory Rua had been shot in the chest; he had tickled his last trout, baited his last lobster pot, scoffed his last hare straight from the gun. He stretched the body on the outshot bed, drew the curtains closed, and examined his own clothes for bloodstains. He had been lucky. There was only one smallish splash on the sleeve of his donkey jacket, which he would see to when he got home.

Seized by a brainwave, he went into the room behind the fireplace and opened the drawer of the bedside table. He did not have far to look. Underneath a jumble of socks, was Eales's sex magazine. With any luck it might contain an advertisement for the longed-for lust finger and other exotic little refinements. The fabled finger would make a nice surprise for Susan, he thought as he stuffed the magazine into his jacket pocket. She was one of those girls who appreciated the funny side of sex. He would order her something amusing for Valentine's Day, which was less than two months away.

He switched off the lights, locked the door of the house, extinguished the storm lantern in the byre, closed the farmyard gate behind him, and trudged down the lane, his fingers clutching the rifle in involuntary spasms. He tried to think but his mind kept whirling incoherently with excitement. He was steeped in luck. No one, least of all McGing, would ever work out why Rory Rua had died. He was surprised when he reached the culvert by the Minister's Bridge because he had not been conscious of going there.

TWENTY-TWO

It snowed in the night. By morning the lightly floating, whirling flakes were still muffling the air in their descent on the whitened glen. From his upstairs window Roarty watched them blowing against the rough boles of the garden trees, forming white, silent bells on the knots and galls and loading the branches above, leaving their dark undersides looking like impossible shadows. The snow lay in great daubs along the eastern side of the dead conifer, white blooms like June roses, as if the sapless wood had unexpectedly burst into flower. As a picture, it looked more exotic, arresting and original than anything he had ever seen in an art gallery.

In the distance the whitened south mountain was scored in black where streams ran down its side, and the fenceless road that descended from Rory Rua's cottage had vanished in the general whiteness of field and hill. It seemed to Roarty that the whole glen had become overgrown in a single night by a beautiful but deadly fungus threatening to smother all things that moved and breathed. He sighed. Though the warmth of the first drink was stirring and spreading its probing tentacles within him, he sensed that he, too, was being smothered by a fungus against which there was no earthly protection.

He would never have guessed that the blackmailer was Rory Rua; he had been so certain it was Potter. He would miss Potter's genially elliptical conversation, his way of leaving things hanging in mid-air, as if what he had been saying was so obvious that he'd lost all interest in saying it. Before leaving to dine with Gimp, he'd promised to look in for one last drink. The world was fast becoming a place of absent friends. Now he'd be alone with the ghosts of Eales and Rory Rua, and with Potter gone there would be no one left to keep Cor Mogaill in his place. If Rory Rua had been telling the truth in his last letter, the story of the murder and the whereabouts of Eales's body would be known to the police within days. More investigation, more tom-fool questions. He would sit tight, keep his nerve and, as Asquith said, 'wait and see'.

Circumstantial evidence alone, even two trout in the milk, would not convict him. Evidence, he knew, was not the enemy. The true enemy was spiritual weariness, the *taedium vitae* his old professor of theology used to ramble on about. To every man comes a time when the game is no longer worth the candle. The curious thing now was that Florence occupied more of his thinking time than McGing. His only bulwark in the war of attrition she was waging against him was Susan. Without her, he'd go under. It was such a shame that it was not given him to make her happy. He'd always blamed his impotence on Florence's sexual rapacity and essential frigidity. Susan, God bless her, was imaginative, an enthusiastic dreamer-up of erotic situations. She and he had learned to make do, but one day she would seek fulfilment in greener pastures, and who would blame her? Life was so unfair. You were born with a wound, and all you could do was to devise makeshift strategies for living with it.

When you thought about it, life was only a succession of problems queuing up for your attention. Head of the queue now was Rory Rua. Assuming that there was no evidence of blackmail, even the most astute policeman would never guess why he should wish to murder him. After all he had been one of his best customers, a man with whom he had never exchanged a cross word. The thought came like a flow of oil, smoothing the ruffled surface of his mind. Perhaps the best self-defence lay in what you might call a strategy of postponement; not crossing bridges till you come to them; putting off until tomorrow what you need not do today. Clearly, there was well-tried wisdom in clichés. Wouldn't it be funny if he found the seeds of his salvation in a bromide! It was the kind of nonsense that would make sense to Potter. He would be sure not to register surprise; he would contrive to give his usual impression of saying less than he might. His departure strategy would be interesting to observe. Crubog, Cor Mogaill and Gillespie had all promised to get up in time to see him off. He was one of those men who inspire goodwill wherever they go while remaining blithely unaware of the doing of it.

He went downstairs and breakfasted off a kipper before throwing the backbone to Allegro. With a momentary sense of luxury, he lingered over a second cup of coffee, pleased that Susan was busy polishing glasses in the bar. He had come within an ace of committing the perfect murder. For all he knew he might have committed two. It was a hollow achievement, however. Though he had so far escaped the retribution of the law, his life had changed irrevocably. He was no longer the Roarty he used to know; he was now an imposter posing as Roarty, a pretender people took for Roarty and in their insistence on the old nomenclature confirmed him in the illusion that he was indeed the true, never-changing, evergreen Roarty, good for a laugh and now and again a drink on the house if he was in a good humour and you were the only customer in the bar. All that was so much outward show. To be a successful murderer, you needed the temperament and constitution of an ox. He himself had always been strong of limb but strength of limb alone was not enough. His Achilles heel lay elsewhere; not in an over-tender conscience that brooded on a rooted sorrow but in an obsessive cast of mind that hadn't given him a moment's peace from either the blackmailer or McGing. His suffering was not a visitation from above but a constitutional flaw; the seeds of suffering had sprouted inside his skull.

Now he was faced with a war in two theatres simul-taneously: a war of images in the head and a ground war in that flabby assemblage of anarchic parts called the body. Of the two, the war in the head was the one he feared. Compared with it, the war in the body was laughable in its banality. He would be going to Sligo Hospital for a check-up tomorrow, where he would be seen by men who lived in a universe of cause and effect and would discover nothing they had not already encountered in someone else's body. The things of the spirit, the ghosts that kept him from sleeping at night, were not generic; they belonged in a universe that was unique to him, a universe beyond the bourn of what could confidently be asserted. There was only one Roarty, just as there was only one Lear.

Smiling at his folly, he told himself that he did not care anymore. His joy in life had shrivelled up. Each drink had become a wearisome turnstile through which he had to pass to reach the next. Cecily, once an angel, had left him, and he had nearly murdered the man whom he would like to have called a friend. Now he found his only pleasure in the touch of Susan's skin. It was extraordinary, the effect it had on him, smooth and pale, almost white. He often wondered what it would be like to sit with her in the garden naked under a full moon on a warm summer night. The moonlight on those thighs, on that silken skin, just imagine. He'd thought of telling her about his fantasy once or twice but of course she'd never understand. She simply had no conception of her own ineffable glories, which was why she wasted her sweetness in the desert that was his bed. He had not forgotten her. He had seen his solicitor and made the necessary adjustments to his will.

The thought of having performed a good act sent a pleasant little frisson up his spine, almost sexual in its intimation of vernal renewal. Giving pleasure to her, even posthumously, brought an unexpected tear to his eye. It was strange to think that he was still capable of such goodness, and a shame that it all had happened too late. Before she came, he used to wonder where the old Roarty had gone, the Roarty he prized most, the reclusive would-be scholar who memorised whole articles in *Britannica* and listened to Schumann in the small hours. In her first week Susan revealed to him that he had not died entirely.

They were alone in the bar at the time, when she said, 'That Crubog has a lively eye'. At that moment he felt a quickening of the blood he had not felt in years. It was St Paul again on the road to Damascus and the beginning of his rebirth, looking forward all day to the night and to the jokey ways she had of recalling him to a life that was less than perfect for her, yet for him unique and therefore without equal. He'd never loved Florence in this unhurried, happy-go-lucky fashion; there was something derivative and predictable about the way she'd made him feel. Susan, on the other hand, was one of nature's philosophers. She once ran her hand down the length of his penis and told him affectionately that half a loaf was better than no bread. In the warmth of her whisperings he found poetry, even a sense of afflatus. Once or twice she'd made him think he knew what it was like to be Catullus. That was absurd, of course. Perhaps it was only because she'd begun telling him one night about a lame sparrow she'd spotted in the garden.

The most important thing she'd taught him was that he'd been wrong all these years to judge women by their figures and faces. The surest sign was that summer-morning light you see in some women's eyes no matter what their age, and of course that heart-quickening fizz in your blood as they put two seemingly simple words together in a way you've never heard before. These were things he did not know till he'd met Susan. If only he'd known them as a young man, what a feast his life would have been. Instead he had met Florence.

He washed his cup and saucer and went out to the bar to get himself a drink. It was still snowing. The morning went by slowly as he sat by the turf fire sipping well watered whiskey and reading the newspaper. At half-past eleven Crubog came in, stooping under the weight of two overcoats and complaining about how difficult walking in wellingtons had become since he was young. Shortly afterwards Cor Mogaill arrived with a drift of snow on his knapsack, which left a pool of water on the floor flags as it melted. The postman called at mid-day with a letter from Cecily. She was coming home for Christmas with her new boyfriend who, to judge by the accompanying photo, was an insubstantial wisp of a youth you'd blow off your fist and wonder where he'd gone. He would not prejudge him. He would wait and see if the deletion of Eales had been in vain. It was all too painful to contemplate. Life was so full of irony that he found himself asking if it was nothing more than a trick played on humanity by a Grand Illusionist with a black sense of humour.

Potter arrived at one and placed a pair of woollen gloves and a burgundy scarf on the counter. Having spent an hour with Nora, sitting in the car by the parochial house gate, he felt pleasantly detached from Roarty, Crubog and Cor Mogaill. The cards might be stacked, and the dice loaded, but he would never give up his seat at the gaming table. She'd told him she loved him, and that God never closed one door without opening another. He left her, feeling truly inspired. He would play a waiting game, in which life itself would be his invincible partner. If the worst came to the worst, he would not be found lacking in contrivance.

'You're for the road today?' Roarty said, placing his Glenmorangie next to the scarf and gloves.

'If I can make it out over the hill.'

'The bus made it this morning. You won't have any trouble in your car. No, that's on the house.'

'A *deoch a' dorais,* as you say! Cheers everyone!'

'Well, I hope you enjoyed yourself here,' Roarty smiled.

'It had its moments, I must confess, and I'm leaving as sound of limb as when I came. Some might say I was lucky, I suppose.'

'It's a pity you didn't discover enough barytes, Mr Potter,' Crubog said with genuine regret.

'No, it would have been the ruination of all of you. What is a pity is that you dropped the Anti-Limestone Society. I'd had great hopes for it.'

'Sadly, it has now become one of the great ifs of ecclesiastical history,' said Cor Mogaill from behind his newspaper.

'As I see it, the only man with cause for satisfaction is the Canon,' Potter reminded them. 'He outwitted the whole bang lot of you.'

'Once we had the Protestant ascendancy,' Cor Mogaill said. 'Now it's the Catholic ascendancy. And they both rule with the same mixture of self-interest and cynicism. The Canon knew there would be no barytes but he also knew the power of avarice. He doesn't make his living by the seven deadly sins for nothing.'

'Where is Gillespie?' Potter asked, looking round.

'He's probably busy writing a purple passage about you for next week's notes,' Roarty said reassuringly.

Cor Mogall banged his palm twice against the wall and emitted a long, high-pitched sound not unlike a horse's whinny. 'Gimp has done it again,' he shrieked, holding up his copy of the *Donegal Dispatch*. 'Listen to this:

"Householders in Glenkeel are mounting watchful vigil on their flocks of hens, geese and turkeys from now until Christmas, fearful that their fattening fowls may be in dire danger from turkey rustlers who raid the pens in search of prize birds for the lucrative yuletide trade."

He's put in that paragraph every year since someone stole Crubog's pet turkey for a joke nearly a decade ago. But listen to this as well, will you:

"During the past week the Gardaí under the energetic leadership of Sergeant McGing have been raiding the homes of poteen-makers, many of whom are busier than farmers should be in winter. The

raids were described by one seasoned poteen-maker as the most intensive in the long history of the still. It is reported reliably that as much as a hundred gallons of wash and as many pounds worth of equipment have been impounded."'

'The man is nuts,' said Cor Mogaill.

'He was in fine form over dinner last night, reeling off poetry by the yard,' Potter said. 'I couldn't keep up with him.'

'Poetry!' said Cor Mogaill. 'Didn't I tell you he's nuts.'

'We were just beginning to wonder if you were snowed in,' Roarty said as McGing's overcoated form filled the doorway. 'A black-and-tan?'

'The very thing.'

Just then a black cat with white paws came in and looked all round the bar.

'That's Andante!' Cor Mogaill said. 'I'd know him anywhere.'

Roarty in his astonishment allowed McGing's pint to overflow.

'That cat's been on the tiles or in the wars,' Potter said seriously. 'Look at his face and fur.'

'He's a shagged cat,' Crubog agreed. 'He's barely able to walk.'

'It is Andante,' McGing said. 'You couldn't mistake those white paws. Where on earth can he have been?'

'Obviously with Eales, to Hades and back,' Cor Mogaill said, going to the window. 'Would you believe it, here he is. If Andante comes, can Eales be far behind?'

'It isn't funny, Cor Mogaill,' McGing reprimanded, going to the window to look out, nevertheless.

'Poor Andante, you look famished.' Roarty chucked the cat under the chin. 'I'll go and get you a bite of breakfast.'

He felt rattled. Unexpectedly, things had veered out of control. He could only do his best to behave normally but didn't quite know how. Absentmindedly, he opened a tin of sardines in the kitchen and put them on a plate, though on an ordinary day he wouldn't dream of giving good sardines to a cat. He poured a drop of milk into a bowl and laid both the plate and the bowl on the floor of the bar in front of Andante. The cat lapped up the milk with dainty appreciation, sniffed at the sardines, and turned his back on them.

'Isn't he the pernickety wee devil, the feline replica of Eales himself?' Cor Mogaill said.

They all watched as Andante crossed the floor to scratch his neck against the cuff of McGing's trousers.

'He's taken a shine to you, Sergeant. He's trying to tell you something,' Cor Mogaill explained. 'If that bucko could talk, his amorous adventures would be worth a fortune.'

Allegro wandered in from the kitchen and raised a friendly paw, as if in salute. He went straight to Andante and began licking his wounded face.

'Tomcats are funny,' Cor Mogaill mused. 'Now if two men began licking each other's faces, you'd say they were taking things a bit far.'

Impatient of Cor Mogaill's attempts at humour, Potter put on his gloves and picked up his scarf.

'Will you be having another?' Roarty asked as McGing drained his glass. Everyone knew that McGing never had more than one, but the question was a matter of established practice like the Canon's 'My dearly beloved brethren' as a signal to listen to a sermon.

'Duty before pleasure.' McGing gave the historic reply. 'I'm about to arrest the most callous and perverted murderer in the history of Irish criminality.'

The silence was so sudden that it froze the air. Roarty picked up a towel, wary lest a single word should betray him. He was the only man who moved.

'And who is it, may I ask?' Potter put back his scarf on the counter.

'Rory Rua. I'm on my way to arrest him for the murder of Eamonn Eales, itinerant barman, and for the attempted murder of Kenneth Potter, English gentleman.'

'I don't believe it,' said Potter. 'Rory Rua is one of nature's gentlemen. Ever since I've had his cottage, he has given me more turnips, parsnips and carrots than I could eat, all for nothing.'

'He was fattening you only to kill you,' said Cor Mogaill.

'He wasn't at home this morning when I called with the key. His door was locked, and curiously enough there were no footprints in the snow.'

'Rory Rua wouldn't hurt a fly,' Roarty said, recovering from the shock. 'Do you have any evidence against him?'

'As much as I need. I've brooded over it in the silent watches of the night, and I've put off the arrest until I could bear the certainty of his guilt no longer. You see, I must tread more carefully here than an inspector of the Yard. In the vastness of London a policeman can forget his mistakes, but not in the country where the relationship between the criminal and the lawman is keenest.'

'I'm astounded,' said Potter. 'You still haven't mentioned the nature of the evidence.'

'It's mainly circumstantial,' McGing conceded. 'But then most criminals are trapped by what a famous barrister once called "the probative force of circumstantial evidence". The thing to remember if you are intent on crime is that most criminals confess when they need not.'

McGing, adopting his most upright bearing, wheeled with military precision and strode out of the bar. He had left his bicycle behind at the barracks. Roarty watched him turn at the crossroads and head up the fenceless road.

'He means it,' Roarty said. 'He's heading for Rory Rua's.'

'I'm sure he's wrong,' said Potter.

'It can't be Rory Rua,' said Crubog. 'He's going to buy my farm.'

'Right or wrong, he's given us a grand topic of conversation for the winter nights,' Cor Mogaill reminded them.

'Sadly, I shan't be able to enjoy your deliberations. I must make tracks before I'm served with a subpoena.' Potter picked up his scarf again and wound it twice round his neck.

'Give my regards to Churchill or whoever is your Taoiseach these days,' Cor Mogaill smiled.

Ignoring him, Potter went with Roarty to the door.

It had stopped snowing and the sunlight was blinding. As they emerged from the porch, whiteness leaped at them from every side. The cold came down with the sunlight out of a windless sky, nipping their ears and ankles and stiffening the roots of their beards. It was a day for reading a book or sitting by the fire with a drink. Further up the street a gang of workmen were unloading the new limestone altar outside the church. They were intent on the job in hand, and who would blame them? Work was work. Without it we'd be done for. It made the world go round. Potter looked down at the blank windows of the parochial house. He'd lost a battle against vanity and vacuity but not the war. That would go on; and if necessary, on and on.

'What will you say when you get to London?' Roarty asked in his facetious way.

'I'll say I went to Donegal for the winter and came back again, and it was very cold weather.'

'Is that all?'

'Is there something else?' Potter looked reflective for a moment.

'I'm sorry to be losing a good customer, not to mention a good friend. If you're ever within striking distance of these parts again, be sure to look in. A welcome and a Glenmorangie will be waiting.'

'No need to wax lyrical, I'll be back. This morning for the first time I got the flavour of Cor Mogaill's conversation. Not even Loftus at his most xenophobic can now keep me away.'

Was he joking? Roarty wondered. Perhaps not. It was typical of Potter to leave a question mark hanging in the air behind him. Roarty turned and slowly climbed the stairs to his bedroom. It was something he'd done many times before. Watching his broad, blank back, Potter was reminded of Loftus. They were both physically forceful men.

The sunlight was so sharp now that for a moment he did not recognise Gillespie, who appeared in a tall furry hat and a dark-green overcoat that reached down to his ankles. There was something ambiguous in his bearing that contradicted his enthusiastic smile. He spoke as if he'd had no recollection of the previous evening and the excesses of his after-dinner conversation. He looked so exuberant that Potter felt he was about to slap him on the back for no discernible reason. Truly, Gillespie was a man of extremes. One day he could be the most genial of boon companions; the next, the rudest man in Europe.

'You're off today. It's goodbye, I suppose?'

'More *au revoir*, I think. I have unfinished business here. I'm one of those men who like to get to the bottom of things.'

'An interesting phrase — I mean, thought. We must keep in touch. If you leave me your address, I'll keep you posted on the state of the game. The biggest mistakes in life come from knowing too little too late. The game we do best here is hurling. It's older and faster than your cricket.' Gillespie smiled broadly and punched Potter on the arm.

'I'll be sure to drop you a line.' Potter sought to put him off without offending him. 'And thanks again for... everything.'

A shot echoed behind them and rolled away over their heads.

'Was that a rifle?' Gillespie wondered.

'A shotgun by the sound of it,' Potter said.

'Maybe we should investigate. Who knows, it could well make a story for the *Dispatch*.'

'Sufficient unto the day... Some things are best left uninvestigated,' Potter said. 'As Roarty once observed to me, the biggest mistakes in life come from knowing too much.'

Gillespie started across the street to the pub. Suddenly he stopped, stricken by a thought.

'That makes no sense, Potter. How can anyone know too much? What on earth could he have meant?' In his ludicrously long overcoat he reminded Potter of a foot-soldier just returned from the Crimean war.

'We all meddle too much in our own affairs, in things we know too much about,' Potter sought to explain.

'Well, isn't that typical! On the brink of departing you raise another hare, and a really big one, too. You failed the barytes test, Potter, but now I think you may have struck gold. It calls for another dinner party. No fewer than the Graces, isn't that what you said?'

'Next time I'll cook dinner,' Potter promised. 'To make up the number, we'll invite Roarty.'